"Oh, I'm sorry. I [...] move my work downs[...]

"Oh, I'm ready to go to bed." The anger in his voice was unmistakable, fueled by a string of lonely nights and several strong Japanese ales. "In fact, I wanted to go to bed hours ago…with my wife."

"Will, I'm not in the mood to—"

"Can you really be this self-absorbed?" He laughed sarcastically. "Can you really be this inconsiderate of other people's feelings?"

"I can't help it if I have a deadline, Will. I would think you of all people would understand—"

"Three hours ago you were completely exhausted. So much so that you wouldn't even let me touch you. So what did I do? I left you alone, just as you requested. Believe me, it's not what I wanted. Then I come up here and find you working? Do you really think that little of me?"

What started as sarcasm quickly grew into a war of words, with Will hurling a slew of hateful comments at her with expert precision. Rebecca stood her ground firmly, determined to keep her cool and the upper hand in the exchange. But the argument escalated into something she wasn't prepared for, and she soon found herself on the darkest side of hurt.

Praise for Suzy England from readers

"Read the whole story in one sitting. It's beautifully written. Stayed up all night. I couldn't put down my phone. You are blessed with a talent, don't let anyone tell you otherwise!"

"You're an amazing writer, with the ability to show people in such a relatable and realistic way. Danielle Steel, move aside, here comes Suzy England!"

"You have this engaging way of going deeper than the surface with real life experiences, yet entwined in the fictional world. Your stories give hope…and we need hope."

"Wonderfully written! The way you capture marital struggles and how easily imperfect people can fall into temptation, just … yeah."

"You unravel a story so wonderfully that it almost always makes me crave more."

Perfect

by

Suzy England

Perfect

Contact Information: info@thewildrosepress.com

Cover Art by *Lea Schizas*

The Wild Rose Press, Inc.
PO Box 708
Adams Basin, NY 14410-0708
Visit us at www.thewildrosepress.com

Publishing History
First Edition, 2023
Trade Paperback ISBN 978-1-5092-4607-6
Digital ISBN 978-1-5092-4608-3

Published in the United States of America

Dedication

To my beautiful mother.
I miss you every day. You were truly perfect.

Acknowledgements

Immense thanks to my brilliant editor, Lea Schizas, at The Wild Rose Press. Computer woes and eighteen (!) pages of galley edits later, we did it!

A very special thank you to Lisa Kamprath, for calling out my passive voice when needed and for always being my cheerleader.

Special thanks to the University of Southern Queensland's Editing & Publishing program, in particular Rachel Marchesi, Siobhan Doig, Abby Rose, Madeleine Warburton, and Shayla Olsen.

Forever thankful to my Wattpad readers, who loved this story from the get-go and helped elevate it on the platform. Y'all are the best!

Finally, to those closest to my heart: my husband, Jeff; our children, Jack and Meredith; my extended family and my close friends. Without all of you, I would not be living my author dreams. I love you infinity and thank you for supporting me.

Chapter One

Rebecca Albright could sum up her marriage to ex-husband, Kelly Glass, with two sentiments: great sex and hellacious arguments. Now, holding fast to his bony arm as they walked in lock-step toward the security checkpoint in Sydney Airport, she could make one unexpected addition to their current relationship: unwavering loyalty. She said not a word, afraid of releasing a floodgate of emotions.

They had ushered in their final morning together, sharing a quiet meal prepared by his hands. She'd watched him closely, observing the rigidity with which he shuffled around the kitchen of his luxury high-rise apartment. His body was no longer that of the once robust sailor who stole her heart many years before. That dark-haired young man with rugged looks and a flair for the unexpected was now gray and thin. A sad shadow of his former self.

The feelings they'd expressed to one another the night before had not been discussed, though their tender moments beneath the starry Australian sky sat like an anvil on her mind. In the handful of days they had spent together, she'd shared more of herself with him than she had during their entire marriage. She couldn't deny it—her ex-husband had changed, and because of their time together, she had as well.

She stopped walking and turned to face him. Her

hands were shaking. He reached and held them, rubbing his sun-baked thumbs over her pale, silky skin. The pain in his eyes was obvious, yet he managed a sweet smile.

"You don't have to say anything. Just let me look at you." He squeezed her hands. "My God, Rebecca, you are so beautiful. Even more beautiful than the day we met."

"Please come back to the U.S. with me. There are doctors who could—"

"Shhh…" he whispered, then leaned forward and pressed his lips to hers in a soft kiss. When he pulled away, another smile graced his lips.

"Promise me you'll take care of yourself," she said.

"I never have. Why start now?" he teased. "You better go, or you'll miss your flight."

"You're a good man, Kelly Glass." She gazed into his deep brown eyes, fighting back tears.

"Only because you've made me want to be," he said.

A throng of travelers swirled around them. An enormous lump formed in her throat at the thought that she'd probably never see him again. With both arms around his waist, she pulled him close and held him one last time.

"I love you, Becks. I never stopped, and I never will," he whispered, resting his chin on her head.

"I love you, too." Tears held at bay finally tumbled free.

****

"We'll be landing soon. May I take that?" the flight attendant asked.

"Yes, thank you." Rebecca surrendered her empty

wine glass to the young woman's outstretched hand.

"Is there anything else I can do for you?"

"No, I don't think so."

Rebecca watched the flight attendant disappear behind a dark blue curtain, wishing she had time for another glass of wine. The day-long trek across the globe had been exhausting despite the perks of First Class and the generous efforts of the flight crew. She'd drifted in and out of sleep, finding only the deepest rest minutes before touching down in New York. Fumbling through the airport, she'd made her connection with only minutes to spare. Now, in less than fifteen, she'd find her feet planted back on home soil in Austin, Texas…and into the abyss she once called a marriage.

"Excuse me, Mrs. Albright." The flight attendant reappeared, speaking now in a whisper. "I know this goes against the policy of our airline, and especially with our most special guests, but would you mind?" She held out a book, along with a black, felt-tip pen.

"Are you kidding? This is the best part." Rebecca smiled, this time more enthusiastically.

"I wouldn't have asked, it's just that I'm an aspiring author, and the fact that you've had such incredible overnight success…and your writing is just so…well, I just really admire you and your work." The woman struggled to get the words out, red flaming her cheeks.

"Thank you very much." Rebecca autographed her best-selling novel. She capped the pen and turned back to the flight attendant. "If I can inspire even one person, then I've achieved something truly worthwhile."

"May I ask you one question?" She took the items back from Rebecca.

"Of course."

"How did you come up with the idea? It's so real."

"Someone once told me that life writes the best stories. You just have to pay attention."

"But the characters and the dialogue—it was all so real. I could see and hear everything. It's like the reader is right there in the room. I instantly fell in love with Jack. He's every woman's dream—strong, sensitive, and sincere. But Zander…" She shook her head with an impish grin. "Zander was a bit of a devil. So rugged and matter-of-fact."

"That's Zander. All force and no finesse," Rebecca added.

"Exactly. Even though he's what some would call a bad boy, I was still a little sad that he and Holly didn't end up together. I mean, Jack and Holly are the perfect couple. But I think every woman is drawn to a bad boy at some point in her life. Guess that's why part of me will always love Zander."

Rebecca sucked in a deep breath, her mind returning to the touching scene that played out with Kelly in their final moments inside Sydney Airport hours before. She glanced up at the flight attendant.

"Part of me will always love him too."

****

"Rebecca! Over here!" a woman hollered, fighting her way through the crowd at baggage claim.

"Georgia!" Rebecca waved.

"Let me help you with that." She took the large suitcase from Rebecca's hand.

"Where's Will?" Rebecca glanced around.

"Didn't you get his message? He said he was gonna text you."

"He didn't."

"He couldn't make it. Had a last-minute meeting. He promised me he'd text you," she repeated.

"Guess he forgot." Rebecca looked at her watch, finding it was still on Sydney time.

"You feel up to grabbing something to eat? We could hit that little dive you love so much, the one with the killer salsa—that is, if you're not too jet-lagged."

"All I really want to do is go home and crawl into bed."

"Then let's get home. Once you're rested, I'll whip up something fabulous."

"Thanks, Georgia." Rebecca gave her sister-in-law's arm a friendly pat.

They rode in silence through start-and-stop traffic. Her head against the headrest, Rebecca tried to ignore the throbbing pain inside. Never in all their years together had Will failed to pick her up from the airport. That he'd sent his sister in his place spoke volumes. What exactly would transpire when they saw one another again? Would he apologize, or would they continue in silence, as they had in the days before her departure? Phone in hand, she debated whether to text him. They hadn't spoken in twelve days, aside from the short text message she'd sent reminding him of her arrival time. He'd responded with a brief acknowledgement only, giving no indication that he would be MIA upon her return. A heavy sigh and a prayer helped her brace for an icy reunion.

The conditions under which she left were among the worst they'd ever experienced. The harsh words spoken by both were weeks of tension waiting to erupt. A combination of her sudden success, the extensive travel involved with a nationwide book tour, and the press junket. All the while, Will was knee-deep in a massive restructuring of his company, designing his new corporate headquarters just west of the city.

"Did Will mention when he might be home?" Rebecca asked.

"No. He's hardly said two words since you left." Georgia sighed heavily. "He's working around the clock. One night he never even made it home."

"He didn't come home?" Rebecca raised an eyebrow. "Where was he?"

"At his office. Crashed on his couch. I drove down early the next morning with a change of clothes. He looked like hell."

Rebecca's eyes closed. Memories of their exchange just minutes before she'd left for the airport bubbled to the surface. Though nearly two weeks had passed, his angry accusations still created a knot in her stomach. Knowing how she felt about Kelly, the knot pulled even tighter.

****

"You're still here?" Whitney peeked into his office.

"I live here, remember?" Will Albright kept his head down, focused on the contract in front of him.

Whitney stood uneasily at the door, unsure if her boss was making a joke. Something had happened to the smiling, relaxed, confident man she'd worked alongside for several years. The man who never sweated a detail or second-guessed himself had become someone unrecognizable.

"Are those for me?" He motioned to the collection of folders in her arms.

"Uh, yes, but they can wait until Monday."

"I'd rather look now."

She crossed his office with a stack of items in need of Will's attention. They spent several minutes reviewing documents, replaying the highlights of the week, and crafting a game plan for the coming one. He dictated one final memo before going silent. He stood and moved to the window behind his desk, watching the city below with a despondent stare.

"Need anything else?" Whitney asked as she closed her laptop.

"No, I think that's it. Thanks for staying late." He spoke in a low voice, keeping his back to her. "Have a good weekend, Whitney."

"You should be going soon, too. Isn't Rebecca flying back from Sydney today?"

"She was scheduled to land at three. Georgia picked her up. I'm sure she's home sleeping off the flight."

"Well, please give her my best. Y'all have a great weekend."

His assistant closed the door, and Will sighed. It was now after six and the inevitable couldn't be delayed any longer. It was time to go home and face the music.

The elevator was empty, as was the parking garage. He popped the trunk to store his jacket and briefcase, catching sight of the tire jack. Guilt reverberated inside him with deafening clarity as the lid quietly closed.

Light rain fell. Will took it as a sign—a grim one at that. Friday night traffic would be impossible now. He took the scenic route to their home in the hills west of the city, hoping the additional miles might help organize his thoughts. Mind racing forward, he anticipated the painful turn his life was about to take. Whatever happened, Rebecca would not bear the blame for any of it. This was his mistake to bear.

The windshield wipers moved back and forth, creating an irritating squeak. He reached for the volume to drown out the annoying sound, and it only took a second to recognize the song playing on the radio. His palms began to sweat, and he felt sick as the haunting lyrics brought the image of her face into the forefront of his mind. A loud car horn forced him back to reality, and he swerved back into his lane. With a flick of his wrist, he silenced the radio and turned his attention back to the road.

An hour later, he pulled up their long, narrow driveway and sat in his car for several minutes, eyes turned up toward their bedroom window. The sun was setting and he wondered if she'd taken her jet-lagged body to bed. Could his confession wait until morning? With a prayer, he retrieved his things from the trunk and quietly unlocked the front door.

The house was silent, and he immediately noticed her large suitcase at the bottom of the staircase. He dropped his briefcase and jacket on the floor beside it before tiptoeing into the kitchen.

"Jesus, Will. You scared the living shit out of me." Georgia jumped in surprise.

"Sorry. I didn't want to wake Rebecca in case she was sleeping."

"She crashed the minute we hit the door. She's exhausted."

"Well, let's not wake her. Maybe she'll sleep all night," he mumbled.

"Maybe you should join her. You don't look like you've seen a bed in days."

"I'm fine." Will sighed, scanning the refrigerator for something cold to drink.

"You sure?"

"I'm just tired."

"Then why don't you go lie down?"

"Look, I'm too keyed up to sleep. Anyway, it's too early. If I go to bed now, I'll be up in the middle of the night." He twisted the top off his beer, taking a drink as he loosened his tie.

"Are you sure you're okay?" She shot him a sideways look.

"Yeah. Why?"

"It's Friday night. You never drink beer on Friday. It's always highballs on Friday." Georgia pointed to the bottle in his hand. "You never work past five o'clock. You never spend the night at the office. You—"

"What the hell? Suddenly you're my goddamn mother?" Will said in a sharp tone.

"No, I'm your goddamn sister, and all I'm saying is you have a gorgeous woman in your bed—one you haven't seen for almost two weeks. It's time you apologized to your wife."

"No, Georgia, it's time for you to stay the fuck out of my business. Seeing as how your marriage ended, you're hardly in a position to be giving advice."

Chapter Two

Will slammed the back door and marched with deliberate steps down to the pool. He settled onto an oversized chaise, immediately regretting his outburst. He'd let anger build to such a degree that he was now lashing out at innocent bystanders. Poor Georgia. He'd hardly had a nice thing to say to her in weeks. In true form, Georgia had tried her best to be supportive despite the wall Will had built around himself. Of course, she knew that something was wrong. She was his twin. His closest confidant, aside from Rebecca. How could she not know?

Cool your jets, finish your beer, then go back in and apologize to your sister. She's done nothing to deserve your shitty attitude.

As the night air blew ripples in the pool, his thoughts drifted elsewhere. Another place in time, though it had only been a couple of weeks according to the calendar. The exact moment Will turned into the man he swore he'd never be...

"I say we call it a day." He examined his watch, *pushing a stack of papers to the side of his desk.*

"But it's only two o'clock." Charlotte checked hers *as well. "Not even close to quittin' time."*

"It's quittin' time somewhere. Let's pretend it's here."

"Well, how can I possibly argue with that logic?"

She smiled.

"You can't. I'm the boss, remember." He gave her a playful wink. "And my word is the law."

"Aye, aye, Captain." She gave him a friendly salute.

Those blue eyes had gnawed on his mind for days. There was something behind them he couldn't quite put his finger on. It had been there from the start, as he'd watched her with complete intrigue on a rain-soaked Friday evening. She was one of the boys, but then no— the creamy skin and silk dress said otherwise.

"What do you say we grab a bite?" he suggested.

"Are you kidding?" She consulted her timepiece once more. "We just had lunch a couple of hours ago."

"Then what do you say we grab a drink at my favorite watering hole?" He made his way to a long, narrow credenza across his office. Seconds later, he transformed its top into a small bar—complete with cocktail napkins printed with the company name.

"You're a bartender, too?"

"I have many talents."

"So I'm learning. Your ability to blindly identify a host of foreign beers and remember random stats for every major league pitcher is second-to-none."

"I told you, I'm a compendium of worthless information." He filled a glass for her. "I bet you have some hidden talents, aside from your stint working in an Indy pit crew, of course."

"Actually, I do have one." She snatched a napkin from the neatly fanned stack.

"You're a magician, right?"

"No."

"Origami?"

"Un-uh." She held out her hand. *"May I borrow a pen, please?"*

Will grinned and reached inside his jacket pocket. Within seconds, he fulfilled her request, placing an expensive pen on her palm.

"I got it. You're a fortune teller," he said, giving his fingers a snap.

"Now hold still. And turn your head this way." She motioned to the left.

Now seated at his desk, she studied his profile briefly, then began sketching on the back of the napkin. Will felt his heartbeat increase, and he fought the urge to turn his head toward her. His office went silent for several moments until he heard the snap of the cap back on the pen.

"All done?" he asked, still holding his pose.

"Take a look." She pushed the napkin in his direction.

Will looked down to find an incredibly realistic likeness of himself. Though she'd completed the drawing in just a minute, the detail was amazing. She'd captured his eyes and expression with depth. She surprised him. It wasn't the first time.

"I knew it!" He snapped his fingers again. *"You're a sketch artist with the police department. You know, I think I've seen this dude. I hear he's trouble."*

"That's an understatement," she agreed.

"So you can draw more than straight lines, huh?"

"I was actually an art major once upon a time."

"Really? What made you change?"

"Honestly? I did it on a dare."

"A dare?" He leaned across the desk, still very much intrigued.

"From my brother, Ben, the original male chauvinist pig. We're just fourteen months apart and extremely competitive. He announced at Thanksgiving dinner during my sophomore year that I couldn't make it in a real field of study—certainly not in one dominated by men."

"Well, I guess you showed him." He raised his glass to her.

"I certainly did."

They tapped their glasses together. An unusual moment passed between them as they sipped their bourbons. Something that screamed, yet went unspoken.

"So, what does your brother do for a living?" he asked.

"He works for me now."

"Touché." Will smiled widely.

"My sentiments exactly." She nodded firmly, returning his bright smile.

****

Lost inside himself, Will didn't move until his wife's hand rested on his shoulder.

"Will?" Rebecca whispered.

"Was I asleep?" he asked with a start.

"Looks like it."

"What time is it?" He tried to read his watch.

"Just after eight," she answered. "Georgia told me you were home. I didn't hear you come in."

"I didn't want to wake you, so I came out here."

She sat down beside him, their bodies touching for the first time in weeks. Will's heart pounded inside his chest. She was so close. He drew a deep breath, taking in the comforting scent of his wife's clean skin. It was all he could do not to sweep her up into his arms. He wanted to hold her as though nothing had happened, to feel her hair on his fingertips, and to taste her kiss. To lie in bed beside her, giving her every reassurance of his love. But masking reality with a physical exchange, no matter how deep or sincere, would only make his confession that much harder. And only confuse her more.

"Dinner's ready," she said.

"I'm really not that hungry."

"I'm not either, but Georgia has gone to a lot of trouble to make something really special for us."

"Then I guess we should head in." He stood with a stretch.

With their crazy work schedules and constant travel, they hadn't enjoyed a meal together in weeks. But sitting in the dining room, it appeared Georgia's efforts were wasted. The conversation lagged to a painful degree, as Will sat quietly, pushing his food around his plate. Rebecca contributed little, giving only an occasional nod. Georgia tried her best to get them to engage but finally gave up, excusing herself from the unbearable tension and leaving them alone.

Will and Rebecca sat at opposite ends of the table, both with a million confusing thoughts and nothing to say.

"How was your meeting?" Rebecca asked, finally breaking the silence.

"Long," he answered.

"Georgia said something about some permits?"

"It's all been taken care of."

"Oh, that's good."

Will shifted focus between his plate and his wine glass, stopping occasionally to reposition the napkin on his lap. His mind wandered to a time when the dinner hour was filled with laughter and conversation. It didn't matter the topic; from discussing world events to the latest celebrity gossip, they'd always been completely focused on each other. Now, there was no sound between them aside from the occasional clanging of pots and pans as Georgia cleaned the kitchen.

"You know, I almost didn't recognize Dizzy," Rebecca said.

"Yeah, the groomer was a little clipper-happy this time." He took a sip of wine. "When Georgia brought him home yesterday, I was convinced she had the wrong dog."

"It's been so long since I've seen those big brown eyes."

"He's due at the vet's next Tuesday. I don't know if you saw the reminder card…"

"No, I haven't had a chance to go through the mail yet."

"I don't think you missed much."

"I missed you," Rebecca replied, her eyes locked on his.

He twisted his wedding ring around his finger. He'd committed murder, for lack of a better analogy. Stabbed his beautiful wife in the back with the dullest of knives, leaving a gaping wound that might never heal. Only, she didn't know it yet. He couldn't hide the truth much longer. Soon he'd have to master his fear and ask her to swallow the most bitter pill of their relationship, knowing it would be the greatest challenge of his adult life.

What have I done? What in God's name have I done?

"I have some work I need to finish up."

He pushed his chair away from the table, avoiding her remark as well as her eyes. He dropped the napkin in the center of his plate and exited the dining room without another word.

****

The activity in the kitchen ceased for a moment. Rebecca strained to hear what exchange, if any, might occur between her husband and sister-in-law. But the silence continued, broken only by the sound of Georgia loading dishes into the dishwasher.

Rebecca sat alone at the table for another five minutes, head in her hands, quietly crying the tears she'd held in for weeks. The days with Kelly had helped her see just how stupid she'd been and how desperately she needed Will. They'd let themselves drift to an unimaginable degree, finding solace in their work instead of one another. How long would she have to endure his angry silence?

They spent the remaining hours of the evening in separate rooms. Will parked himself at the desk in the study, clicking away on his computer and taking an endless string of business calls. Rebecca returned to the quiet confines of their bedroom, taking a long shower before curling up with her laptop. The house began its symphony of late-night creaks, and with each noise, she looked toward the door, hoping to see his face.

The antique clock chimed from downstairs, signaling the arrival of midnight. Rebecca turned over just in time to see Will close the bedroom door before slipping into their bathroom. Heart racing, she sat up and took one deep, cleansing breath. In seconds, he would round the corner and crawl into their bed. He'd said almost nothing since dinner. Not one question or comment about Kelly, her time in Australia, or the hurtful exchange that left her aching before her departure. The silence was brutal. As much as she hated the thought, she was ready to fight it out. Pick up where they'd left off and come clean about the lie they'd been living for the past two months. She was ready to face his cold eyes—eyes that had sharply avoided hers all night.

She heard the sound of running water, followed by the tap of his toothbrush against the side of the sink. A minute later, he bypassed their bed and took refuge across the room. Standing by the window, he appeared completely lost in his own thoughts, not acknowledging her presence. Rebecca studied him, her heart beating wildly. His normally confident posture was missing. His body slumped against the window frame with hands thrust inside the pockets of his pajama bottoms. Hands that hadn't touched her in weeks. The distance between them was immeasurable. Rebecca struggled to find some way to bring him back—to reclaim the one true constant in life.

Without a sound, she went to him, arms encircling his waist tightly while her head rested against his back. His body tensed, unresponsive to her touch. She held her breath, wishing they could delete the last few miserable weeks of their lives. In all their years together, they'd never lied to each other. Theirs was a marriage built on trust, respect, and unconditional love. Fighting to keep all emotions in check, Rebecca prayed that rock-solid foundation would be enough to hold them up.

"Rebecca, I..." He turned to face her.

She buried her head against his chest. The beat of his heart mirrored her own—loud and strong.

"Let's just get in bed and hold each other," she whispered.

"I can't—I can't do that to you." He took a step back, closing his sorrowful eyes for a moment. "It's not fair."

"If I could take it all back...Kelly and the funeral..." she started, bringing her body back to his. She reached for him, but he pulled away again.

"Rebecca, please, don't—"

"Why won't you let me touch you? Why won't you look at me?" Her chest tightened.

"Because you'll only be making this harder on yourself. I'm trying to protect you."

"Protect me? From what?"

"From the truth, because I don't want to hurt you."

"Will, what's happening to us? We've always been able to work through anything. We can fix this. Just tell me what you want me to do, and I'll do it."

"It's not that easy—not this time."

"Is it the book? The funeral? Because if it is..." Her bottom lip quivered, and the tears fell harder.

His arms wrapped around her and held her with the same touch that swept her away twelve years earlier. Her body responded immediately. He pressed his lips to her forehead for a full minute before pulling away.

"Can we sit down?" he asked.

The look in his eyes was one she didn't recognize. Pangs of fear coursed through her. Something was wrong. *Really* wrong. Something beyond his building project, her travel, and Kelly. She sat beside him at the end of their bed. Will took a deep breath.

"These past couple of months, I've watched two people drift further and further apart. It's like I was watching us from outside myself. We'd become other people. Another couple. Those people we swore we'd never be. The ones who live separate lives." He stopped for a moment, head shaking in confusion. "My God, I'm not even making sense. I've prayed that the right words would come to me, but there are no right words. Not for this."

He buried his head in his hands. Rebecca draped a supportive arm around his shoulder, but he pulled away and returned to the window, resuming his defeated stance in silence.

"Just say it," she demanded, terrified by what he was holding inside.

"Her name is Charlotte," he whispered, bringing his guilty eyes back to hers.

Chapter Three

Six weeks earlier

Will stepped from the shower and wrapped a towel around his midsection. Their bedroom was quiet, giving his mind a chance to rest for the first time all day. He'd spent most of his workday poring over the final proposals. He had a pretty good idea of what he was looking for and was confident his inner circle would confirm his selection. *How hard can it be*, he'd joked weeks before at a regular meeting. *There are reputable architecture firms all over the place. Just pick one.* He quickly learned that his little project was painfully extensive and specific, well beyond pulling a name from a hat.

He stood at the sink and hummed softly, studying a collection of colognes before going with one he'd worn for years. A freshly pressed tuxedo waited on his bed. *Georgia, what would I do without you?* After quickly dressing, he retrieved his watch and wedding ring and examined himself in the mirror. His bowtie hung loosely around his neck. He'd always struggled with tying a perfect bow, mostly because it was something he hadn't had to worry about in years. That was Rebecca's job. She'd always taken care of the little details in his life—adjusting his bow tie, finding the perfect cufflinks, making sure his tuxedo was pristine. But tonight, Will was flying solo; tonight would be the third event his wife would miss, forcing him to make more excuses for a string of absences. Not that any excuse needed to be given to anyone. Those within their circle were fully aware of Rebecca's newfound literary success. How could they not be? Her name was on everyone's lips, and her image was plastered across magazines and talk shows coast-to-coast. The rumor mill was beginning to churn, however, and he couldn't deny the feeling that it created. With a sigh, he took the silky ends of the tie in his hands to make himself presentable.

He found Georgia in the living room watching Food Network, staring intently at the newest episode of Chopped.

"Well?" Will smiled, making a once-around turn. "What do you think?"

"Chinese swamp eel and Gummy bears. No idea what I'd do with that."

"No, I mean the tux."

Georgia looked up and studied him for a minute. "Your tie's crooked. Want me to get that for you?"

"The tie's fine. Look, I don't know how long this party's gonna run."

"I wasn't planning to wait up."

"No big plans tonight?"

"Just studying for a test in my Restaurant Operations class."

"Well, if you need me to taste test anything later…"

"It's the business side only. Nothing to eat, unless you have a craving for a spreadsheet."

****

Drizzle that had covered the windshield as he exited their property was now pelting rain. Will strained

21

to see in front of him, finding the white lines on the asphalt had disappeared under the heavy downpour. He drove for several miles, relying solely on the taillights of the vehicles ahead as his guide. His hand gripped the steering wheel and with the radio silenced, his full attention focused on the road.

Oh, Rebecca. What the hell are we doing? The short, hurried conversation they'd shared earlier that day popped forth. She'd started in New York with back-to-back appearances on national news shows. Will caught the tail end of one, enough to see the effects of travel on his wife's face. Not that anyone else would notice. She looked absolutely beautiful, dressed in a rich purple sweater and dark gray pants. But the eyes? The eyes told the real story—one that only a husband could read. The sparkle inside those soft green eyes was missing, and Will silently questioned how long Rebecca could keep the current pace. With some mental figuring, he guessed that she'd probably checked into the next hotel. Waking up in the Big Apple, she'd now be bedding down in Boston. Or was it Baltimore? The constant plane hopping, book signings, and the like were taking a real toll. Whether she would admit it or not, true rest was needed—and he needed the same. Not just a respite from his overly demanding schedule, but some real time to reconnect with his wife. His thoughts returned to a recent argument during one of her brief stops back home…and the telling way it summed up the present state of their relationship.

"I'm sorry I'm late. Have you been waiting long?" she asked.

"As a matter of fact, I have, so I started without you."

"Oh," she answered with surprise.

"You know, if you were gonna be this late, you could've called me," he huffed.

"You're right. I should have called. I'm sorry."

"Yes, well, I'm sure you were..."

"Sure I was what?"

"Never mind." He took another bite of salad.

"No, you were going to say something." Her tone changed from apologetic to annoyed.

"Look, Rebecca, just order, okay?"

"No. I want to know exactly what you were going to say."

"No, you don't." He shook his head and looked away.

"Why not?" Her voice rose.

"Because you can't handle that much honesty right now."

Strong words had forced Rebecca out of the restaurant, leaving Will embarrassed, alone, and late for a very important meeting. He'd been the one to offer up the first apology later that evening. Rebecca didn't deny her side of wrongdoing, but there was still an indescribable tension between them, which remained ever since.

The SUV in front of him slammed on its brakes and swerved sharply to the right. Will, deep in thought, had no time to react. In seconds, he identified the sound of screeching tires, followed by an unnerving echo of metal on metal. And in the next second, he felt it: a blown tire on the driver's side after colliding with a large piece of unidentified debris on the slick roadway. *Goddamn it!*

The rain continued to fall. He looked for a safe

place to exit the highway. Slowing down the car, he flipped hazard lights on while considering his options. Up ahead, an overpass offered temporary relief from the rain. It wasn't an ideal stopping place, but he signaled anyway, pulling onto the shoulder to inspect the damage.

He exited the car, cursing at the discovery—the majority of a back tire missing. The cause of the blowout remained a mystery, being only a brief flash of silver in the headlights. Time was slipping away. Eyes on his watch, Will made a couple of quick calculations. *Save the tux, call the auto club, and wait for what could be as long as an hour? Screw the tux, change the tire, then be back on the road in less than fifteen minutes? Or, take it as a sign from above, forget the whole damn thing and go back home?*

A black Mercedes sedan rolled up behind him. The heavily tinted windows coupled with the rain kept the identity of the driver from him. The hairs on the back of his neck bristled to attention. *Great! I'm about to be carjacked in the pouring rain in a tuxedo.*

"Sir, are you okay?" A woman emerged from the driver's side.

"I'm fine. My tire, however…" Will pointed down to the rubber remnants still clinging to his rim.

"Do you need me to call someone for you? A tow truck maybe?" she asked.

"Maybe just the dry cleaners. My tux will be toast when I'm done changing this."

Will took off his jacket and tossed it across the driver's seat. The rain was now beginning to slow somewhat. *If I hurry, I can still make it to Mark and Julia's in time.*

"Let me get that for you." She closed her car door and approached him.

"Oh, no. I got it. I'll be back in business in a few minutes. It's no big deal, really."

"You hit that bumper back there, didn't you?" She bent down, inspecting what was left of the tire.

"So that metal monstrosity was a bumper, huh?" he asked. "It all happened so fast I had no idea what I hit."

"From a Camaro, I think. Looks like maybe an old Rally Sport."

"A Rally Sport?" He gave the stranger a hard look.

"I'm not one hundred percent sure. I only saw it for a couple of seconds."

"Well, I appreciate you stopping, but I got this." He rolled up his sleeves.

"I'd hate for you to mess up your tux. Why don't you let me change it for you?" She looked down at herself. "Obviously, I don't have any big plans this evening."

Will stopped and focused on the woman. Dressed in black yoga pants and a plain white tee that highlighted her small, toned frame, he guessed she was en route to or returning from a workout class. Chin-length dark hair peeked out from underneath a baseball cap. She wore very little make-up, and it only took him a second to decide that she really didn't need any. Her blue eyes were bright, with an expression that made him smile.

"Absolutely not." Will shook his head with a chuckle.

"C'mon. Pop the trunk," she insisted. "You can time me. I bet I have you back on the road in under ten."

"Listen, this is very nice of you but never in my life—"

"Have you let a woman change your tire?" She finished his sentence. "Is that because you're a chauvinist or a gentleman?"

"Well, I'd like to think I'm the latter."

"Then be a gentleman, and kindly open your trunk, sir."

He granted her request and removed the jack, which she promptly took from him. She placed it on the ground beside the damaged wheel, then turned and made her way back to her car. By this time, the rain had all but stopped, and Will shifted his weight back and forth, unsure what to do or say at this point.

She returned a moment later with a towel, which she spread neatly on the ground near the back bumper. Will stood watching, completely dumbfounded, at the rate and skill with which she worked. In minutes, his car was back in full working order, and she smiled as she stored what was left of his tire back in the trunk.

"That was amazing." Will grinned. "How'd you learn to change a tire so quickly?"

"My grandfather was in A.J. Foyt's crew back in the late sixties."

"*The* A.J. Foyt?"

"The only man to win Indy, Daytona, and LeMans."

"Your grandfather taught you well. And you were right—under ten minutes."

"Looks like you're all set."

She closed the trunk lid and turned back to him. It was then that Will noticed a small black smudge on her cheek. He quickly retrieved his jacket from the driver's seat and fished a fresh handkerchief from its pocket.

"Here." He held it out to her.

"What's this?" she asked.

"You've got something…" He pointed to her cheek. "A little smudge right there."

"Oh!" She grinned, taking the cloth and wiping her face. "Did I get it?"

"You got it," he said with another smile.

"Thank you."

"You don't need to thank me. I'm the one indebted here."

"It's my pleasure. How could I not assist a fellow member of the Benz Nation?" she joked.

"Well, because of you, I might just make my dinner before all the dishes have been cleared."

"I'm glad I could help." Her eyes twinkled as she draped the towel over her arm.

"I hope I haven't made you late for your yoga class."

"Yoga? Are you kidding? Contort my body into ungodly poses? No, I'm a spinner. And I just finished."

"Spinner?"

"Stationary resistance cycling?"

"Oh, right!" He nodded, again unsure what to say. "Well, I guess I should be on my way."

"Enjoy your evening."

"Thank you. And be careful out there," he cautioned.

"You too. Goodnight," she said with a wave.

Back in his car, Will waited until the woman rejoined the flow of traffic. He pulled his cell phone from his pocket and made two calls. First, a quick call to touch base with the host and hostess of the dinner party to explain his unavoidable delay. His heart pounded as he placed his second call. It was answered on the fourth ring, but to his disappointment, it was only her voicemail.

"Hi, this is Rebecca. You've reached my voicemail. Please leave your name and number and a brief message, and I'll return your call at my earliest convenience."

Will listened, waiting impatiently for the beep.

"Hi, babe, it's me." He paused as an uncomfortable feeling settled in his gut. "I just needed to hear your voice."

Chapter Four

"There he is! Better late than never." Mark swung open the door of his home with flair.

"Listen, I'm so sorry." Will shook his hand. "Is Julia about to kill me?"

"Of course not."

"I hope you didn't hold dinner on my account."

"You haven't missed a thing. We're just now sitting down. I've got a fresh drink with your name on it waiting at your spot." The man welcomed him inside with a pat on the back.

He followed the host into a large, formal dining room. The other guests were already seated. After quick greetings, Will sat at the table.

They'd barely made it through the first course when the conversation took the inevitable turn. He knew it would and was fully prepared, having a slew of stock answers on hand to satisfy the curious masses. He'd played this game for the last month or so, from the day Rebecca's novel hit number one on the New York Times best-seller list. *Yes, she's still traveling. Yes, she did look beautiful, didn't she? No, she's still negotiating with the studios. Reese Witherspoon's book club? You know, I'm not sure. Another book? Well, I really can't say anything at the moment. Her agent would crucify me. Sorry, no free copies. Hey, I'm looking to retire early. Yes, of course I'm extremely proud of her.*

Was he really able to sell his enthusiasm anymore? Or had his enthusiasm become something else? Something dark, hidden deep inside?

"You know, Will…" the wife of a colleague began. "I hate to admit it, but your wife's book has made me do something shameful."

"Shameful?" Will questioned. "And what would that be, Caroline?"

"She made me root for adultery," the older woman teased.

Will was given no time to respond when the wife of another executive chimed in, as if on cue. Only this time, he had no pat line in his arsenal to fire back on her unexpected commentary.

"You must be one understanding husband, Will," the other woman said.

"In what way?" he asked.

"Reid would have a fit if I wrote about the intimate particulars of our past life for the entire world to see."

"I'm not sure what you mean." Will looked around the table, noticing he wasn't the only one feeling uncomfortable.

"Oh, c'mon. It's so obvious," she answered with an insistent tone. "The characters, the relationships. Everybody knows you're Jack Steele. He's you. You're him. And then there's Zander—just substitute polo for sailing and there's no question he's Kelly. Everyone's talking about it, only we had no idea that Mrs. Albright was still Mrs. Glass when she fell into your arms."

"Madelyn, that's enough," the man beside her said firmly. He turned to Will, clearly embarrassed. "I should have cut her off after that second martini."

"No, it's all right." Will smiled, trying to retain his composure. "You're not the first to make the supposed connection." He lied. "I'm sorry to disappoint you, but the characters in Rebecca's novel are just that—characters." He looked around the table with an air of nonchalance. "They say that truth is stranger than fiction, but that's not the case this time."

The second course arrived, and Will breathed a sigh of relief, knowing he'd survived another round of questioning. The conversation thankfully moved away from Rebecca and on to other topics. It was almost ten before coffee and dessert were served. Will shook his head and declined the offer of fresh tiramisu, ready to sign off on the deal and call it a night.

"Oh, c'mon, Will. Italian desserts are your favorite," Julia said.

"I'm gonna pass. I think it's time you people went to bed so we can all go home."

Several guests chimed in, seconding Will's motion to wrap up the evening. They spent the next ten minutes saying their goodbyes. Phones out, the group synched their collective calendars with things like rounds of golf or spa days before exchanging hugs. Finally, Will and his contemporaries disappeared into the library for a moment while the ladies retrieved their handbags.

"Well?" Mark asked, closing the large double doors behind him. "Time to cast the final ballot."

"It was one helluva process, but after looking at all the proposals, there was one that stood out above all the rest. Way above. I think it's the right firm," Will addressed the group of executives around him. "I hope you'll be in agreement."

"Charlie Cross and Associates?" Garrett asked

hopefully.

"Yeah. How'd you know?" Will could not hide the surprised look on his face.

"Because CCA was our first choice too," Mark confirmed. "Unanimously."

"You're kidding?" Will looked at the faces of his trusted inner circle. "All of you?"

"Across the board," Jonathan answered.

"Then make the call and get the wheels in motion," Will said enthusiastically.

****

The rain had moved on. With minimal traffic, the roadways were now clear, unlike Will's mind, which was a jumble of thoughts. The unexpected twist of the dinner conversation left him with a headache that had nothing to do with multiple glasses of Texas red. Was Madelyn truly trying to start shit? Probably not. They'd been friends for years. Still, her words had backed him into a corner, causing tiny sparks of resentment he wouldn't soon forget. Where might the conversation have ventured had their dirty little secret been revealed? *I thought everyone knew about our affair? Wow, Madelyn, for a woman who prides herself on being the go-to source for gossip, looks like you're dead-last this time.* Will laughed to himself, imagining her face had he made such a declaration. Thankfully, the conversation drifted in another direction and an embarrassing scene was avoided—for now. To his knowledge, no one had made a comparison between Rebecca's novel and their affair twelve years earlier. They'd worked hard to keep it that way.

Will replayed the night that changed the course of his life, finding a peaceful place for the first time all day…

"Is white wine okay?" he asked, his eyes scanning the nearly empty shelves of the mini-fridge.

"I'm fine, thank you," Rebecca answered, staring out the window at the sunset.

"Are you sure?" He noted the sudden change in her body language.

"Yes. Why?" She turned to face him.

"Because I worry about you."

He closed the distance between them and stood just inches from her. He could smell her signature perfume, a lethal combination of sparkling floral with a hint of mandarin and woody undertones. Instantly, his senses were transported back in time. She'd lured him in before they'd even touched as that same scent swirled around him. Her hair was much longer then, grazing her shoulders. Never had his willpower been so challenged, as hundreds of eyes watched them move around the dance floor, including those of her husband.

Unable to resist, he gently ran his fingers through her hair. Months of crossing paths at charity events had given rise to an unlikely friendship, one that had escalated into something more. The past few weeks, they'd met for lunch and dinner, discussing a partnership in philanthropy and their desire to better the world. But now, alone on his yacht in a quiet marina, their partnership was about to take on new meaning.

"I worry about you all the time because I can't stop thinking about you."

A wave of heat flowed through his body. Harmless flirtation and pushing the moral envelope created an inner struggle that he'd been secretly losing for weeks.

"Will, I don't think I can…" She took a step back. "This is wrong. I should just go."

"Hey…" He reached out and took her by the hand. "It's okay. I just want to be here with you. Right now. In this moment."

"But what are we doing?" She exhaled heavily.

"According to the world? We're committing adultery. According to me, we're falling in love."

"I can't do this." She shook her head firmly and tried to pull away. But he held fast, keeping a tight yet loving grip on her wrist.

"Because of Kelly?" he questioned.

"No, because I can't say goodbye to you. Not again. Every night ends in goodbye and it's not enough for me," she confessed. "It's just not enough."

"Then don't say goodbye. Just stay with me. Stay with me forever."

He started at her fingertips, kissing each one before moving up the length of her arm. He stopped briefly to nuzzle her neck before finding her lips. He kissed her softly with the realization that his search was finally over. He'd found the woman he longed for all his life. It didn't matter that she belonged to someone else. Tonight, she was his to love.

Heart beating with emotion, he called Rebecca again. A heavy exhale of relief escaped when she finally answered in a sleepy, disoriented tone.

"Will? What's wrong?"

"Nothing. I'm on my way home from Mark and Julia's big shindig. I'm sorry I woke you. I tried to call you earlier…"

"My phone was on silent when Drew and I were at dinner and forgot to turn it back on. I didn't get your message until midnight but didn't want to call and interrupt the dinner. How was it? Actually, you don't have to answer because Julia always outdoes herself from year to year. I'm so sad I missed it. I love getting all dressed up for her yearly dinner party."

"It was great. And yes, our hostess put the Julia in Julia Child again this year."

"Did y'all make a decision? About the winning firm?" she asked.

"We're going with Charlie Cross and Associates."

"They're supposed to be one of the best," she said with a yawn.

The pain in Will's head moved to his chest in an uncomfortable tightening. Small talk and empty pleasantries had been the focus of their conversations for too long. He was ready to put an end to the charade.

"I miss you," he said after a lengthy pause.

"I miss you, too," she whispered.

"You know, I was just thinking about the marina."

"The marina?"

"Our first night together—the first time we didn't say goodnight at a valet stand or inside a hotel lobby."

"It's amazing how one night can change the whole course of your life," she said.

His eyes left the road for a brief moment and snagged momentarily on the opposite side of the highway as his silver Mercedes cruised beneath a now-familiar overpass. The image of the dark-haired woman with engaging eyes flashed across his mind and again, he was overcome with a very unsettling feeling.

"It certainly is," he responded softly.

Chapter Five

Jack Steele leaned confidently against the bar, his right hand wrapped firmly around a glass of Scotch. Though he'd tried for two hours, he couldn't take his eyes off her. He'd seen her early that morning, leaving the hotel in what appeared to be a rush. There was something about her he couldn't quite put his finger on. She'd rested in a quiet spot in the back of his mind all day.

"Hey, Ken, who is that woman? The one at the table in the corner," Jack asked.

"The blonde?"

"No, the brunette. In the red dress."

Ken strained his eyes, focusing on the figures in the corner of the pavilion. It only took him a moment to confirm the object of his friend's desire. He laughed loudly when he identified the woman in question.

"What's so funny?"

"You," Ken replied.

"How am I funny?" Jack questioned.

"Because you're so goddamn predictable, that's why."

"I point out a gorgeous woman and that makes me predictable?"

"You could have any woman in the world but you hone in on the one woman you can't have here. It's classic."

"What's that supposed to mean?"

"It means take a good, long look, Jack, because that's all you're gonna get." Ken downed the last of his highball. "She's spoken for. I'm surprised you don't recognize her."

"Who is she?" Jack asked.

"Holly Mitchell."

"Holly Mitchell?" His head snapped sharply in Ken's direction. "As in Holly Mitchell, the journalist?

"Holly Mitchell, as in property of Alexander Deming. You should see the rock on her hand."

"Yeah, right," Jack said sarcastically.

"I'm not kidding. She's Zander's wife."

"How do you know?"

"I was introduced to them last year at some fundraising dinner—starving artists of Soho or some such bullshit, I can't remember. But they are Mr. and Mrs."

"Holly Mitchell is Holly Deming?" Jack questioned once more, looking back in her direction.

"Ladies and gentlemen, he's smarter than he looks," Ken teased, turning toward the bar to secure the bartender's attention.

Jack shook his head in denial. "How did an arrogant sonofabitch like Deming land a woman like that?"

"How does any arrogant sonofabitch land any woman? No one knows, but somehow, they all do." Ken shrugged.

"Maybe she doesn't know what she's missing." Jack placed his drink on the bar and then turned on his heel.

"Where the hell do you think you're going?" Ken

grabbed his arm.

*"To congratulate Mr. Deming on his big win."
Jack pulled free from his friend's grasp.*

*"You're making a huge mistake. Zander Deming is
not the type of man who likes to share."*

*"Well, let's just say I'm giving him an opportunity
to be a gentleman. A chance to move from sonofabitch
to stand-up guy." Jack straightened his tie before
running a hand through his dark, thick hair. "His team
beat us into the ground today. The least he can do is let
me dance with his wife."*

*Jack crossed the formal event tent of the Westbury
Polo Club, trying his best to retain an air of
nonchalance. Crowded around him were at least two
hundred of New York's wealthiest. Moguls.
Entertainers. Politicians. Top international polo
players. All well-spoken, well-educated, beautiful
people...and all leaving him bored to tears. Of course,
his bank account was right in line with the tuxedo-clad
mass that surrounded him. The night was alive with
pretense, propositions, and an endless flow of Veuve
Clicquot. It was the exact atmosphere Jack Steele
generally avoided, but he'd signed up to represent the
U.S. in a series of tournaments around the
globe...which included the grand soirees that filled the
evening hours following most events.*

*He stopped every few feet, accepting a handshake
or friendly pat on the back. Bits and pieces of
conversations reverberated in the air, blending
seamlessly with the clinking of champagne flutes and
the nine-piece orchestra. As he passed various groups,
his name fell in whispers from the mouths of numerous
party goers. By the time Jack made it to his destination,*

Zander Deming had returned to the corner table, busy holding court with a group of a dozen or so onlookers.

Zander was a large man, standing at least six foot four. An all-around athlete, he picked up a polo mallet in his mid-twenties at the urging of a family friend. Like everything in Zander Deming's world, he excelled to an almost painful degree. He'd amassed a sizable fortune in real estate and timely investments across Australia. In addition to his conquests in the boardroom, he spent years enjoying the company of some of the wealthiest and most influential women in the world.

Jack strolled casually up behind him, giving the woman beside him a knowing look before making his presence known. To say they were old friends would be a lie. No one was ever a friend to Zander Deming. Not truly. You could be a business associate or competitor. A select group might qualify as old acquaintances. Zander trusted few and his inner circle was small, which suited Jack just fine. They had very little in common, save their desire to be the best at everything. Yet where Zander clamored for the limelight, Jack avoided it at all costs.

"I see you haven't lost your touch. Once a bullshit artist..." Jack whispered from behind his back.

"Well, well, well..." Zander Deming turned and locked eyes with him. "Jack goddamn Steele." A sly smile broke across his lips, and he offered an outstretched hand.

"Good to see you." Jack shook his hand.

"Wow! How long's it been? Two? Three years?"

"About three. I think the last time was at Ascot Park."

"The Cartier event?" Zander spoke after a moment

39

of memory searching.

"That's the one." Jack nodded.

"Has it been that long?"

"At least." Jack paused and nodded at the beautiful woman beside him. "I just wanted to personally congratulate you on your big win. You played a hell of a match today."

"Only because you're on the injured reserve list." Zander pointed to the Ace bandage covering the majority of Jack's left hand and wrist.

"I should be back in business by the time Saratoga rolls around."

"We're gonna miss that tournament this year, aren't we, darling?" He turned his head, giving the woman beside him a wink. "It's too bad. I'd really love to see what you've got."

"It's not much, I can assure you."

"Same old Jack. Always so goddamn humble." Zander's comments were tinged with sarcasm. "I don't believe you've met my wife." He wrapped his arm protectively around the brunette at his side.

"No, I don't believe I've had that honor." Jack held out his hand. "Jack Steele."

"Holly. Nice to meet you." She shook his hand warmly, staring into his eyes.

"Are you still here in New York?" Zander asked.

"I bounce between here and London. How 'bout you?"

"Still grinding away in Australia."

"And how are things down under?"

"You know, Jack, it's just like Hell. Full of fire and brimstone—two things I can't get enough of." He smiled, giving his wife a playful squeeze.

They spent several minutes playing all the obligatory games that were conducted at such affairs. Formal introductions were made to those at the corner table. War stories were exchanged. Drinks were refilled. Self-deprecating remarks were offered, all at Jack Steele's expense of course. He feigned interest in Deming's tales for nearly half an hour, just for the opportunity to converse with the man's wife. It was a lot like chess, he decided. When Mr. Deming was at his weakest, nursing yet another fine Kentucky bourbon with his mouth in full gear, Jack carefully lined up for a quiet attack in the hopes of taking his Queen.

"Would you care to take a spin on the dance floor?" Jack smiled. "That is, if it's all right with your husband." He glanced toward Zander.

"Sure. What the hell...just have her back by midnight," he replied with a grin before resuming a lively tale with those around him.

"Mrs. Deming?" Jack offered his elbow, unsure if she'd accept.

"I'd love to," she answered, linking her arm through his.

They walked without speaking to the middle of the pavilion and the large parquet floor that waited. The night was growing old, and as the drinks and conversation continued to flow, the number of dancers diminished. The large chandeliers suspended from the oversized tent dimmed suddenly, making Jack smirk. With his bandaged hand on the small of her back, they danced into the dwindling crowd. The band played an old Jimmy Webb tune and his mind raced with sinful thoughts, making him fight to keep a respectable distance between himself and the married woman in his arms. But the scent of Holly's perfume got the better of him and in a moment, the pavilion went dark. His eyes closed, he increased his grip and pulled her closer.

"I don't know if anyone's told you this tonight," he whispered in her ear, "but your confidence is showing."

"My what?"

"Your confidence."

"I'm not sure I follow."

"Red sequins at a black and white ball?"

"Too dramatic?"

"Word is, you're vying for attention, Ms. Mitchell."

She laughed. It was a sound that made him smile.

"Tonight, it's Mrs. Deming. And I think my husband has the attention-seeking angle completely covered."

"Your words, not mine." He squeezed her hand.

"How long have you known Zander?"

"About fifteen years."

"Via polo?"

"Polo. Business. Our paths have crossed several times, but that was years ago."

"Before he moved back to Sydney?"

"Yes."

"So what do you do, Mr. Steele?" she asked.

"A little of this. A little of that."

"A true Jack of all trades?"

"I like to think so. Of course, nothing I do comes close to the mark you're leaving on the world."

"I hope that's a compliment."

"For you, I've nothing but compliments. Which brings us back to the subject of this evening's wardrobe

choice." He gave the sleeve of her dress a gentle tug.

"Since I was a last-minute attendee, my choices were extremely limited. It was this or a turtleneck and sweatpants."

"Which I'm sure you'd make look equally beautiful."

"Thank you very much." She smiled warmly.

"No, thank you." He stared into her eyes. "And I speak for the majority of the men under this tent."

"May I ask you a question, Mr. Steele?" she asked after a moment of silence.

"Of course."

"Are you always this flirtatious?"

"Only with confident women," he said with a smirk.

"I'll make note of that." Holly winked.

They stayed on the dance floor until the band played its final song of the evening. He hated to relinquish his grip after only three dances, but the night was coming to a close. Jack escorted her to the bar where the last call was ordered. They stood chatting amid several other couples, discussing a host of topics. They talked non-stop and it didn't take long for them both to realize that their paths had unknowingly crossed before. They carried torches for similar causes and had attended many of the same events over the past few years.

"So the big gala in LA for the SPCA last year?"

"Yes, I was there in a more official capacity. I was covering it for the news agency that I sometimes write for," she commented.

"I don't remember seeing you there. And believe me, I'd remember."

"Well, I wasn't wearing this little number. I was slightly more camouflaged."

"Trust me. You stick out. Red sequins or no."

He looked over her shoulder just in time to see Zander down the last of his drink. He turned and made his way toward them, stumbling slightly and grabbing the back of a chair to keep his balance. In a minute, his arm was back securely around his wife's shoulders, and he began his goodbye speech.

"Steele, thanks for minding the store for me." He gave Holly a squeeze.

"Anytime." Jack's glance connected with hers. "It was my pleasure."

"Hey, good luck at Saratoga. That is, if you're back in the saddle by then." He extended his hand once more.

"I'm looking forward to it. Just sorry that you won't be there," he lied, giving his hand an extra firm shake.

"Yeah, paybacks are hell. Glad I'll miss out on that one." He laughed and turned to his wife. "Baby, are you ready?"

"Whenever you are," she answered.

"Take care, Jack." Zander gave a nod.

"You do the same," Jack answered.

The couple turned and Jack watched them walk away. They were just about to exit the tent when Holly turned around one last time, frantically scanning the crowd. Jack took several steps in her direction, giving a genuine smile and a wave. Her soft green eyes sparkled, and she returned his wave with an equally large smile.

Will placed a worn valet ticket in between the

pages and snapped the book shut. He dropped it on his bedside table and leaned back with a heavy sigh. In twenty-four hours, Rebecca would return, which gave him only one night to sort out a gamut of emotions that covered everything from pride to betrayal.

Chapter Six

Will gripped the steering wheel tightly, maneuvering through mid-afternoon traffic. He checked his watch for the third time, silently cursing himself for leaving the office so late. He pictured her standing with her luggage at the baggage claim area, wondering if he would show up. They'd spoken just a couple of times over the weekend, and had she not been meeting with a popular screenwriter early that morning, she would have returned home the previous day.

He'd vacated their estate under the cover of Monday morning darkness, hoping to get a jump start before meeting the architectural design team at the building site. His exhaustion was more than just the early start time to his work week. A best-selling novel had captured his attention in the quiet hours of Sunday evening. He'd fought for sleep, battling disturbing feelings while Madelyn's dinner comments still resonated in his head.

His cell phone buzzed, snapping him out of his thoughts.

"I'm about fifteen minutes away," he answered.

"Don't rush. They've lost my luggage. I'm waiting to fill out the paperwork now," Rebecca replied with an annoyed tone.

"All of it?"

"No, I have my carry-on bag. The rest is on its way

to the Bahamas. At least, that's what they're thinking."

"Why don't I meet you out front? By the car rental shuttles?"

"Fine. If I'm not there, just take it once around the park. I'll call you back."

"All right."

Thirty minutes passed before they were able to rendezvous at the designated spot. Rebecca stood, raincoat draped over her arm, purse on one shoulder, and a small designer duffle bag at her side. Will pulled up in the No Parking zone and quickly popped the trunk, eager to store her things and get back on the road.

"What happened?" She examined the remains of the mangled tire.

"I hit a bumper on the way to Mark and Julia's Friday night."

"A bumper?"

"On the highway. Fell off someone's car. It was raining and the car in front of me swerved to miss it, but I tapped it with my back tire."

"That looks like more than a tap," she said with concern.

"I made it under an overpass. Had it changed and was back on the road in about fifteen minutes. It was no big deal," he fibbed.

Rebecca had little to say on the trip home. She was exhausted, and the look he noted in her eyes matched the same one he'd witnessed a couple of days before on a morning news show. Normally, they made a detour to a small diner to celebrate homecomings with a favorite dessert. Today, Will didn't even bother to ask and drove on in silence as she sat with eyes closed in the passenger seat beside him.

As traffic slowed and eventually stopped, he took advantage of a quiet moment to look at his wife. She'd reclined the seat with her face turned toward him. Both arms were folded neatly across her chest. Her face held no real expression, other than a desire to get home. Even though he'd started the day with anger in his heart, the look of her skin and the shape of her nose made it difficult to feel that way now. He recalled the passage he'd read the night before. It was almost a verbatim account of what had occurred many years ago. Sure, the names, dates, and places had been changed to protect the innocent, but it didn't matter. It was their life—written, published, and distributed for the entire world to see. At some point, tired wife or not, it had to be addressed.

They made it home in time for dinner, finding that Georgia had left them an Italian feast before departing for a movie with a friend. They ate in the kitchen, making small talk and keeping to safe topics of discussion. Sitting across from her, he now realized how much he'd missed her. Their professional lives had taken separate roads, leaving them with little time for anything else.

Rebecca's cell phone rang twice, and she excused herself both times, leaving Will to finish the majority of his meal alone. Her lack of communication troubled him. She seemed to have limitless words for everyone else—her agent, her editor, the press. But in those rare times when they found themselves alone, they shared little in the way of meaningful conversation. Were they suffering as all married couples do at some point? Was this just a phase? A low spot? He wasn't sure, but he opened a bottle of port following their meal, hoping to entice his distant wife out of her shell. They'd just settled down in the living room when her cell phone rang again.

"Just let it go," he begged.

"It won't stop. Let me take care of it now and be done. All right?"

"That's what you said with the last call," he muttered.

Will busied himself with a task he actually enjoyed, and by the time she returned, the glow of a warm fire filled the room.

"Who was that?" he asked, brushing a bit of soot from his hands.

"Drew," she sighed.

"Where are you jetting off to now?" he asked sarcastically.

"I don't even know," she answered flatly. "I wasn't really listening. London, I think."

"What? London? Are you kidding me?"

"He got a call from some executive. They want my novel for a film. They're offering me a chance to collaborate on the screenplay."

"Novel?" Will laughed. "You mean your dirty diary."

"What's that supposed to mean?" she asked, giving him a hard look.

"Ask Madelyn. She knows. In fact, I'm sure the majority of North America knows."

"Ask Madelyn what? What are you talking about?"

"Look, just forget it."

"No, I won't forget it. You brought it up. And frankly, I'm getting really tired of these little snide

49

comments you keep making. If you have something to say, then say it. I don't have time to play games with you."

"Yes, I know. You'd have to actually be here to do that," he snapped.

"I cannot even believe that you just said that."

"The truth hurts, doesn't it?" His eyes pierced her heart.

"You want the truth? Let's take a look at the big picture, shall we?" She glared back at him. "Just pick a year…any year since we've been married, and I'll show you the truth. Take eight years ago, when you decided to expand into the European market. You were back and forth to London for almost a year. You lived there for a solid month while I sat here like the perfect wife and waited patiently for your return."

"We decided that together. You weren't ready to close your practice then anyway," he argued.

"*You* decided, Will. I wasn't given a choice." She breathed deeply before continuing. "And five years ago, when your eastern interests took a hit, you spent six months jockeying between here and Tokyo, trying to get back on track. I hardly saw you then. I think it was three years ago when you and your team spent months scouting all over the US for industrial space for God knows what reason. And last year, you decided that your office needed some sprucing up. But oh no, you couldn't hire a designer to make a few changes. You spent months personally searching for just the right firm to build you your very own Taj Mahal. You have people to do that, Will. Dozens of people. Then the retirements and the interviews and the last-minute jaunts across the pond, and all the while I never said a word, Will. Not one goddamn word!"

"What the hell do you expect me to do? It's my job, remember? That 'Taj Mahal' as you call it? Don't forget that's what puts this gorgeous roof over your head and a closet full of designer clothes," he yelled.

"Of course, I understand it's your job, and I think I've been extremely understanding. What I can't figure out is why you demand respect for your job, yet you can't show me the same respect when it comes to mine?"

"Writing is not your job, Rebecca. It's a hobby. It's not even close to the same thing. I have hundreds of employees with families who depend on me—"

"I depend on you!"

"I think you've proven over the last few weeks that you don't need me," he mumbled.

"Oh, Will, you can't be serious!" She shook her head in disbelief.

"You want to know how I spent my weekend? Alone. Just like last weekend. And the weekend before that, and the weekend before that. I'm tired of showing up for this party and that dinner without my wife. I'm tired of making excuses for you and being backed into a corner every time your name comes up in conversation."

"And how many times have you been missing in action over the years? Leaving me to attend your events? How many times have I had to accept this award or that honor on your behalf because you were on a plane somewhere? I don't see how this is any different." She stopped, summoning her most sarcastic tone. "Oh wait, I do... *I* was the one who never complained."

"I knew you wouldn't understand." He brushed past her, heading toward the front door.

"I don't know how my absence has backed you into a corner," she yelled. "I've lived in that same corner for years, and I managed to make out just fine."

"Yes, but you didn't have to defend our private life to the rest of the world while you were there, did you?" he shouted back.

"What does that mean?"

"You couldn't have been more discreet? It's so blatantly obvious. Just substitute polo for sailing." He borrowed Madelyn's words. "Did you honestly think no one would make the connection about your book?"

"Wow! Now there's something I wasn't expecting." Her arms folded across her chest. "I guess I should be honored that my husband was finally able to carve out a small sliver of his busy life to read it."

"Yeah, I finally read it. And I'm mad as hell," he countered.

"Why? Because you *can't handle that much honesty right now*? Or you just hate being the last one to know?" She threw his own words back at him.

"You lied to me, Rebecca. About a lot of things," he yelled. "And how do I find out? By reading some goddamn dime store novel."

"I never lied to you. Had you stopped for one minute and taken interest in what I was doing with my career, you would have known every detail before a single word was published."

"Your *career* is being a marriage counselor. At least, it was. How we doin', huh?" he asked with overt sarcasm.

Rebecca looked away, staying silent while

lowering her arms to a less defensive position.

"I can't believe you'd betray us like this. All our private conversations—"

"It's not a betrayal. It's a story. That's it."

"And you're still lying! There are things in that book—private thoughts that I shared with you—and I don't appreciate that you've advertised it to the—"

"How would anyone know? Were they there? Was the whole world there with us? I don't see how you can be so upset by—"

"You went back to the hotel and slept with Kelly immediately after you left me at the pier? After all the things we said to each other?" Will looked at her with eyes full of hurt. "And you continued to sleep with him even after you decided to leave him?"

"And there it is. It all comes back to sex. We were married, Will. What would you have had me do? I tried to go on as though nothing had happened. Do you think it was easy for me? Do you have any idea what it was like to have Kelly touch me when all I wanted was to run to you?" Tears built in her eyes. "You want to talk about lies? You didn't have to live one, but I sure did. For almost a year. You weren't married. You were Will Albright, Mr. Carefree and Completely Unattached. No one would have given it a second thought if you decided to bed a married woman. But put the shoe on the other foot, and it's an entirely different story. I had everything to lose, and you had nothing. So don't talk to me about lies. If anyone's put themselves out there, it's certainly not been you."

A trail of tears crept down her pale cheeks. She turned and moved toward the fireplace, taking a seat on the hearth. With her back to him, she wiped her eyes with the cuffs of her sweater. Seconds later, his hands were upon her shoulders, gripping her with a tender touch.

"I don't want to fight anymore. If I clear everything for a long weekend, do you think you can do the same?" he asked.

His breath touched her ear as he kneeled behind her, his arms now wrapped tightly around her. He rested his chin on her shoulder and prayed she'd say yes.

"I'll try." She turned to face him, and he wiped away the trace of a tear with his thumb.

Chapter Seven

Zander Deming rolled over, looking for comfort in the form of his wife. When he reached out for her warm skin, he found her side of the sheets cold and empty. He quickly sat up in bed. Across the suite, he studied her silhouette against the large picture window. Seeing her there reminded him of the first time he'd seen her, looking just as beautiful now as she did years before.

He didn't speak for a long time, studying her body language. Many times, he'd wake to find she'd disappeared sometime during the night. Well, he couldn't really say 'many'. The actual nights they spent together were sporadic at best. Zander's grip on the world of finance kept him plane hopping regularly. His wife's success in the world of journalism created a hectic schedule as well.

His eyes focused on her slender frame, draped in pale blue French silk. He'd purchased the peignoir on his last trip to Paris, knowing it would look incredible on her. Seeing her form against the window, his intuition was confirmed. No other woman made his heart race the way Holly did. There was something about her quiet confidence that made him want her. Sadly, he knew their relationship was more or less one-sided. He'd known it from the beginning, and the nature of their careers only compounded the problem. He needed her much more than she needed him.

There'd never been a true level of security in their relationship. The jealousy he felt when it came to the roving eyes of other men reared its bright green head often. On the few occasions he'd quieted his jealousy with a bottle, the nights ended in a shouting match. Tonight was no exception. The drive from the polo club to the hotel had been filled with angry words, fueled by a fair quantity of bourbon that still pulsed through his veins. To say it was a fight wouldn't even be an accurate description. He yelled. She stayed silent. That's how it was when Zander was clearly in the wrong...and obviously drunk.

He joined her at the window. His arms encircled her waist, but she didn't move, keeping her eyes focused on the world beyond the glass.

"I'd ask what's wrong, but I already know the answer." He nosed at her neck, drinking in her familiar scent.

She took a deep breath and released it slowly.

"If I could take it all back..." he started.

"But you can't."

"And therein lies the problem." He released her and returned to the bed. "Because the word 'forgive' doesn't exist in your vocabulary."

"Why should I? It was a dance. One dance, Zander."

"You can't even count. It was three dances," he corrected. "And you didn't even have the courtesy to come back to our table. I stood there like a complete idiot while my wife—"

"We waited in line at the bar to get something to drink, with at least five other couples. You make it sound like we took a cab back to his hotel. I was never

out of eyeshot. By the time our drinks arrived, you were already standing beside me saying goodnight."

"Well, you don't know Jack Steele. If he thought he could, he would've had you in a cab back to his hotel room as soon as he—"

"If you didn't want me to dance with him, then you should have—"

"What? Said no? And how would that have looked?"

"Since when have you ever worried about what others think of you?" she countered. "And I'll tell you exactly how it would have looked. It would have looked like a man wanting to spend time with his wife instead of letting another man babysit her on the dance floor."

"Well, you certainly didn't appear to be suffering," he shot back. "In fact, you two looked quite cozy."

She folded her arms across her chest. "Wow! I didn't think you were capable of pulling yourself away from your audience long enough to pay attention."

"Holly, please, let's not start this up again. Look, I said I was sorry. I had a little too much to drink, and you know how my mouth starts running."

"A little?" She chuckled sarcastically. "Alcohol is not an excuse. You've worn that one out. Why can't you just admit that you're—"

"Jealous? Is that what you want me to say? That I'm jealous of every man who looks at you? Hell yeah, I'm jealous. Do you want to know why? Because I've been in their shoes. I've been the man to pursue you...and I said goodbye to a wife and daughter in the process."

"Now, wait a minute! You'd been separated for a year and were two weeks from finalizing your divorce *when we met. Don't even think about playing that card."*

****

Whitney jumped, startled by his presence behind his desk.

"Sorry, Whitney. I didn't mean to scare you."

"I had no idea you were even here. I didn't expect to see you until next week."

"My plans changed at the last minute." He turned his gaze back to his laptop.

"I thought you and Rebecca were spending a few days at that Hill Country resort?"

"Rebecca had some unexpected travel come up at the last minute so no trip after all."

"Oh, I'm sorry."

He glanced over to the oversized cardboard mailing tube in her arms. "What is that?" he inquired.

"This was sent over by courier after you left yesterday. It's from CCA." She placed the container on his desk.

"Really?" He whistled, clearly impressed. "I had no idea they'd get these finished so quickly. We just walked the site a few days ago."

Whitney backed quietly out of the office. Will waited until the door was firmly closed before examining the contents of the tube. His heartbeat quickened with eagerness to see how the vision for The Albright Group world headquarters translated to paper in a formal architectural rendering. He removed the contents, carefully spreading out the collection of drawings. With a careful eye, he studied each one, his expression morphing from optimistic anticipation to dissatisfaction. Expectations had not been met. In fact, nothing Will expressed to the lead architect during their last meeting had been addressed. A whole day walking the site, totally wasted.

What happened to the fountains? And the underground parking access? The facade is entirely wrong. What the hell?

Without missing a beat, he reached for the phone, eager to express his extreme disappointment.

"Charlie Cross and Associates, how may I direct your call?" a cheerful operator asked.

"Seth Culver, please," he said firmly.

"One moment while I connect you."

Will waited, tapping his fingers impatiently on his desk. In another moment, his call was answered, but not by a human.

"This is Seth Culver. I'm away from my desk at the moment. Please leave a detailed message and I'll return your call as soon as possible. Thank you."

Will left a very detailed message, actually running out of time before he was able to nail down all his concerns. He hung up and sat in silence for another minute. *Should I call him back? Finish up my message?* He decided the urgency in his voice was enough to get his point across. He checked his watch against the clock on the wall and noted the time on his day planner. *If I haven't heard from him by lunchtime, I'll call back.*

The plans were rolled up and returned to the cardboard tube. His attention returned to his computer until his thoughts were interrupted by the phone a few minutes later.

"Will, you have a call," Whitney announced.

"Seth Culver?" he asked hopefully.

"No. It's Preston Patton. Would you like me to take

a message?"

"No, I'll take it," he sighed with disappointment. He depressed the button for the call. "General Patton," Will greeted the voice on the other end.

"Just calling to confirm."

"Confirm?" Will repeated, confused.

"Tennis? Tomorrow? Our court is reserved for—"

"Eight-thirty. No, I didn't forget," Will lied, scribbling a reminder on a Post-It note.

"Loser buys lunch?"

"I won't be able to stay for lunch, Preston."

"A sign of true cowardice. That's all right. I accept cash and personal checks."

"Fine. I'll see you in the morning."

"Listen, why don't you bring Rebecca along? I'm sure I could talk my wife into some mixed doubles."

"I would, but Rebecca is out of town."

"Don't tell me she's still soaking up the limelight on the press junket?"

"Not exactly. Just away on some other book business."

"Well, I guess it's for the best."

"What makes you say that?" Will inquired.

"It's bad enough you two are younger and better looking than me and Annie. You also smoke us every time we step on the court."

Will spent the remainder of his workday trying to get ahead for the following week. Lunchtime came and went, and eventually, he forgot all about the plans and the message for Seth Culver. It was after three o'clock before he remembered to call back. He reached for the phone, hoping to schedule a meeting for the coming week. He wanted to cash in his chips early and head home, leaving this loose end for Monday.

"Charlie Cross and Associates," a different but equally pleasant voice answered.

"Yes, my name is Will Albright. I'm trying to reach Seth Culver."

"Mr. Culver is out of the office until next Tuesday. Would you like his voicemail?"

"I left a voicemail message earlier and still haven't heard back from him."

"I can transfer you to his assistant if you like. She may be able to help you."

"That would be great. Thank you."

"One moment, please."

Will listened, amused by the choice of music that played on the line while he waited. It was anything but standard elevator, and he found himself tapping along to the beat of a club remix. But the high-energy sound disappeared in a few seconds, replaced by the sound of a woman's voice.

"This is Kris."

"Hi, Kris, my name is Will Albright and I—"

"Oh yes, hello, Mr. Albright. What can I do for you?" she asked enthusiastically.

"Well, I was going over the initial renderings this morning and—"

"You don't sound pleased."

"I'm not. In fact, to say I'm displeased would be a huge understatement."

"I'm so sorry to hear that. Could you be more specific? I'd like to take some notes to forward to Mr. Culver."

"Well, to be perfectly blunt, the whole thing is wrong. None of my requests have been addressed."

"Such as?" she probed.

"Everything. The entry. The parking. The facade. There are just too many items to list."

"I see." The woman said, sounding intrigued. "Would you mind if I put you on hold for a moment?"

"Of course not."

Again he waited. This time, the upbeat music he'd tapped along with before had been replaced with a soothing song from the seventies. He hummed along for a couple of minutes, curious as to what the woman's response would be when she returned to the line.

"Mr. Albright?"

"Yes.

"We'd like to schedule a meeting for Monday morning. Would you be available to come in around, say, eight o'clock?"

"Monday would be great, but the receptionist mentioned that Mr. Culver will be out of the office until Tuesday."

"You won't be meeting with Mr. Culver. After a mistake of this magnitude, the big boss wants to address your needs personally."

Chapter Eight

"Where'd everybody go?" Will asked, scanning his living room with a puzzled look.

"Home," Georgia answered.

"How was the bake-off? Think you're ready for tomorrow?"

"My croissants were perfect, but my focaccia was a little on the dry side."

"What time is your exam?"

"Not until one. I thought about maybe getting up early and giving it one more go, but I'm tired of bread. It's been my life for the last two weeks, and I'm done.

"So, you're toast?"

"Very funny." She rolled her eyes. "Listen, there's a ton of food left. My friend Lori made her famous southern pecan pie."

"I'm really not that hungry, Georgia."

"You haven't had much of an appetite lately." She gave him a hard stare.

"No, I guess I haven't."

Georgia continued to study him, not saying a word. She knew that if he waited long enough, Will would make the first move. He needed to talk. Georgia had known it for days.

"Can I ask you a question?" Will spoke after several moments of quiet reflection.

"You know you can ask me anything."

"When you and Danny were married—"

"I'm gonna stop you right there," Georgia interrupted. "What happened between me and Danny doesn't matter. Comparing you and Rebecca with us is beyond laughable."

"Don't say that."

"What? It's the truth. First off, you and Rebecca didn't come into your marriage dragging steamer trunks full of baggage behind you. Danny and I were doomed from the start. Two recovering addicts joining forces? Like that was going to work."

"It worked for a while. You were really happy for the first few years."

"Oh sure, we had some great times together. We loved to cook, we loved to travel. He had his music and I had…" Georgia stopped mid-sentence. "Will, listen to me. Danny and I never had anything like what you and Rebecca have. Did I love him? Absolutely, I loved him. He was the sweetest, most gentle soul I've ever known. Was it the kind of love to last a lifetime? Like what you and Rebecca share? Well, I think my singular presence answers that question."

"At what point did you start to question?"

"Question? Question what?" Georgia gave a confused look.

"Your life together. Your relationship. Your marriage." Will glanced down.

"What exactly are you saying?"

"I don't know. Things between me and Rebecca lately…it's hard to explain. All I want is to be with her. Then when we're together, all I want is to be somewhere else. Does that make sense?"

"You can love someone without liking them all the

time. Happens to everyone."

"There's this thing between us, tension or something. God, I don't know what it is." He exhaled heavily. "Every talk turns into a serious discussion and every serious discussion turns into a fight. On the rare occasions when we do talk, it's empty. It's like we don't even know each other anymore."

"Because of her book?" Georgia asked after a long pause.

A full minute of silence grew between them, and the delay of a response confirmed the validity of Georgia's question.

"This thing going on between the two of you won't last forever, Will," Georgia replied, trying her best to show encouragement. Only Will, preoccupied and confused, saw it from another perspective.

"That's exactly what I'm afraid of." He stood and left without another word.

****

"That's Patton...with two T's," Preston joked.

"Nice try." Will signed his name to a personal check and then ripped it carefully from his checkbook. "Please give Annie my love." He placed the check on the bench in front of the older gentleman.

"She doesn't want your love. She's fine with American currency."

"Now Preston, whether you acknowledge it or not, your wife works very hard. You know Rebecca and I are longtime supporters of the Symphony League. We're happy to donate. "

"She only does these fundraisers so she can buy something new to wear. Can't be seen in the same thing twice when it comes to all these events."

"I think you're getting off cheap. She has to live with you." Will smiled, tucking his pen back inside the inner pocket of his jacket.

"You know, I think we met Rebecca for the first time at a symphony event. You two were either newlyweds or just about to get married."

"Yeah, I remember that. It was the Jewel Ball, I think."

"I remember Rebecca wore this red sequined number." Preston Patton whistled. "Damn, Will. That woman of yours turned some heads that night."

"She does that quite a bit."

The man smiled. "What an amazingly striking couple the two of you were."

"Were? You mean we're not anymore?" Will teased.

"I didn't mean it like that. Of course you are. Just look up perfect couple in the dictionary and there you are, Mr. and Mrs. Wonderful." The man reached for his sports duffle. "What do you say? Meet back here in two weeks? With the ladies?"

"I'll have to check with the boss first, but that sounds great."

"Think she can hit a backhand in that red dress?" He gave Will a friendly elbow to the ribs.

The two friends emptied their lockers and exited the men's area, continuing to laugh and joke as they walked to the entrance of the tennis club. As was customary, the sunny skies and cool temperatures had prompted many outdoors, eager for some fresh air and exercise. Swinging his racquet by his side, Will now wished he'd taken up Preston's offer of lunch. He hated to go home to a quiet house. The comments Preston had made about a certain red dress conjured up some painful pictures in his mind.

"Hey, listen, does that lunch offer still stand…?" Will fished.

"Sorry, but I'm meeting the girls for lunch—some fancy tearoom."

"Well, have a good time." Will extended his hand.

"I'll probably hit Whataburger on the way home. Man cannot live by tiny cucumber sandwich alone."

He watched until his colleague disappeared from view from the double glass doors of the club. Standing alone in the entryway, he debated for a moment before beelining toward the restaurant. He took a seat at the bar and perused a menu, finding nothing that appealed to him. He watched the bartender for a minute as he mixed several pitchers of healthy, fruity drinks.

"What can I get you?" the bartender asked.

"What do you have on tap that's imported?"

"Nothing. Only domestic beer on tap."

"You got Guinness?" Will inquired.

"Nope. Sorry. No Guinness."

He considered his options for a moment, then slid off the back of his barstool. "I'll pass. Thanks, anyway."

Gear in hand, he headed toward the main doors. The restaurant was too crowded and noisy for his taste, anyway, making Patton's suggestion of a drive-thru burger sound better with each step. He searched his pockets for the keys to his car, ignoring the comings and goings of others around him in the lobby. He'd just made it to the reception desk when he bumped right into her.

"Excuse me, I'm so sor—" Will stopped,

immediately recognizing her.

"Well, hi." The dark-haired woman smiled.

"Hey! If it isn't Roadside Assistance?" he said playfully. "How are you?"

"Really good. And you?"

"High and dry at the moment."

"Did you make it on time? To your dinner, I mean?"

"Sat down right as the first course was being served."

He took advantage of the full daylight to examine her. She looked as though she'd stepped from the pages of a magazine and his heart beat a little faster than normal.

"I'm Will, by the way." He extended his hand.

"Charlotte." She shook his hand warmly. "Nice to meet you—officially, I mean."

****

Will sat alone at the breakfast table, polishing off the last of his burger. Without the uber health-conscious eye of his wife on him, he could do so without repercussions. An unnerving quiet filled their home, with Georgia away for the afternoon and Dizzy hiding out somewhere upstairs. It was becoming almost routine, spending the weekend hours trying to keep his mind occupied until Monday. He'd fought for sleep the previous night, replaying the short, disturbing conversation with Georgia. What had he been saying, exactly? The D-word? Call it quits? All because of a book?

With a sigh, Will mentally calculated the time difference while debating on whether to call Rebecca. Would she even answer? If she did, then what? More arguing? Luckily, fate decided for him, and his heartbeat kicked into high gear when her name appeared on his Caller ID.

"I was just about to call you," he answered.

"I wanted to check in and let you know that I made it all right." Rebecca's tone was soft and much calmer than when she'd exited his car at the airport.

"Have you eaten dinner yet?" he asked.

"We're on our way out now. I don't feel like going out, but Drew is running this show, not me."

"Are you meeting with the TV people?"

"Just the one executive that Drew's been working with. He'll make his pitch. We'll think about it. Then comes the counteroffer, and so on." She yawned. "How about you? It's what? Lunchtime now?"

"Yeah. Just finishing up a big salad."

"A big salad, huh? One with or without fries?" she asked after a moment.

"How'd you know?" he asked, dumbfounded.

"Because at lunchtime today, I committed the very same sin," she confessed with a laugh.

They talked for a few minutes. Will was surprised by the somewhat playful quality of their conversation. There were even a couple of occasions that elicited laughter, something neither had shared in a long time.

"Do you remember that time when we met for drinks at that little hole-in-the-wall bar?" he asked.

"Remember it? Are you kidding? That was the beginning of us."

"You left at least a dozen messages for me under the name Stefania. You walked into the bar with your hair pulled back, wearing that hideous blouse."

"It wasn't hideous. And besides, I was

undercover."

"Undercover?" Will laughed."More like over-cover. From head to toe. Like you'd just come from a 1940s librarians convention."

"I was going for tastefully conservative."

"It was conservative all right. Like a nun. But that's not what I remember. I remember dancing with you at that little club and thinking, God, how much longer do I have to play hide and seek with this woman?" He paused once more, summoning a much more serious tone. "I'm still wondering the same thing."

"Will, I have to be downstairs in five minutes. I can't have this conversation right now because it will just end in a fight."

"How much longer are we gonna do this, Rebecca?" he asked firmly.

He surprised himself with the directness of his question, and his heart started to pound. Looking down at his wedding ring, tears welled. He remained silent for a minute, praying she would offer up a truthful response.

"I honestly don't know," she said in a whisper.

****

Will walked confidently through the revolving door of the building. Housed on a busy corner downtown, the firm occupied an entire floor of offices. He took the elevator to the sixteenth floor, checking his watch. *Five minutes 'til eight. Right on time.*

The elevator doors opened to a wall of glass, bearing the familiar company logo. Behind it, a hub of activity loomed, as quick-paced people moved in and out of view. He gripped the chrome handle and made his way inside. A petite blonde woman sat behind a large reception desk and greeted him with a smile.

"Good morning."

"Good morning," he answered, recognizing her voice from Friday's call. "I'm Will Albright. I have an eight o'clock meeting."

"I'll let them know you're here." She reached for the phone.

"Thank you."

He took a seat on a leather sofa to the left of the entry, selecting a trade magazine from the sleek Lucite side table. He'd only flipped a couple of pages when the receptionist called his name.

"Mr. Albright, you can go through. It's down this hall, the last door on the left."

"Thank you." He stood and smiled, dropping the magazine back on the table.

His feet carried him down a long hallway. Glass walls revealed more employees busy at work, none bothering to look up. Reaching the last door, he paused for a moment to straighten his tie. Running his hand through his hair, he took a deep breath and grabbed the door handle.

A large desk, similar to the one in the reception area, filled most of the space. Behind it stood a woman, her back turned to him as she rifled through a drawer of pocket files.

"Good morning," he spoke, breaking the silence.

"Good mor—" She turned around, stopping cold when her eyes met his.

"Now wait just a minute…" He shook his head. *This is insane. Three times in a couple of weeks?*

"Well, well, my suspicions are confirmed. You, sir,

are a stalker."

"I can't believe this." He gave her a large grin.

"So, you're Will Albright?" She folded her arms across her chest, trying to hide her smile. "Future Hollywood stunt driver and wannabe tennis pro?"

He stood in silence for a minute, stunned by the unexpected twist of fate. "Not exactly. I can't believe you work for Charlie Cross."

"We've been together for years."

"I have to say I'm a little confused. Shouldn't I be meeting with my project manager?"

"Well, sometimes Charlie likes to meet with really important clients in person, just to get a sense of what the client is looking for. It helps keep the entire firm running smoothly. Charlie's big on oversight privileges."

"Well, it is his firm," Will answered. "I don't suppose you have any tips to share before I go in and face the old man?"

"Tips?" she repeated, confused.

"I have to say I'm a little nervous. I feel like I've been called to the principal's office."

"Really? And why is that? After all, we're here to please you, not the other way around."

"From what I've been told, Charlie Cross meets with no one. I understand he built this firm from nothing, and now he just sits back and lets his name do all the work."

"I can personally guarantee that Charlie's a little more involved than that. Shall we?"

She led him into a beautiful office that was even more impressive than he anticipated.

"Why don't you make yourself comfortable?" She

pointed to a large sitting area with inviting sofas and chairs. "Charlie will be here in just a minute. Can I get you something to drink? Some coffee maybe?"

"Coffee would be great." He nodded.

"Black? Cream? Sugar?"

"Straight up, thank you."

"I'll be right back." She backed out of the office with a nod.

Alone, Will tried to occupy himself with the elegant artwork and furnishings around him. He knew he had to do something. His heart was now beating a loud, guilty rhythm brought on by the sight of her serene blue eyes.

The office was nothing like what he'd imagined. It wasn't overtly masculine. It was tasteful. Elegant. Classy. Along one wall, plaque upon plaque of design awards. On the others, simple yet beautiful framed charcoal drawings, reminiscent of Picasso. He was just about to take a closer look when the door opened.

She entered with two steaming mugs, offering one to Will before placing the second on the coffee table.

"Thank you." Will smiled again.

"Anytime."

She positioned herself on a French period chair across from Will, offering yet another smile. An uncomfortable silence settled between them. Will's gaze bounced between the ornately carved door and the beautiful woman sitting before him.

"Cross is a coffee drinker, as well?" He tried to make polite conversation.

"An addict really, but with a little cream and sugar," she responded.

"You must get tired of sitting in on these meetings,

huh?"

"Well, I don't have much choice." She looked him squarely in the eyes and extended her right hand. "I'm Charlie Cross."

"You're Charlie Cross?" Will took her hand, shaking it cautiously.

"It's Charlotte, remember? But all my friends call me Charlie."

"And all this time I thought that you were—".

"A man? Don't worry, you're not the first and you won't be the last."

Will was utterly dumbfounded. He grinned, impressed by this smart, attractive woman yet again.

"So why 'Charlie Cross and Associates' and not 'Charlotte'?"

"It's a man's world, Mr. Albright. I don't have to tell you that. The fact is that clients tend to respond better when they think a man is at the helm."

"But isn't that deceitful? Some kind of reverse sexism?" he questioned.

"Not at all." She reached for her coffee with a smirk. "I like to think of it as beating the boys at their own game."

Chapter Nine

"You really saved us today, Steele. Great job," a dark-haired gentleman said, offering an affirming pat on the back in passing.

"Thanks, Ross."

"That last shot was bloody brill."

"Not really," Jack smiled. *"I just got lucky."*

"Glenrothes Eighty-Five or Old Pulteney's?" The man turned and hollered, just steps from the paddock door.

"What's that?"

"What's your preference? I'll have one waiting for you."

"No circus tent for me tonight."

"You're not staying?" the man asked, surprised.

"I'm afraid my presence is required elsewhere."

"With a much smaller party, I assume?"

"Actually, I've got a business meeting. And if I'm not on the road in five minutes, I won't make it."

"Don't you ever take a night off, Jack?"

"Never," he confirmed with a large grin.

The sun had set, and again he found himself last out of the paddock. Well-wishers and nouveau fans held him up following the match, all eager to offer congratulations. He knew that if he didn't pack up quickly, he'd never make it back to the hotel. The faint sounds of the band warming up beneath another canvas

75

tent echoed in the distance. The tournament sponsor, a well-known German automobile corporation, had spared no expense on the match's extracurriculars. But tonight, he planned to disappear into a glass of single malt and a pair of green eyes instead of the wealthy crowd now beginning to assemble on the other side of the field.

It had been almost two months since they'd danced together at Westbury. The scent of her hair and the glow of her skin were etched indelibly on his mind. He'd searched the crowd feverishly at Saratoga, hoping that perhaps she and Zander would make the event after all. Methodically he'd worked his way through the crowd, hoping to glimpse her dark hair or the shine of her smile. But every face belonged to a stranger, and he'd returned to his hotel feeling an emotion he rarely encountered: disappointment.

Gear bag swinging at his side, he walked to his car with a brisk gait. He checked his watch, trying to determine his ETA. A quick shower, then a cab to the address on the card she'd sent to his office the week before. With luck on his side, he'd make it to his destination on time. She'd given no real indication of why she wanted to meet. Only that she needed to discuss a benevolent cause. There'd been no other correspondence. No phone call or email to confirm whether or not he'd show. He chuckled, thinking about the last line of her handwritten note: I know you won't let me down, Jack.

He pushed open the heavy door and stepped in out of the wind, ducking his head to avoid a large wooden sign hanging from a low rafter. It took a moment for his eyes to adjust as he scanned the dimly lit pub. Standing just inside the doorway, he silently questioned her choice of location. Jack had spent years crawling the pubs of London, but this was one stop he'd never made. In fact, from the outside, he wouldn't have known that a drinking establishment operated behind the building's shabby facade. He'd even questioned the cab driver— twice. But checking the number on the door against the card in his hand, he was in the right place.

It was an intimate space, dark and smoky. A large group of what he supposed were regulars were stacked two deep around the bar, lifting pints and telling stories. In the far corner, another group assembled around a dartboard, quiet for several moments before erupting in laughter and cheers with each dead-on shot. Several gents at the bar turned to give him the once-over. With a hand through his hair and a slight smile, he made his way toward the back of the pub and the single empty table that remained. He was almost there when he felt the light touch of a hand on his shoulder.

He turned and instantly his heartbeat increased. As beautiful as she'd looked in red sequins two months before, she was now even more so, dressed in a black cashmere turtleneck sweater. Her hair danced on her shoulders and framed her face in soft waves.

"Mrs. Deming?"

"Tonight, it's Holly," she corrected gently, taking his outstretched hand in hers.

She directed him to another table where her jacket lay draped over the back of a chair. On the table sat the remains of a Black & Tan alongside a flickering votive in a dark green hurricane lamp.

"I'm sorry I'm late." He pulled out her chair. "But I'm glad you didn't wait."

"I knew you'd be here, eventually. How was the match?"

"We won." He sat down across from her, careful to keep a cushion of space between them.

"Congratulations."

"It wasn't our best effort, but when you stick a bunch of aging executives on horseback and put them up against the best and the brightest...well, you've seen it firsthand."

"You're an excellent player, Jack."

"So is your husband. Just where is the honorable Mr. Deming this evening?" He looked around the bar. *"His team could've used him out there today."*

"Back in New York. He had some business come up. Last-minute thing. You know how it is."

"And he left you here all by yourself?" he teased.

"Well, I've been in London for over a week, finishing up some of my work."

"The environmental article?" He motioned toward the bartender. *"For National Geographic, right?"*

"How did you know I was—" she started, completely stunned.

"I do my homework, Mrs. Deming." He shared a sly smile.

"What am I going to have to do to get you to call me Holly?" She returned his smile.

"I don't know," he said, unable to control his flirtatious nature. *"How about we make a list?"*

****

Rebecca stood waiting inside the restaurant, watching as her agent tried to secure a cab in the downpour. She'd been met with rain when she landed three days earlier, and unfortunately, it continued to fall. They had finally settled the particulars of the deal, and she had a week to mull over the final proposal. Drew was elated, having several offers to entertain. Truth be told, she was ready to be done with the whole thing. What started as a silly experiment on a dare had quickly become a monster—one which had driven a wedge between herself and her husband.

A cab pulled up to the curb outside and she watched a young couple, laughing and smiling, quickly file out. They ran to the safety of the restaurant's entrance, not even bothering with their umbrella. It wasn't until they were inside, removing their raincoats, that Rebecca recognized the beautiful young woman.

"Lily!" Rebecca called out to her.

"Rebecca?" she responded with surprise.

They exchanged a hug and a kiss on each cheek. Rebecca took a step back to examine the young woman fully.

"Lily!" Rebecca shook her head. "It's so good to see you. What are you doing here in London?"

"We live here. This is my fiancé, Maks." She gave the tall man beside her a smile. "Baby, this is Rebecca, my wicked stepmother. Well, former stepmother, that is."

"I think you made a mistake." He held out his hand. "She looks more like the Fairy Godmother type."

"Fiancé? But you're not old enough to get married. And why aren't you in school?"

"Because I'm not six years old anymore," she said with a smile.

The two women chatted for several moments before they were interrupted by the sound of Drew's voice calling out.

"Rebecca, the cab's here." He stuck his head back inside the door of the restaurant.

"Oh, Drew, I want to introduce you to someone…" She motioned for him to join her.

Introductions were made and the party of four blocked the doorway for another five minutes. Rebecca listened as Lily shared the goings-on in her life in the years since they'd seen one another.

"So, you're acting now?" Rebecca confirmed.

"It's a small production, but I love it."

"Well, that's truly all that matters. How is your mother?"

"She's fine. She found spiritual enlightenment and moved to Sedona about two years ago. She lives on a reserve with a group of hippies—extremely privileged, wealthy hippies, of course. I'm sure she meditates on a Gucci mat or something."

"Wow. And Kelly?" Rebecca dropped her ex-husband's name.

"What can I say? Kelly is Kelly. You of all people should know that better than anyone."

"He's still living in Sydney?"

"I wouldn't exactly call it living. It's more like existing."

"What do you mean?"

"He's sold off most of his major interests. He spends as much time on his boat as he can, like some old reclusive Papa Hemingway type. I don't see much of him. In fact, no one does."

"So, his obsession with the corporate world…?"

"Is no more. We talk several times a week. I think he's happy to be out of the rat race."

"Well, well." Rebecca smiled. "Good for him. I

honestly didn't think he knew the meaning of the word 'retirement'."

"Rebecca, we really should be going." Drew glanced out the window at the waiting cab.

She reached for Lily's hands. "It was such a treat to see you, sweetheart, I'm thrilled that you're so happy and I pray you always will be."

The two women embraced. Drew helped Rebecca into her raincoat, and they made their way to the door. She turned around one last time and called out her name.

"Lily?"

"Yes?"

"Take care. And the next time you talk to your father, please give him my best."

****

"So, what did you think?" Charlotte asked, searching her purse for her keys.

"I think that I've had a fabulous day," Will said.

"I'll get right on those ideas that we discussed first thing tomorrow. I should have something ready for you by Thursday."

"Anytime is fine. I'm just honored that you're handling the project personally."

"Well, again, I'm so sorry about the mix-up. Switching your specs with another company's project is—"

"Would you stop apologizing? Please? It was an honest mistake." Will paused. "Hey, listen, if you're hungry, I know this great little diner where we could—"

"Mr. Albright, it's a quarter to midnight."

"I told you, it's Will. And it's okay, it's a twenty-four-hour joint."

"I certainly appreciate the offer, but you've spoiled me enough for one day."

"Well, I can't thank you enough for sharing your work and your insight with me. The field trip was a great idea."

"It didn't hurt that you just happen to have a private plane at your disposal either."

"I'm blessed to have a few good friends who are obsessed with flying. They've given me carte blanche with their aircraft whenever I need it."

"Why can't I find friends like that?" Charlotte laughed.

"I really enjoyed myself today and I learned a lot. Scale, urbanism, fenestration, spandrel. You're an excellent teacher." He studied her bright blue eyes.

"I want you to be happy with the final product. I'll do whatever it takes to see that happen."

"So you're thinking Thursday, huh?"

"If I don't go home and get some sleep, it'll be Friday."

"I'm sorry. Forgive me." He opened the car door for her. "Please drive safely."

"I will. And thanks again for a wonderful day." She slid in behind the wheel.

"Keep an eye out for falling bumpers."

"You too. Goodnight." She looked up at him and smiled.

"Bye, Charlie." He smiled back.

Will closed her door firmly and watched until the taillights of the car disappeared into the night. He slipped his hand inside his pocket for his keys and headed toward his car.

"Mr. Albright?" a voice called from behind him.

"Yes?" He turned around.

"You forgot your cell phone."

He took the phone from the pilot's hand. "Thank you. And thanks for working overtime tonight. I really appreciate it."

"Happy to do it."

"I'm sorry again about the last-minute notice."

"It's no problem, sir. Anytime."

In minutes, Will was on the highway, making his way home from a long yet productive day. Very productive, in fact, and full of surprises. Sitting in Charlie Cross's office that morning, he'd had no idea what he was going up against. In fact, he still couldn't believe it, though he had spent the entire day with the head of the prestigious firm. A consummate professional, she played personal tour guide, showing him several buildings around the Dallas area that she had designed. They discussed everything from architecture to microbreweries in their time together and shared a lot of laughter in the process. The day had flown by. After seeing her work firsthand, Will gained a better sense of what he wanted and was certain that he'd made the right choice. Listening to her expansive knowledge of her field, he was more impressed than ever.

Monday quietly ticked over to Tuesday as he turned his key in the door. Dizzy sat waiting and barked loudly as Will, still wearing a smile, entered the house.

"Where the hell have you been?" Georgia rolled off the sofa, questioning him with a sleepy yet accusatory voice.

"I told you. We flew up to Dallas for the day."

"And you couldn't answer your goddamn phone?"

"The battery's dead, and I didn't have a charger on me."

"Rebecca has called here at least a dozen times."

"What's wrong?"

"Her father had an accident. He fell down the basement stairs. He was out cold when they found him. I don't know if he blacked out or what. Maybe he just slipped. Anyway, he's got a pretty bad gash on his head. Fourteen stitches. Probably a concussion. And he broke his hip."

"Which hip?"

"The other one this time. They'll probably have to replace it, too."

"When did this happen?"

"I don't know. Rebecca called around four o'clock."

"What would that have been? About midnight in London?" He tried to make a quick mental calculation.

"There about." Georgia nodded. "She's taking a flight directly to Atlanta."

"I need to get a flight, too." He pulled his cell from his pocket, forgetting that it was dead. "Georgia, would you mind—"

"I'll take care of it. Why don't you call Rebecca and let her know you're home?" Georgia held out her cell phone to him.

Will made his way upstairs with the dog on his heels. Inside their bedroom, he closed the door and breathed a heavy sigh. He patted Dizzy's head and then called Rebecca's cell. Instead of his wife's voice, he was directed to her voicemail instead.

"Babe, it's me. You're probably in the air right now. Georgia is working on getting me a flight out first thing in the morning. Please call me when you get on the ground, okay?" He paused for a moment, overcome with a sense of guilt. He'd spent the whole day laughing—hell, borderline flirting—with another woman when his wife needed him. "Everything will be okay. I promise."

****

Drew gave Rebecca a supportive hug before parting ways at Atlanta International. She'd only spoken with the hospital once and had no idea the progress, if any, her father had made during the night. Thankfully, his injuries weren't life-threatening, but his failing health made the idea of surgery frightening.

She'd checked her phone while waiting at the baggage claim area but hadn't had a chance to return Will's call. The tone of his message had been one of genuine concern. Of course, he would want to fly out to offer whatever support might be needed. Will had a wonderful relationship with her father and would be there despite their marital tensions—tensions that hadn't been addressed before her trip to London. Phone to her ear, she waited, thankful when he answered on the second ring.

"Are you on the ground?" he asked.

"En route to the hospital now."

"You sound exhausted."

"I am, but I'll be okay once I get to see him."

"He's doing all right. He actually had a pretty good night."

"You talked to the doctor?" Rebecca was surprised.

"No, I spoke with the man himself. I'm here at the hospital."

"You're already there? But how?"

"I wanted to be here when you got here. Between Georgia and Nick Garland's private plane, we made it happen."

"I should be there in about an hour."

"I'll let him know his favorite person is on the way."

"He's really okay?" she questioned.

"He's in and out. Obviously, the painkillers have taken control, so he's not himself. The doctors are very optimistic."

"And his head? The concussion?"

"Very minor," he assured her.

"I'm glad you're there," she said. "Not just for my father...but for me, too."

"I'm not the only one. There's someone else here who can't wait to see you."

"Georgia came with you?"

"No. Hold on." There was a pause as Will handed the phone to someone.

"Darling, it's me," a woman said.

"Mom?" Rebecca whispered.

Chapter Ten

"I had no idea the Angel of Death would be so beautiful," Leland Graham whispered as his daughter entered his hospital room.

"How're you feeling, Dad?" Rebecca asked softly.

"Much better now that you're here." He focused on his daughter's face.

"If you wanted me to come home, all you had to do was ask," she teased, taking his hand as she sat on the edge of the hospital bed.

"What can I say? I've always had a flair for the dramatic." He gave her hand a light squeeze.

"Yes, I know. Is that why you decided to sneak down to the basement by yourself?" She gave him a hard stare.

"I've already endured the third degree from Dr. Patel and your husband. Should I prepare myself for a sermon from you, as well?"

"But you know those steps are steep. You've slipped on them before. Why didn't you just let Melba help you out?"

"Melba was out, and I wanted a bottle of Shiraz," he cut her off, now visibly annoyed. "And frankly, I'm tired of being treated like an invalid."

"No one thinks you're an invalid, Dad. But there comes a time in life when everyone must face their limitations."

"I've traveled the world. Flown in bombers. Slept in trenches. Watched men suffer and die for God and country. If I want a goddamn bottle of wine with my goddamn dinner, then I should be able to go down and get one without anyone's assistance or permission."

Rebecca lowered her gaze, now focusing on the wrinkled hand she held. Something about her father's hands had always intrigued her. They'd convicted her with heavy judgment and consoled with the softest and most understanding touch. The years were beginning to leave their mark, and his strong hands were now those of a frail man trying desperately to hang on to disappearing years.

"You're right. You're absolutely right." She resumed eye contact with him, looking to pursue a different angle.

"Damn right I'm right." He nodded.

"I mean, you're Leland Graham. You're the man who became one of the youngest war correspondents in the Korean War, right?"

"Yes, I did." He gave a nod of confirmation.

"The man who stood bravely behind enemy lines, snapping shot after shot of the hellish demons of war, right?"

"Scariest days of my life," he added.

"The most celebrated photojournalist of his time and the man single-handedly responsible for the success of National Geographic magazine?"

"According to some circles. Very small and heavily liquored up circles, but still…"

"You've been everywhere and have seen everything?"

"I racked up quite a few miles in my day, yes. And

that was *before* frequent flier miles."

"Well, far be it from me to tell you what to do," she said with an undertone of sarcasm.

"You know, your reverse psychology has no effect on me whatsoever," he said after a long pause.

"Then maybe my straightforward psychology will." She locked her eyes on his, speaking with a tone that rivaled her father's. "Keep your goddamn ass out of the goddamn basement."

Leland's haughty expression quickly transformed into a smile, and he gave his daughter's hand another squeeze.

"It's hell getting old, you know?" He sighed.

"But it certainly beats the alternative," she countered.

"That it does, my dear." He smiled once more. "I'm sorry. I'm just a grumpy old man who's feeling sorry for himself, I guess."

"It's time you stopped. You're going to be fine. Dr. Patel is very confident."

"That's because Dr. Patel is not an old man with two bum hips."

"Do me a favor? Do yourself a favor?"

"What?"

"Just be pleasant. Please? And let us help you."

"No offense, sweetheart, but I've seen your idea of help." He rolled his eyes.

"What's that supposed to mean?"

"You brought my ex-wife to my deathbed."

"I did not bring your ex-wife here. Melba called her, and she flew down. I didn't even know she was here until I spoke with her on my way in from the airport. In fact, I didn't even know my husband was here." Rebecca shared another serious look. "You, of all people, should know that no one manipulates my mother into anything."

"She's a master manipulator." He rolled his eyes.

Rebecca reached and brushed a strand of white hair off his forehead. "She's here for the same reason you flew to New York and sat in her hospital room for two days last year."

"Well, you know what they say. Keep your friends close and your enemies closer."

"Dad, I hope you haven't—"

"I've been a perfect gentleman, I promise."

"Well, just remember that she did give birth to me, so she can't be all bad." Rebecca winked.

"Where is she?"

"She's down the hall in the waiting area with Will working on the game plan."

"Game plan?" The old man raised an eyebrow.

"How best to take care of you once we get you out of here."

"I don't expect you to stay here and play nursemaid to an old man. You've got more important issues to deal with. Your book and the—"

"Nothing's more important than you, and I won't be doing it alone. Mom and Will will be with me. They've already arranged to have a hospital bed delivered. We'll set you up in the study since it will be a while before you can navigate the stairs and—"

"Your mother's planning to stay? With me? I mean, with us?"

"Of course. It was her idea to move you into the study. She may not be your wife anymore, but she still cares about your wellbeing."

"And if I doth protest?" he asked in a staunch voice.

"An intelligent man like yourself? You know better." She grinned.

****

Rosalie Graham stood and stretched before taking a short stroll to the windows. The sitting area left much to be desired. She struggled to find a comfortable position in the boxy, unyielding chairs. The entire morning was spent watching her son-in-law do the same while they waited for Rebecca. Ever since her daughter's arrival at the hospital, an unsettling feeling had quietly gnawed at her. It began the moment Rebecca stepped onto the third floor of Regents Hospital. Behind the safety of a magazine, she watched as Will greeted his wife halfway between the elevators and the family waiting area. They hadn't seen each other for days and the reception she witnessed sent up a red flag.

It wasn't the first of such flags. She had the same unsettling feeling several weeks before when Rebecca breezed in and out of New York, finding only enough time to grab dinner. Her normally animated daughter sat with little expression, quietly picking at her food. It only took a few minutes for Rosalie to recognize that Rebecca was completely preoccupied. The demanding pace was wearing on her. Rebecca blamed her mood on extensive travel, but Rosalie now guessed it was probably the product of marital disharmony.

"Rebecca is out of gas," she said to Will, returning to her chair.

"She does look tired," he agreed.

"You should take her back to Leland's. You could both do with a rest. I'll take it from here."

"I think I'll let you pitch that ball to your daughter." Will fidgeted in his chair.

"Why? You don't think she'll leave?"

"Do you?" he asked.

"No," she answered with a heavy sigh.

"I think the best plan would be that we spend the day here and then we *all* go back to Leland's this evening. We won't do him any good tomorrow if we're all exhausted."

"You're right."

"I've been telling you that for years." He winked.

The small talk continued until the door to Leland's room opened and Rebecca made her way toward them.

"Well?" Rosalie asked, standing and dropping her magazine on the chair behind her.

"It's all settled. I told him that he has the three of us at his beck and call," Rebecca said.

"And he's okay with it? My staying in the guest house?"

"Okay? He's thrilled." She smiled.

"Babe, your mother wasn't born yesterday." Will gave her a look.

"He's right. Thrilled is a little strong, don't you think?" Rosalie folded her arms across her chest.

Rebecca held her hands up in concession. "Okay, okay…but he did promise to be on his best behavior."

"We'll see," Rosalie said, her eyebrow now cocked.

They spent the afternoon hours gathered around Leland's bed. Will and Rebecca enjoyed real laughter for the first time in weeks as the former Mr. and Mrs. Graham entertained them with their unique brand of humor. A late visit from Dr. Patel answered their questions and affirmed their makeshift schedule.

Surgery would be followed by a minimum of three days in the hospital. After being discharged, Leland was required to attend daily sessions at a physical therapy rehab unit. Rebecca watched her father's face screw into disappointment as the doctor spelled out the coming weeks of his life. Leland Graham thrived on self-sufficiency. Handing over the reins was not his nature and asking for help was ordinarily out of the question.

The doctor excused himself, suggesting they all do the same. Will stood and stretched, exchanging a knowing look with his mother-in-law. She quickly followed suit, taking her purse and coat before moving beside her ex-husband's bed.

"Is there anything you need before we go?" she asked in a soft, sincere tone.

"Youth," Leland answered sarcastically.

"Well, I can't help you there. I'm afraid I'm running low on that myself."

"I beg to differ. You're as beautiful in your seventies as you were in your twenties."

"We really should go." She locked eyes with Rebecca, sharing a large grin. "The drugs are starting to kick in."

"I'm glad you're here, Rose." Leland held out his hand to her. "I mean it."

"We'll see you as soon as you're out of surgery." She gave his hand a tight squeeze.

"Dad, are you sure you're okay? I can stay here tonight if you think—"

"Absolutely not. Will, take her home," Leland commanded.

"Yes, sir." Will gave a salute.

"If you need anything at all during the night, no matter what time—" Rosalie added.

"Will, can you get them out of here? All this constant mothering—" Leland repeated.

"We're going, we're going, " Will answered with a smile, draping Rebecca's coat around her shoulders.

****

The ride back to Rebecca's childhood home was painfully subdued. Rosalie sat in the backseat of Will's rental car, silently watching his eyes in the rearview mirror. Rebecca sat beside him, her face and thoughts turned toward the landscape out her window. Their interactions at the hospital would have fooled most but they couldn't fool her. A certain spark that usually shined brightly between them was barely a flicker and the lack of physical contact confirmed her suspicions.

"Why don't you two take the guest house? I can stay in Leland's room—until he's home from the hospital."

"We can stay in my old room. We usually do anyway."

"There's so much more room out there. It's much more private. There's only one of me, and I hate—"

"I'd actually feel better if we were all under one roof," Will offered.

Rebecca agreed. "Me too. The guest house isn't exactly convenient, and they're still working on the new stone pavers out front. The last thing we need is you slipping and falling."

"Rosalie, you take Leland's room, and we'll stay in Rebecca's old room."

"Well, I just hate to be in your way."

"You won't be, but if you're feeling guilty, you can

make it up to us by whipping up some of your famous crepes in the morning before we head out." Will shared a wink in the rearview mirror.

The idea of dinner at a nearby eatery was vetoed in favor of a quick stop at a local market where Rosalie snagged ingredients for her world-famous clam chowder. The three sat around the large farmhouse table in the oversized kitchen where Rosalie happily assumed the role of hostess in her former domain. Together, they chopped vegetables and revived precious memories of Rebecca's younger years on the vast country estate.

"Mom, do you remember that time that Dad and Uncle Alford rode into town to the bar?"

"Of course I remember it. I had to go and bail them out."

"When was this?" Will asked, again intrigued by another classic tale.

"I guess you must have been about eight." Rosalie looked at her daughter. "We'd had a few friends over. It was during the holidays. Just an impromptu little dinner party."

"'Little' meaning about forty people," Rebecca added with a wink in her husband's direction. "And the word impromptu is a lie. This woman plans everything down to the nth degree."

Rosalie continued. "Anyway, Leland and Alford had a little too much to drink that night. When they ran out of spirits around eleven o'clock, they decided they were going to go make a run into town. But Claudia and I hid their car keys because they were in no condition to drive. So what did they do? They saddled up two horses, rode into town and right inside the Red Carpet

Lounge."

"They rode the horses inside the actual bar?" Will grinned.

"Right up to the bartender, where Leland Graham proudly placed his order—Johnny Walker Black for everyone in the house."

"He's got style. And good taste," Will confirmed with a nod.

"You know, the arresting officer said the very same thing." Rosalie smiled at him.

"Do you ever hear from Alford and Claudia?" Rebecca asked.

"No."

"Who are Alford and Claudia?" Will inquired.

"They were our closest family friends at one time. Claudia was Mom's business manager."

"Here in Atlanta or New York?" Will asked.

"Here. This was years ago. We met through a mutual friend," Rosalie said.

"She bought Mom's very first painting. Promoted her work to everyone."

"Eventually she ran my gallery," Rosalie added.

"Are they still down in Florida?" Rebecca asked.

"I have no idea. I don't keep tabs on Claudia anymore." By the tone of that response, Rebecca decided to change the subject.

"I'd go for a third helping, but I'd only make myself sick." Will stood, collecting empty bowls around the table. "Once again, Rosalie, you've outdone yourself."

"Here, let me get those." Rosalie stood.

"Absolutely not. Go put your feet up, Mom. We've got this," Rebecca said.

Chapter Eleven

Will stood at the sink in silence, rinsing glasses and trying to decide how to address the subject that had weighed heavily on him all day.

"What time would you like to roll out in the morning?" he asked.

"His surgery isn't until ten, so maybe eight-thirty? That should give us plenty of time to see him before he goes under."

"Your mom and dad are quite a pair," he offered after another moment of silence.

"I think you mean a handful." Rebecca smiled.

"Why do they do it?"

"Do what?"

"Argue ad nauseam. I mean, it's obvious they still love each other."

"Oh, they're crazy about each other," Rebecca stated matter-of-factly. "The arguing is just for show. Have to keep up the appearance that they're happy in their solitude."

"Did you see the way they were looking at each other?" Will began. "At one point, I thought your mother was going to crawl into that hospital bed with him. And that comment about how she's still as beautiful as ever?"

"I've been telling you for years, only you swore it was my imagination."

"I guess I haven't been around the two of them together enough to notice."

"For a couple that's been divorced as long as they have, they certainly keep a close eye on one another."

"I think it speaks volumes that neither one of them remarried."

"I think they both secretly hoped they'd get back together. In fact, I have indisputable evidence that my father is still deeply in love with my mother. Come with me."

She led him to her father's study, a private oasis where he spent the majority of his time. Standing in the darkened doorway, she turned to her husband.

"Take a look at this…" She flipped the light switch on.

Leland's study filled with light. Above the mantle hung an enormous black and white photograph housed in a simple black frame. The subject was a beautiful young woman in a black, sleeveless dress. The shot was candid, the young woman having no knowledge that she was being photographed. The image was a contradiction in itself; her innocent, distant expression contrasted against the long slim cigarette in her hand.

"What's Audrey Hepburn doing hanging in your father's study?"

"Right? She was very Audrey, wasn't she?" Rebecca's eyes locked on the photograph of her mother.

"Wow!" Will took a few steps closer. "Does your mom know it's hanging up in here?"

"I don't think so. Takes your breath away, doesn't it?"

"Where's he been hiding this?"

"I don't know. I haven't seen it in years."

"What was hanging up there before, when we were here over the fourth of July?"

"I don't even remember. A shot from one of his safari trips, I think."

"When was this taken?"

"Back in the sixties. Dad was vacationing in Venice. He just happened to be taking a coffee break at a cafe across the street from where my mother was sitting. He shot an entire roll of her that afternoon. She had no idea, of course. Want to know a surefire way to piss off my dad? Tease him about being a stalker."

"I wonder why he decided to put this up now?"

"I'm not sure but it all makes sense."

"What makes sense?"

"At the hospital, I mentioned that we'd made arrangements to have a bed delivered and that we'd set him up in here. I said it was Mom's idea, and she'd be staying here." Rebecca sighed. "And then suddenly my father seemed very nervous."

"Because his secret would be revealed."

"Exactly." She nodded.

"Well, the composition is fantastic. It looks like an old movie still."

"She was beautiful, wasn't she?" Rebecca regarded her mother's image with admiration.

"Gorgeous." Will turned to his wife. "Like mother, like daughter."

Just that one small compliment and Rebecca felt the weeks of icy distance start to melt away. He took a step toward her and held out his hand. She reached out and took it, a familiar warmth enveloping her heart. He led her over to the small loveseat near the fireplace and they sat side by side, fingers intertwined.

"I sat in that hospital room today watching two people who clearly love one another struggle with some very intense issues. People dealing with strong feelings of regret. I don't want to end up like those people, Rebecca."

"Will, I—" she started, but he cut her off.

"Please, let me finish. I sat there today and thought about all the regrets in my life—the vast majority of which have been the result of my recent behavior."

Rebecca focused on the sincerity in his eyes.

"I didn't read your book. Not all of it anyway. Just to the point where I was mad as hell. That's my biggest regret to date—not taking a genuine interest in your work. Especially when you have always been supportive of mine." He paused and took a deep breath. "Babe, I am so very proud of you. I guess I've just been too jealous to show it."

His admission took Rebecca by surprise. Not the fact that he hadn't finished her novel; she'd suspected as much, knowing that if he'd read it cover to cover, he would have seen that it was indeed a true work of fiction. It was more that her self-assured, always-confident husband was feeling something that he rarely encountered—jealousy.

"I want you to know that I finished it, read the whole thing on my flight out here," he confessed.

"Okay." Rebecca held her breath, curious to hear his honest opinion.

"It's a beautiful story. Hauntingly beautiful." He gave her hand a loving squeeze. "If I'd just taken the time to read a couple more chapters, I would have seen that the similarities ended when the story took a whole new twist. Was I mad that some of our more private moments found their way into it? Yes, I was. Those are our moments. Our feelings and our words."

"Maybe I was wrong to include some of the things I did. I'm sorry that it upset you. That was certainly not my intent. The challenge was to write an amazing love story…and I only know one," she said in a whisper.

"I'm honored that you felt my words were worthy enough to find their way inside your book because I meant them when I spoke them, just as I mean them now."

"It was never about hurting you, Will."

"I know that. And I'm sorry. For so many things."

They curled up together on the loveseat and quietly studied the photograph of Rosalie for several minutes. Will spooned his body beside hers, his arm draped across her waist. Rebecca's feet found the warmth of his and it didn't take long until they found themselves in that loving, secure place.

"I'm sorry I had to cancel our weekend getaway," Rebecca whispered.

"There'll be other weekends," he said, placing his hand atop hers.

Silence filled the room once more and Rebecca listened to the sound of his breathing. Nothing relaxed her more than lying beside him and feeling his arms around her.

She didn't move until she felt the light touch of her mother's hand on her shoulder.

"Sweetheart?" Rosalie whispered.

"What?" Rebecca sat up with a start, waking Will in the process.

"What time is it?" he asked, trying to read his

watch.

"It's almost midnight," Rosalie answered. "Wouldn't you two be more comfortable upstairs?"

Will yawned then stood and collected his shoes from the floor. "I'll see you in the morning. Don't forget my breakfast order." He placed a kiss on his mother-in-law's cheek in passing.

"I'll be right up," Rebecca said with a yawn.

She stretched and motioned for her mother to join her. Rosalie smiled and snuggled up close to her grown daughter. Rebecca reached out for her hand, wrapping it tightly inside her own. She examined it closely, just as she'd done with her father's hand earlier that day. It looked very much like her own. In fact, many swore she was a replica of her mother. Almost everything about them was similar: their frame, their smiles, the way they moved and gestured. Leland was forever stopping her when she told a story with her hands, swearing how much she resembled her mother.

Rosalie wore very little jewelry. Just an understated yet expensive watch on her left wrist and a simple diamond-encrusted band on her right pinky. The ring had been a gift from her father many years before. It was sort of an inside joke between the two of them, one that Rebecca had never been able to get the full story on. The ring finger on her left hand was bare and had remained so for almost thirty years. There had been one man in her life besides her father, just a couple of years after they'd divorced. She remembered spending a series of holidays with them on her visits home from college. Bill Parker, Rebecca suddenly recalled his name. He had been nothing like her father. He was quiet, passive, attentive, and compliant to a fault. Even his name was nondescript and safe. Maybe that was why her mother sought his company.

When the subject of marriage eventually came up, Rosalie promptly ended the relationship and stopped seeing him. Aside from the odd dinner date over the years with a host of successful gentlemen, she never made a lasting connection. Rebecca knew there was only one relationship in which her mother would willingly invest her energy. When that ended abruptly decades earlier, she'd thrown herself into the only other relationship that brought her comfort—that of her artwork.

They held hands for a long time without a word between them while Rebecca silently replayed her husband's observations in her mind.

"I hated to wake you. You looked so peaceful."

"I'm glad you did,"

"Are you okay?" Rosalie asked.

"Yes."

"You're sure?"

"Yes. Why?"

"Because I'm worried." She pulled back and looked her daughter squarely in the eye. "About both of you."

"We're fine, I promise." Rebecca turned her eyes back to the photograph above the mantle. "Tell me about that girl."

Rosalie studied the image of her former self for several moments before speaking.

"Well, for starters, that girl had no idea about the dangers of smoking. No one did back then. Of course, she wasn't really smoking. I think the few times she did inhale she was sick in bed for days, but she thought it made her look very sophisticated."

"What else?" Rebecca probed.

"She was trying to convey an air of confidence, but only because she felt so incredibly inadequate."

"That girl?" Rebecca pointed at the picture and laughed. "That girl doesn't have an insecure bone in her body."

"She did back then. Oh, darling, she was very naive. Like a country mouse in the city."

"Well, she certainly played the part because she's the picture of confidence."

"They say the camera never lies, but it did that day." Rosalie sighed.

"No, it didn't. You just never saw yourself as others did. Or the way Dad saw you—and sees you still."

She waited for her mother's response, hoping to draw something deep and emotional from her. She knew those feelings were in there, having witnessed them throughout the day in Leland's hospital room. In classic Rosalie form, she side-stepped the comment and pulled the conversation back to the original topic.

"You know something? She spent every cent she had on that dress. And it fell apart after two washings," she said with a chuckle.

"So, what do you think about it?" Rebecca pressed once more.

"About the photo? Or the fact that it's hanging there?"

"Both."

"It might be the greatest compliment your father has ever paid me."

"I think so, too." She squeezed her hand.

"You haven't told me about your trip?" Rosalie changed the subject.

"It was fine. I ran into Lily."

"Lily?" Rosalie searched her memory for a moment. "Kelly's Lily?"

Rebecca nodded. "She's living in London now. She's an actress, engaged to a very handsome European chap named Maks." Rebecca gestured for dramatic emphasis. "She's absolutely beautiful. Looks just like her mother."

"I wonder what her mother's up to these days?"

"I asked her that very question. She's living in Arizona at some spiritual enlightenment camp."

"And did you ask about Kelly?" Rosalie inquired.

"She said that he's officially checked out of the rat race. Spends all his time on a boat in Sydney."

"Kelly Glass?" Rosalie looked at her daughter with confusion. "He actually stopped working?"

"I said the same thing. Lily says he's quite content and pretty much a recluse these days."

"Another Howard Hughes?"

"Well, I wouldn't go that far." Rebecca laughed.

"What about Gloria? Did she mention how she's doing?"

"No, we only chatted for a few minutes. They were coming into the restaurant just as we were leaving. Drew had a cab waiting, and it was pouring rain—"

"Gloria adored you." Rosalie smiled. "You know she still sends me birthday cards and Christmas cards every year without fail? She's never missed one."

"She sends them to me, too," Rebecca confessed.

"What a beautiful, giving person. Always so gracious and thinking of others. How she could raise such a self-absorbed son…" Rosalie shook her head.

"Mom, I'd rather not." Rebecca held up a hand in protest.

"All right." Rosalie gave her daughter's hand a loving pat.

"We really should get to bed," Rebecca said just as the quarter-hour chimed from the clock in the hall. "I told Will I'd be right up."

"Are you sure everything's okay between the two of you?" her mother asked once more.

Rebecca looked away, not wanting to say it out loud. "The last few weeks have been really tough."

"He's having a hard time with the success of your book, isn't he?" Rosalie gave her a hard stare.

"It's not just the book, Mom. He's got a very full plate right now. His entire starting line-up retired, and he's had to field a new team from scratch. Then there's the new HQ. But you know Will, he won't turn it over to someone else. He has to personally oversee every single detail. He's working very hard and—"

"And isn't it just like the good wife to make excuses for her husband's bad behavior?"

"I'm not making excuses. It's the truth. We're being pulled in opposite directions. And yes, it's been difficult, but we'll get through it."

"I hope he's as understanding about your workload as you are of his."

"I'm not going to lie. There's been some jealousy."

"Well, just remember that there are worse things in a marriage besides jealousy."

"Really? Like what?" Rebecca asked.

"Pride," Rosalie answered firmly.

Chapter Twelve

"*Ms. Mitchell?*" *the man inquired with a heavy Brooklyn accent.*

"*Yes?*" *Holly answered from behind her locked hotel door, trying to hide the alarm in her voice.*

"*Flower delivery for you.*"

"*Would you just leave them outside?*" *She stared out the peephole, but her view was obscured by an enormous collection of sunflowers, lilies, roses, and snapdragons.*

"*I would, lady, but I gotta have a signature or my boss will have my head. Know what I mean? I'll be outta your hair in two seconds.*"

"*Uh, all right.*" *She sighed and looked down, quickly taking note of her less than appropriate appearance. "One minute.*"

She darted around her suite in search of the robe that matched the cream silk nightgown she wore. After a moment, she found it hanging on a hook in the bathroom. Pulling it tightly around her, she secured the sash at the waist and opened the door.

"*I'm sorry, it's just that—*" *she began.*

"*I'm not interrupting anything, am I?*" *His head popped out from behind the large bouquet.*

"*Jack! What are you—*"

"*I got your note. I just wanted to stop by and check on you and to bring you these.*" *He held out the large vase.*

"They're beautiful."

"Beautiful flowers for a beautiful woman."

"You certainly didn't need to."

"I wanted to," Jack insisted with a grin.

"You're wicked good at accents. I really thought you were a delivery guy."

"Just one of many hidden talents."

They stood in the doorway of her luxury suite for a minute, surrounded by silence. Holly knew there was only one way of escaping the magic of his expression. Just say thank you and politely close the door. You can do it.

"Are you feeling better?" he asked with genuine concern.

"A little." She nodded.

"Is there anything I can get for you? I think I passed a twenty-four-hour pharmacy on the way over."

"I'm fine, really."

Their conversation quieted once more. Seeing him there, dressed in a classically-cut tuxedo, she could feel her resolve melting away with each second that passed between them.

"Listen, I know you need to rest, but there's some unfinished business to address. I know you have an early flight and—"

"Unfinished business?" she repeated, confused.

"The fine print, as they say."

"I'm sorry but I don't quite follow."

"That night in the bar? The night you talked me into participating in this little soiree?"

"I didn't realize that we'd—"

"Would you mind if we had this conversation

inside?" He gave a stealthy glance over each shoulder. "I try not to discuss contract particulars in hotel doorways."

She smiled. "I'm so sorry. Please come in."

Holly retreated and Jack's eyes scanned the elegantly appointed room as he entered, stopping at the closed bedroom door.

"Would you like something to drink?" She crossed the room toward the small corner bar.

"I've met my quota for the evening."

"Please, sit down."

She motioned to the large sofa in the center of the room. Jack gave another smile before taking a seat. Holly followed suit, taking her place beside him but leaving enough distance to keep them honest. They sat staring into each other's eyes for several moments. Holly felt her heartbeat increase, and the intense migraine she'd fought earlier that afternoon showed signs of returning.

"When I got your message, I thought that maybe Zander made it in and—" Jack began.

"Zander's idea of a charitable contribution is allowing his wife to carry the ball for such affairs."

"Not one for crowds, huh?"

"You can have Zander's time or his money but not both."

"Can I add your name to that list as well?"

A searing heat rushed through Holly's body, head to toe.

"I don't think I ever told you how disappointed I was when I showed up for the Vaquero Cup in Dallas last week and found your husband flying solo. I was hoping to see you again before tonight."

Holly's heart pounded as she recalled feeling a similar disappointment when a last-minute assignment from her news agency kept her from attending the polo match—especially when she'd dreamed of a face-to-face reunion with Jack for weeks.

"Your presence was sorely missed tonight, too," he added.

"I'm sorry. I hope you know that."

"There's no need for an apology. I'm just glad you're feeling better. We raised a lot of money that will benefit a lot of underprivileged children. I wish you could have been there to witness the fruits of your labor firsthand. I'm also sorry the public was deprived of seeing you in whatever fabulous dress you'd planned to wear."

He inched closer. Holly fought hard against the current of his blue eyes. "So, these contract particulars you mentioned..." she said, desperate to change the subject.

"Ah, yes, the fine print." His smile was questionable.

"Why do I get the feeling I'm about to be had?"

"Hey, they're the terms we mutually agreed upon. I'm just making sure this venture is above board."

"I still don't know what you're talking about."

"When the fine folks over at Steele and Company signed on to help sponsor this charity event, we did so for two reasons."

"Reason one?" she inquired.

"We believe in giving back to the community. Without community, we don't exist."

"I see. And reason two?"

"Oh, I'm afraid you won't like reason two." He shook his head with a serious look.

"Why not?"

"Because it's incredibly egocentric and self-serving. You promised me a dance."

"A dance?" She laughed.

"That's what sealed the deal, remember? I said I'd help foot the bill if you agreed to one dance." He held her eyes, putting all humor aside. "Now I kept my end of the deal, and I'm here to see that you follow through with yours."

"Oh, Jack..." She shook her head. "You can't be serious."

"I've never been more serious in my life."

Jack stood and held out his hand with a determined look in his eye,—one that told Holly he wouldn't take no for an answer—not that she could ever see herself turning him down. His face was the first thing she saw in the morning and the last thing she saw in the seconds before she fell asleep. Months of emails and phone calls in preparation for the charity gala had catapulted Jack Steele from casual acquaintance to the center of her most private thoughts. With each passing correspondence or contact, the pictures she'd created in her head became exponentially clearer. A life with Jack Steele. That was all she wanted.

"Well, I'm hardly dressed for a spin around the dance floor." She reached and took his hand.

"Why don't you let me be the judge of that?"

With his right arm around her waist, he slowly danced her around the suite. Softly, he hummed a familiar tune in her ear—the same Jimmy Webb song they'd danced to months before after the polo match.

"Red sequins or white silk," he whispered, his hands gently massaging her back. "You look and feel

incredible."

"*Jack...*" *She stopped and pulled back.* "*I'm married.*"

"*Married women don't dance?*"

"*Not when they're alone in a hotel room, no.*"

"*Am I making you feel uncomfortable?*" *he asked.*

"*You're making me feel too comfortable.*"

"*And what's wrong with a little comfort?*"

"*I don't think I can do this.*"

"*Do what?*"

He traced the line of her bottom lip with his thumb, silencing any chance of a reply as his lips pressed against hers. She'd dreamed of this moment from the time he'd held her under the white canvas tent at Westbury.

Holly Mitchell had done what no other woman had been able to do, though many had tried. She'd captured him.

"*I can't tell you how long I've wanted to do that,*" *he whispered.*

Chapter Thirteen

The lighthearted antics that filled Leland's hospital room before his surgery followed them home. Despite his obvious pain, the old man put up a brave front on his first day out of the hospital, determined to keep them entertained. Will could see it was time to let the patient rest. He exchanged knowing glances with both his wife and mother-in-law, protectively positioned on either side of Leland's bed. Will parked himself in the corner of the study, dividing his attention between a copy of *The Wall Street Journal* and the conversation in progress.

"Thoughts for dinner? What sounds good to you, Leland? I can run and pick up whatever you want," Will asked.

Rosalie stood. "Way ahead of you, Will. I've already got dinner planned. In fact, I better get started."

"Really, Rose, that's not necessary," Leland interjected.

"I want to." Rosalie smiled. "Besides, I miss my old kitchen."

"We'll help you, Mom," Rebecca offered.

"Why don't you get some rest, and I'll make sure these two stay out of trouble? Call my cell phone if you need anything." Will stood, giving his father-in-law a wink.

"Is Rack of Lamb Persillade okay?" Rosalie asked,

standing in the doorway of the study.

"Rack of Lamb?" Leland asked, surprised. "You mean your mother's recipe?"

"Just the way I used to make it for you," she said proudly.

"With the roasted potatoes? The ones with rosemary?"

"As a matter of fact, yes."

"What's the catch?" The old man raised a wary eyebrow.

"There's no catch. I just thought you might enjoy one of your old favorites for your first night home."

"Actually, I've been enjoying one of my old favorites ever since she flew in from New York," Leland responded with a genuine smile.

****

They were just steps into the kitchen when Will's cell phone rang.

"Well, that didn't take him long." Rebecca laughed.

"It's not your father calling, it's Georgia." Will checked the display screen. He answered cheerfully but his playful expression changed, and Rebecca stood frozen beside him, knowing the call didn't bring good news.

"My name is Albright. Will Albright. Yes, she's my sister." He spoke with a serious tone. "And what time was this?" Will motioned frantically for paper and pencil, which Rebecca produced in a matter of seconds. "What hospital? Thank you very much." He ended the call and turned to his wife.

"Will?" She scanned his eyes.

"Georgia was in a car accident."

"What? Who was that?"

"One of the paramedics on the scene. He found Georgia's cell phone in the car and called the last number on her phone log."

"Oh my God." Rebecca's hand shot to her mouth. "What happened? Is Georgia okay?"

"I don't know. The guy said that she was in an ambulance on the way to the hospital now."

"Was it just Georgia? Or were other drivers involved?"

"He didn't say. I don't know anything." He stared through her, making mental notes.

"Oh, God, Will, I'm so sorry." Rosalie took a step closer and touched his arm. "I'm pretty sure there's a nine-thirty flight on United. If you two hurry, you can—"

"But what about you and Dad?" Rebecca began.

"I took care of your father for years before you came on the scene. I think I can manage."

"But he's got therapy every day for the next two weeks—"

"Sweetheart, Georgia needs you and Will. We'll be fine. I promise. Now go upstairs and get your things together. If you like, I can call the airlines to see if—"

"No, I've got my laptop upstairs. We'll take care of it," Will answered.

Rebecca followed her husband upstairs in silence, praying for Georgia's safety with each step. She could see that Will was now in crisis mode, quietly going over a multitude of scenarios and preparing for any number of outcomes. Always the picture of calm, though inside she knew fear gripped him.

She darted around her childhood bedroom, gathering up an assortment of items and dumping them on the bed. She was just about to retrieve her suitcase from the closet when he placed his hands on her shoulders.

"I want you to stay here," he whispered in her ear.

"What?" She turned around to face him.

"You know as well as I do that your mother cannot do this by herself. Just getting your father in and out of the car today was a monumental task. If we leave her here alone, she may wind up in the same condition. It's not like Melba can help much either. She's pushing seventy."

"I don't want you to be alone at the hospital, and we don't even know Georgia's condition." Her voice trailed off and the first of several tears slid down her cheeks.

"I'll be fine. Georgia is going to be okay. I just know it."

"But what if Georgia is…I mean, what if it's more serious?"

"Then you can fly back home. Until we know for sure, I think the best thing is for you to stay here. Your mom needs you. I know she says she doesn't, but the last time she took care of your dad, she wasn't a seventy-something-year-old woman with blood pressure issues."

"I know. It's just that…"

"What?"

"I'm tired of living our life between emails and phone calls. I'm tired of always saying goodbye."

The weeks of separation had created a bitter wall between them. Yet, through the misfortune of her father's accident, they'd spent the last few days slowly finding their way back to one another; a knowing look, a tender touch. A soft embrace. Seeing the love that still existed between her parents helped her realize the importance of acceptance and forgiveness within a relationship—two concepts that had become foreign to both of them. While they weren't back to normal by any stretch, it was definitely a start.

"It'll just be for a few days. We're going to have to divide and conquer on this one, babe. I need you to be strong."

"I don't want you to go," she whispered, taking solace in his arms.

They held each other for a long time, neither saying a word.

"Can I tell you something?" He finally broke their silence.

"What?"

"I'll never get tired of hearing you say that."

****

"Excuse me, miss," Will said to the backside of a woman standing behind the counter in the hospital E.R.

"Yes?" She turned around.

"I need some information on a patient."

"Name?" she asked, taking a seat in front of the computer.

"Georgia Albright-Hall."

"Will?" Georgia called out.

Will turned to see his sister emerge from the waiting area just beyond the information desk. There were no visible signs that she'd been injured in any way, which immediately elicited opposing feelings of thankfulness and confusion.

"I'm sorry, sir." The woman shook her head as she clicked on her keyboard. "But my records show that—"

"Never mind," Will interrupted. "I found who I'm looking for."

He thanked the woman, then turned and walked briskly toward Georgia.

"You're okay?" Will inspected her from head to toe.

"What the hell are you doing here?"

"I got a call from an EMT that you'd been involved in a bad accident and had been transported here."

"What? No. It's not me, but a friend of mine—Jacqueline. And why would an EMT call you?"

"An EMT called me on your cell phone and—"

"Because my phone was in my car. Christ, Will, I am so sorry."

"What the hell's going on?"

"It's a long story."

"Where's your car?"

"In a ditch, totaled. My God, Will. I am so sorry for the mix-up."

Georgia's bottom lip quivered. Will pulled her in for a hug. Her body immediately turned into a limp noodle as she released a downpour of emotion.

"How long have you been here?" he whispered.

"I don't know. Hours."

"Have you eaten?"

"No."

"Let's go get something to eat. Then, let's get you home. I'll bring you back and I'll sit here with you for as long as it takes, but you need to rest a bit."

In the car, Will turned on the radio to help diffuse the silence. Georgia was still visibly upset, so he didn't press for details. A twenty-four-hour diner was just a short drive from the hospital, and it was better to wait and get the whole story after filling Georgia with a cup of coffee at the very least.

They arrived in minutes. A friendly woman escorted them to a quiet table in the back. Once the coffee was delivered and firmly in hand, Georgia took a deep breath.

"Jacqueline's in pretty bad shape."

"How bad is 'pretty bad'?" Will questioned.

"Broken femur, ankle, collarbone, and wrist. A lot of cuts and bruises. Not good for anyone, especially not a diabetic."

"What exactly happened? And how did you manage to escape without a scratch?"

"I escaped because I wasn't even in the car."

"But the EMT guy found your cell phone and called me—"

"That's the long part of the story. A group of us got together to practice for an upcoming exam. About an hour into it, I got one of my massive migraines. Like a Mack truck hit me—it was bad. I asked Jacqueline if she'd drive me home because I obviously couldn't drive in that condition. She got me home, in bed, and then I told her she could take my car home."

"And you left your cell phone in the car?"

"Yes, and evidently, Jacqueline didn't have any ID on her…"

"The EMT assumed the phone was hers."

"I guess so. I'm so sorry you dropped everything to come back home."

"That's what families do."

"There's one more thing. My car is totaled, or rather the car you bought me is totaled. I've already spoken with the insurance adjuster and—"

"I don't care about the car. I'm just thankful that you're okay and that your friend is alive." Will reached across the table, resting his hand supportively on hers.

"I know what you're thinking."

"No, you don't."

"You might not be thinking it right at this moment, but I know you were thinking it after you hung up with the EMT. You thought I'd run a dozen lines and plunged off a cliff, didn't you?"

Will held his twin sister's gaze for a long time, knowing full well that she could read his mind.

"The only coke I'm running these days is the cola variety. I'm clean, Will. And for the last three years, happier and stronger than I've ever been. You and Rebecca have given me everything—a home and support to live out my dream of becoming a chef and owning my own restaurant one day. I'm not about to blow it—no pun intended."

****

"Will?" Rebecca answered the call in a sleepy voice.

"We're home," he said with a sigh, falling back against the pillows on their king-size bed.

"Home? She's okay then?"

"She wasn't even in the car. Her friend Jacqueline was driving, lost control, and flipped into a ditch. Georgia's phone was in the car and the EMT thought it belonged to Jacqueline."

"Oh my God, how awful and scary. How's her friend doing?"

"She's got a long road ahead of her. Georgia spent all day at the hospital. She's wiped out and blaming herself. I'm praying this doesn't, you know, cause her to have any personal setbacks."

"Georgia is stronger than she's ever been. She's gonna be okay. Be sure and give her the biggest, tightest hug for me, and tell her how much I love her."

"I will. How was your night?"

"Oh, it was fine. Just great," she answered.

"Do I detect a hint of sarcasm?"

"Well, if I have to hear about that damn cornucopia one more time."

"Cornucopia?" Will asked, confused.

"The subject of the monumental, knock-down, drag-out fight of my childhood. My mother had her florist make an enormous cornucopia every year as the centerpiece for our Thanksgiving table."

"How could a floral arrangement spark the fight of the century?"

"Easy. Take a houseful of guests, one stressed-out hostess, an overcooked Thanksgiving turkey, and one crabby old man who's just polished off his third martini. Shake well and serve."

"Sounds ugly."

"Oh, it was ugly all right."

"And they're still rehashing it?"

"Until I rang the bell and sent each to their respective corners."

"Do you want me to come back out?" he asked. "Just let me get Georgia's car situation settled and I can fly back out in a couple of days."

"My mom and I can handle it. I'm sure you have plenty to do there."

He silently leafed through a stack of phone messages Georgia had slipped him. Just a couple from Whitney and the remainder from Charlie Cross and

Associates.

"Actually, there are a few things in the works that need my attention."

"Mom is planning to fly back to New York in a few days. I should stay here until she leaves."

"Absolutely. I know they'll enjoy having you all to themselves. I'm just in the way, anyway."

"Now, you know that's not true. My parents adore you."

"They adore you. They tolerate me," he teased with another yawn.

"Why don't you say goodnight? You've been up for almost twenty-four hours."

"Rebecca?"

"Yes?"

"Hurry back to me," he requested in a whisper.

"As soon as I can," she whispered back.

Chapter Fourteen

"Good morning." The woman looked up with a cheerful, yet surprised expression.

"Good morning. Is Ms. Cross in?" Will asked.

"Yes, she is," the woman answered. "Do you have an appointment, Mr...?" She quickly checked the computer screen in front of her.

"It's Albright. Will Albright. And no, I, uh, don't have an appointment. Just several urgent phone messages from Ms. Cross." He fanned himself with several small slips of paper. "I've been out of town, and she's been trying to reach me."

"Of course, Mr. Albright. If you'll have a seat, I'll let her know you're here." She smiled and picked up the phone.

"Hey, Houdini!" Charlotte rounded the corner and approached Will with an outstretched hand.

"Houdini?" he questioned with a grin.

"I'm, of course, referring to your great disappearing act."

"I've been in the Atlanta area for the last few days. A family emergency. I apologize for not touching base." He shook her hand.

"I'm sorry to hear that. I hope everything's okay."

"Everything's fine."

"Good. Would you like to see the new HQ for The Albright Group?"

"Only if you're ready to share."

She returned to the desk and pressed the intercom button on her phone.

"Yes?" a voice answered.

"We're ready for the Albright renderings."

"Of course, Ms. Cross."

"Thank you." She turned back to Will. "It should just take a few minutes. Would you like something to drink? Some coffee or hot tea?"

"I've met my coffee quota for the day, but thank you."

They engaged in light discussion while waiting for the plans to arrive. Their conversation was cut short by a rap on the door. A tall man in an expensive suit entered, carrying with him an oversized leather portfolio underneath one arm.

"Will, this is Brooks Schroeder. Brooks, our client, Will Albright."

The two men shook hands and exchanged casual pleasantries. Mr. Schroeder placed the portfolio on a large conference table on the other side of the room and then left them alone.

"Will, would you like to do the honors?" She gave the portfolio a nudge in his direction.

"Of course."

He grinned and reached for the zipper closure. In seconds, he flipped the case open to reveal the plans for his new corporate headquarters. The first page featured the front elevation of what she now referred to as his campus. He studied it silently for several moments, completely in awe of her ability to turn his thoughts and ideas into lines and angles. They more than encompassed the look and feel he was after.

"You don't like it," she said with a slightly deflated tone.

"Are you kidding?" He looked up at her. "It's more than I could have ever imagined. It's fantastic. Exactly what I wanted."

"Are you sure?" she questioned.

"I don't know how you did it, but you pulled together all the different styles that I said I liked and somehow made it work. And that was no easy task."

"Actually, you made it quite easy. You're the kind of man who knows exactly what he wants—all I had to do was listen. After our field trip to Dallas, I had a pretty good idea of what you were looking for."

"This is more than a pretty good idea. It's dead-on."

"Well, I'm pleased that you're pleased. There's more to it than just the outer elevation—much more. Unfortunately, I'm meeting with another client this morning." She quickly checked her watch.

"Oh, I'm so sorry. I didn't mean to keep you."

"I'd reschedule, but this meeting got pushed back two weeks ago and—"

"Please, you don't owe me an explanation. I realize I'm not your only client."

"Could we meet later today or tomorrow? Whatever's good for you?" she suggested.

"I have a four-thirty today and a dinner engagement tonight. I haven't been back in town long enough to know where I'll be tomorrow."

"Listen, why don't you take the plans home with you? Take a good look at them, and jot down some notes too—things you like or don't like. Concerns or changes you'd like to make. We can talk in a day or two and go from there. How does that sound?"

"That sounds like a great idea."

"That's what you're paying me for, remember?" she replied with a wink. "Great ideas."

****

Will walked with a brisk gait across the parking lot. He skipped the long valet line, opting to self-park in the lot next to the restaurant. Their dinner reservation was for seven-thirty, and he'd be on time with only sixty seconds to spare. Inside the upscale eatery, Will's eyes scanned in search of his dinner companion before conferring with the maître d'. He was escorted through the main dining room, where his business associate motioned to him with a discreet wave.

"Where there's a Will…" The man stood and offered his hand.

"Trent. Good to see you." Will shook it firmly.

"Let me guess. You got thrown in jail."

"I got thrown in the middle of a medical emergency," Will answered, releasing his hand and taking a seat. He placed his cell phone on the table and motioned to a member of the waitstaff.

"It's not Rebecca, is it?"

"No, Rebecca's fine. It's her father."

"The grumpy old man with all the great war stories?"

"That's the one. He fell and broke his hip while fetching a bottle of wine from his basement."

"Hey, I can think of worse ways to go."

"Me too." Will smiled.

The two men discussed a multitude of topics before finally getting down to business. They hammered out the details of a merger between smaller divisions within their companies. By the time the check arrived, they'd exchanged another handshake, sealing the deal like gentlemen of a bygone generation.

"Will, please…" Trent tried to snatch the check from Will's grasp.

"Absolutely not." Will handed the waiter his credit card.

"Well, next time then. I insist."

"That makes two of us. We'll bring the wives next time. I know Rebecca would love to see Marisol again."

The words had barely left his mouth when he noticed the sudden change in his colleague's body language. The man across the table didn't respond but pushed his unused salad fork back and forth between his thumb and forefinger.

"Did I say something wrong?" Will inquired.

"Marisol and I separated six months ago," he responded after a long silence.

"What?" Will sat stunned. "What happened?"

"She got tired of waiting around."

"Waiting around? For what?"

"Me," he answered.

"What do you mean?"

"I mean, she is officially resigning her position as corporate wife. Our divorce will be final next month."

"But, Trent…" He forced a smile and lowered his voice as the waiter returned with his credit card receipt. "I don't get it. You're one of the happiest couples I know. You're perfect together."

"There's no such thing as perfect, my friend."

"Damn. I don't know what to say."

"There's nothing to say. I devoted an endless amount of time and energy to hundreds of profitable investments, except the one that really mattered. Leave your wife alone in a cold bed long enough, and she'll find someone to fill your space."

"Wait. Marisol had an affair?" Will whispered, raising an eyebrow.

"As hard as it is for me to admit it, yeah, she did."

"Oh man, I'm so sorry. I had no idea."

"Don't be sorry. It's no one's fault but my own."

"There's no chance that you and she will—what I mean is, have you thought about marriage counseling? You two have been together, what? Fifteen years? Rebecca doesn't have her practice anymore, but I know she'd be willing to sit down and talk with you—both of you."

"Counseling isn't an option. It's not what she wants. *I'm* not what she wants. Not anymore. It was over between us before she got involved with what's-his-name. We'd been living separate lives for a while."

"So that's it? Over and out without a fight? That doesn't sound like you."

"Like the song says, you gotta know when to hold 'em and know when to fold 'em." The man raised his highball glass and downed the last of his drink.

With this comment, Will knew it was time to drop the subject. The two men stood and made their way to the front of the restaurant where Will shared a supportive pat on the back with his dinner guest.

"Let's get the paperwork drawn up so we can put this deal to bed."

"I'll have my team start on it first thing," Will promised.

"Hey, give my best to Rebecca and her father. I hope the old man is feeling better soon."

"Will do."

The men parted ways at the valet stand. Will continued toward his car parked in another lot just a few hundred yards away. He slipped his hand inside his pockets, finding the keys in the left, while the right felt strangely empty. *Damn! My phone!*

Will made a U-turn and retraced his steps back to the restaurant. Their table was being cleared, but his phone sat untouched. He quickly retrieved it, slipping it into his pocket. Walking back through the crowded space, there was another wave of patrons standing wall-to-wall in the main entrance, impatient for a table. The shifting of bodies in and out of the bar area forced Will to stop momentarily. It was then he saw her.

She was sitting alone at a small round table near the bar. Dark hair, which had been pulled back earlier that morning, was now down in loose waves and flipping up ever so slightly at the ends. The conservative suit she'd worn had been replaced with a fitted cashmere sweater in a rich charcoal tone. The burgundy-colored tablecloth fell to the floor, leaving him to wonder if the ensemble included pants or a skirt. Attention focused on her phone, Will guessed that she was in the midst of sending someone a text. Seconds later, his phone vibrated, and once again, his hand slipped into his pocket.

He didn't recognize the number but knew it had to be her.

—Mtg. tomorrow @ 10 just canceled. Can meet if you have the time to discuss renderings.

He smiled while reading, amazed at the coincidence of being mere steps away from her.

Text her a reply...or walk up and deliver my

response in person?

This internal debate lasted all of two seconds. Will loved the element of surprise and couldn't resist. Maneuvering through the swarm of people standing shoulder-to-shoulder, he made it to the table without her ever looking up.

"Ten o'clock sounds great," he announced with a smile.

She looked up, her blue eyes both surprised and intrigued. "But how…"

"I was passing by the bar when I got your message and, well, I just happened to glance in here and that's when I saw you."

"Either that's the greatest coincidence of my life or you really are a stalker."

"I promise, I'm not a stalker. I just finished a dinner meeting with an associate."

"You're on your way out, then?"

"Yes."

The bartender arrived with a selection of at least six different beers—the majority of which Will had never heard of. He gave Will a friendly nod before depositing the bottles and retreating.

"I'd tell you to have a nice evening, but it looks like you're heading in that direction."

"To be honest, this is research."

"Research?"

"When I first moved here about ten years ago, this was one of the very first restaurants I tried. Now I'm sort of a regular around here. And Slats here…" She pointed to the elderly bartender. "He and I have become really good friends. We've established a certain tradition that we celebrate every year."

"A tradition that revolves around beer?"

"I sample all his latest finds every year on this very day."

"Why this particular day? Is it National Hops Day? Barley Appreciation Day?"

"It's her birthday," the old man hollered from behind the bar.

"Slats!" Charlotte's head snapped in the bartender's direction, and she shook a finger at him in reproach.

"Sorry, Chuck. No sense in keepin' it a secret."

"It's your birthday?" Will asked.

"Actually, yes," she said, somewhat embarrassed.

"You're telling me that you sit here every year on your birthday sampling beer from around the world?"

"Some are local craft beers, but yes."

"By yourself?"

"Yep."

"Excuse me if I'm out of line, but why?"

"Well, I guess because I like quiet celebrations…and beer." She laughed. "Would you care to join me and sample a few for yourself?"

"I don't know. I wouldn't want to mess with tradition."

"Take a seat, mister. If you like good beer, it's the finest birthday party you'll ever attend," the bartender called out.

****

It took Will several attempts to get his key in the door. Finally, after dropping them on the ground twice, he unlocked the door and slipped inside where he found a worried Georgia waiting.

"And just where the hell have you been? It's after

one o'clock. I was about to call the cops."

"Jamaica, Finland, Brazil, Norway, the Netherlands." He laughed. "Oh, and Denmark, too. Can't forget our friends, the Danes."

"That must be one helluva deal brewin' between you and Trent. Or maybe just a lot of brew." She locked on his bloodshot eyes. "I'd say you're way past tipsy and now registering in the full-on drunk range. How'd you get home?"

"By the grace of God."

"You mean you drove home? In your condition?" Georgia raised her voice. "Are you insane or just stupid? You're supposed to be the responsible adult, Will. Playing the fuck-up is my game."

"G'night, Georgia."

Will disregarded the third degree, climbing the stairs toward his waiting bed while ignoring Georgia's continuing admonishments from below. He'd spent three hours with an intriguing brunette, surveying an assortment of international spirits and exchanging sports trivia, all while laughing hysterically. When they finally agreed to call it a night, after several toasts and a rousing version of the Happy Birthday song, Will stood up to find he was something that he hadn't been in quite a while—blissfully happy. Visibly drunk, but happy no less.

****

The phone rang a fifth time, and he silently cursed Georgia for not answering it. It was a little game she liked to play—her unique form of punishment when Will had overindulged the night before. Georgia made no attempt to make his environment a quiet one, compounding his hangover.

"Georgia!" he yelled, annoyed. "You win! Answer the goddamn phone."

No response, but the phone stopped ringing. *Finally!* He turned over, pulling a pillow over his head to block out all sound. Seconds later, however, his cell phone rang, forcing him out of bed to silence the infuriating noise. It took a minute, but he found his pants lying on the floor in the bathroom and quickly fished the phone from his pocket.

"Will Albright," he answered sluggishly, with eyes closed.

"Did I wake you?" a woman inquired.

"Birthday or no, let's just say my passport is full." He laid back on the cool tile floor in the dressing area to calm his pounding head.

"Your passport?"

"That last trip to Denmark was a doozie."

"Will, what are you talking about?"

"Rebecca?" He sat up with the sobering realization of the party on the other end of the call.

"Who'd you think it was?"

"Oh, good morning." He hesitated. "I guess I'm still half asleep."

"Are you okay? You don't sound very good."

"I had dinner with Trent last night to finalize the details of the merger. Then on my way out, I ran into, uh, Charlie Cross in the bar. We had a few drinks together and to borrow a phrase from Georgia, I guess I was over-served."

"Over-served in Denmark?" she questioned.

"Danish beer."

"Oh, I see."

"How's your dad this morning? And your mom?"

133

He quickly changed the subject.

"Fine. We're leaving for the rehab center in a few minutes. How's Jacqueline?"

"I haven't gotten today's update yet."

An awkward silence fell between them as the pounding in Will's head moved down into his chest. His heart beat wildly and the alcohol that still pulsed through his veins was replaced with something much stronger: guilt.

"Are you sure you're okay? You don't sound like yourself."

"I'm fine. I overindulged a little, that's all."

"You really should try to get in bed at a decent hour tonight."

"I promise to do just that."

"Call me later?"

"I will. At the usual time."

Another moment of silence developed, and for the first time in their relationship, Will was at a loss on how to end a phone call with his wife.

"Will?" She again broke the silence.

"Yes?"

"I love you," she whispered.

"I love you, too."

Chapter Fifteen

"And this is what I got for Mom..." Hillary held up
a beautiful gold-beaded evening bag. The design was
both exquisite and playful, in the shape of a beehive
with jeweled bumblebee accents. *"I debated between
this one and a black and white clutch shaped like a
peacock. It was gorgeous too, with Austrian crystals.
But the beehive is just too perfect. I mean, every woman
named Honey should carry a beehive-shaped evening
bag, right?"*

Holly sat across the room on a sleek chaise, Irish
coffee in hand, staring blindly into the fireplace and not
hearing a word. Though the flames warmed the living
room of her sister's posh Manhattan apartment, she felt
cold and had since she'd returned from Los Angeles.

"Holly?"

"What?" She continued to stare, lost in thought.

"Mom's gift?" She held the purse up once more.
"Do you think she'll like it?"

Holly's eyes met those of her much older sister.
Sitting amid a mass of festive holiday trimmings,
however, the society-minded elder Mitchell daughter
appeared very childlike. Christmas was, by far, Hillary
Mitchell-Payne's favorite time of year. Her husband's
immense Wall Street success made her the most
generous of gift-givers. Even though she had the means
to hire a fleet of elves, she enjoyed purchasing and

wrapping presents on her own.

"Cute," Holly commented softly.

"Cute? A six-thousand-dollar hand-beaded Judith Leiber? The best you can muster is 'cute'?"

"I'm sorry. It's beautiful. Really beautiful. Mom will love it." Holly forced a smile before taking another sip of coffee.

"Are you okay?" Hillary abandoned her gift wrap duties and joined her sister on the chaise. "It's the most wonderful time of the year..." Hillary sang, trying to lift her sister's spirits.

"Hill, don't. I don't feel like singing."

"What is wrong with you? Ever since you came back from that big charity event, you've been a million miles away."

"I'm just not into it this year."

"You're not into what? Christmas?" She gave a hard look. "Are you kidding me? You love Christmas."

"I'm tired."

"You know what I think? You miss him. You miss him like mad."

Holly didn't respond but turned back toward the fireplace. She couldn't give an honest answer. Not when they'd be talking about two different men. She did miss him. More than she could ever verbalize. From the moment he'd slipped his arm around her waist on the dance floor at Westbury, he'd captured her. And now, every part of her longed to be touched by every part of him. Though they'd shared just the one kiss inside the privacy of the hotel suite, she wanted more. But a wedding ring kept those desires in check, creating a pang of guilt that turned her snow-white holiday to slush.

Hillary continued in a teasing tone. "Of course you miss him. Who wouldn't? I mean, how could anyone resist your husband? That man can charm the pants off anything—animal, vegetable, or mineral."

"Hill..." Holly shook her head.

"And even a few men, I suspect. Not that he'd ever be inclined, of course."

"Just stop it! Okay? Please?" Holly snapped.

"Something is wrong. Listen, if you want to talk about it—"

"There's nothing to talk about."

"Did something happen between you and Zander?" she asked after a lengthy pause.

"Hillary, please." She looked into her sister's eyes. "Let it go? Please?"

"I'm worried about you." She reached and held Holly's hand. "Something's going on. I don't know what it is, and if you'd rather not talk about it, then I won't press you. But I want you to know that I'm here for you."

"I know you are, and I love you for it." She squeezed Hillary's hand.

"Your mood wouldn't have anything to do with Jack Steele, would it?"

A pregnant pause was followed by Holly slipping her hand from Hillary's grasp. She reached for the beaded handbag, pretending to inspect it.

"Of course not! What would give you that idea?"

"Come on, Holly. This is your big sister you're talking to. I walked so you can run, sweetie."

"What the hell is that supposed to mean?"

"It means that you've dropped his name into conversation a few too many times for your relationship

to be strictly platonic."

"I have not!" Holly insisted.

"Jack this and Jack that. At dinner the other night, Jack said... Jack has a knack for picking just the right wine... Yes, Jack mentioned that just the other day..."

A flush worked its way from Holly's neck up to her cheeks. In seconds, she was as red as the bow on her sister's holiday gift box.

"So, tell me honestly." Hillary changed the subject. "Do you really like the beaded evening bag?"

"I love it."

"It's not too pretentious or over-the-top?"

"Everything you do is pretentious and over-the-top, but I still love it," Holly said.

"Good to know...because I heard Santa's bringing you a Judith Leiber, too," she confided with a grin.

****

"Sweetheart, would you give me a hand with this?" Rosalie hollered.

"What is it?" Rebecca asked, now standing in the doorway of her father's bedroom.

"Can you reach this box?" she asked from inside her ex-husband's closet. "I'm not quite tall enough."

"What on earth are you doing?" Rebecca questioned, taking a minute to survey the room. Clothing, shoes, and boxes of all shapes and sizes littered most every surface of Leland's private sanctuary.

"A bit of reorganizing," Rosalie answered, backing out of the closet.

"Well, this confirms it."

"Confirms what?" her mother asked.

"That you have a death wish."

"What are you talking about?"

"When he finds out that you've gone rummaging through his things…"

"I'm not rummaging. I'm editing. Getting his life back on track. Do you know suits are hanging in there that haven't been touched in thirty-plus years?"

"He likes his stuff. He's sentimental."

"He's a hoarder."

"Mom, I really think you're asking for trouble here."

"Once he sees the benefit of a well-organized closet, he won't be able to argue. In a few days, when he's up and around more, I'm taking on that pigpen of a space he calls his study."

"Oh, you definitely have a death wish." Rebecca laughed.

Rosalie sighed as she glanced around his room. "Leland was always so fastidious. I mean, just look at his greenhouse. Everything in its place. But this old house…"

"Has never been the same since you moved out," Rebecca added.

"Help me with this box?" she asked once more, ignoring her daughter's comment.

Rebecca obliged and retrieved the large, dusty old box from the uppermost shelf in her father's closet.

"What's in here?" she asked.

"I'm not sure, but I think…" Rosalie lifted the lid and peeked inside.

"What is it?"

Rosalie handed the box to Rebecca with a smile.

"It's a box of old wine corks. I guess you're right. My father is a hoarder."

"Normally I would agree, but these are very special. I can't believe he saved these."

"Some sort of inside joke?"

"These corks represent every bottle of wine and champagne your father and I shared. Well, I guess I shouldn't say *every* bottle but quite a few." She sighed and took one from the box. "This one is from Christmas Eve."

"How could you possibly remember when you—"

"Your father wrote the date on each one. See?" She held the cork up. "And this one was from a bottle of champagne that we popped back when we found out we were expecting you."

Rebecca selected a cork. "This one says HVD, but I can't make out the date. What's HVD?"

"Happy Valentine's Day." Rosalie sat down on the edge of Leland's bed, balancing the box on her lap. "I remember that cork. That was the last time…" Rosalie stopped.

"The last time, what?" Rebecca sat beside her mother.

"The last time my Valentine's Day was happy." She took the cork in question from her daughter. Silently, she inspected Leland's inscription before dropping it back in the box.

"Because the next year you were alone in New York?"

"That was a very long winter…and a very lonely one, at that."

"But that was what you wanted, remember?" Rebecca added quickly with a firm tone. "The fancy Manhattan apartment. Your own gallery. Legions of pretentious art collectors clamoring for anything with your signature."

"I know it seemed that way to you, sweetheart, but things aren't always what—"

"What do you mean, 'it seemed that way'?" Rebecca mocked her with a chuckle. "I was here, remember? You left us. You were given the choice between your family and your career, and you chose the latter."

Rosalie focused on the hurt in her daughter's eyes with pain of her own. "You make it sound as though I flipped a coin. Surely you know that moving to New York was the most difficult decision I've ever made in my life."

"I just don't understand how things can be fine one minute and over the next. I didn't understand it then, and I still don't understand it."

"Well, I suppose life sometimes happens that way."

"You could have stayed. I know you could have found a way if you'd really wanted to." Rebecca could feel the formation of tears in her eyes.

"We never meant to hurt you. It was never about you."

"Well, of course, you're going to say that. Why do all divorced parents say that? Do the lawyers give you a guidebook or something? Does everyone agree to the same oath?"

"Rebecca…" Rosalie sighed.

"I know I wasn't a little kid when it happened, but I still needed my mother and father together, as one cohesive unit. Just because I'm a grown woman now doesn't mean I don't stop wishing for it." She paused and took a deep breath. "Whether you meant to or not, when you stopped loving my father, you stopped loving a piece of me. See, I am my father, just as much as I am you."

Though her words stung, Rosalie remained strong, careful not to overreact to her daughter's sentiment.

"If you want to know the truth…" She ran her hand lightly across the silky lapel of his old tuxedo jacket. "I never stopped loving your father. I never will. "

****

"Will?" Whitney's voice echoed from his office intercom.

"Yes?"

"Two very questionable characters are standing here at my desk, demanding a quick audience with you. Shall I send them in?" she inquired.

"If you must," he said with a laugh.

Seconds later, the door opened and two men in dark business suits entered.

"Where's Charlie?" Mark inquired. "I thought you and she were working on the—"

"We're done. She left about an hour ago."

"Done? She's already drawn up the revisions?"

"Well, they're just the preliminary sketches at the moment. She'll send over the final specs by courier in a few days like she did when we revised the south end of the complex."

"When you mentioned that Charlie Cross was joining us for lunch the other day, I had no idea that—" Mark confessed.

"She was a woman?" Will interrupted with a grin.

"Well, yeah…"

"You did a good job of hiding your surprise," Will reassured him.

"I can't believe she's developed such a vast

reputation across the country. I mean, for someone as young as she is to be the head of one of the top firms..."

"She certainly doesn't look fifty, does she?" Will asked.

"Fifty? No way in hell she's fifty." Jonathan corrected him. "I doubt she's even forty. And if I was a little younger and a little less—"

"Married?" Mark interrupted.

"Sorry, but Charlie Cross is half a century old," Will replied.

"And just how the hell would you know?" Mark inquired.

"He knows because they've spent a lot of time together ever since he got back into town," Jonathan offered. "All work-related, of course. I wasn't implying that you and she—"

"Actually,"—Will shot him a look—"someone I know attended her fiftieth birthday party recently. That's how I'm privy to her age. And you're skating on thin ice with a comment like that, Jonathan."

"I'm sorry. I didn't mean it the way it sounded, swear to God."

"Now, was there something else you two needed?" Will asked.

"Well, we were going to see if you and Charlie wanted to join us for a drink, but I guess..."

"Another time, gentlemen." Will snapped his briefcase shut. "The airport awaits."

"So, where are you off to now?" Jonathan asked.

"Nowhere. I'm strictly playing Uber driver. Rebecca is flying back from Atlanta. She's been playing nursemaid and referee for the last week."

"You are one lucky sonofabitch, Will Albright," Mark announced smugly.

"And why is that?" Will asked with a smirk.

"You're always in the company of beautiful women."

Chapter Sixteen

Will had just pulled onto the highway when his cell phone rang. He wrestled it free from his suit pants. Glancing down, he didn't recognize the number on the screen.

"Will Albright," he answered.

"It's me."

"Rebecca? Don't tell me you missed your flight?"

"Actually, I just landed."

"You're already here?"

"I took an earlier flight."

"Where are you?"

"I'm in a taxi. The driver let me borrow her cell."

"Where's your phone?"

"At my father's. I was in such a hurry when I left—"

Will noted a distressing tone in his wife's voice. "Are you okay?"

"I don't want to talk about it. I'm tired and ready to be home. I'll see you in a few."

It was after seven when the security box at the main gate sent out an alert. Will buzzed the car in and jogged outside to greet her. They'd talked only sporadically over the last week, and with each conversation, he knew that his wife was growing wearier. It was the most consecutive days she'd spent with her parents in recent years. What started as good-natured ribbing had at times turned ugly between Leland and Rosalie, leaving Rebecca uncomfortably in the middle of a decades-long feud.

The few minutes they did talk were filled with more of the same safe, empty words that defined the bulk of recent communication between them: book talk, corporate restructuring, movie deals, and blueprints. The tiny growth that developed in their time together had all but withered away, making Will question what, if any, reconnection had truly been made during their brief reunion in Atlanta. He made a firm decision on the way home to do everything possible to reignite that flame that once burned bright between them. With a little help from Georgia, he hoped that maybe they could find their way back to one another.

She hadn't even exited the car and already he could see dark circles under her eyes. He opened the door, handed the driver a wad of cash, and then helped her out. Georgia appeared and retrieved the bags from the trunk, leaving them on the bottom stair as she shuffled back to the kitchen. With his arm around her shoulder, Will led Rebecca inside.

"Georgia made your favorite stuffed pork tenderloin. I haven't sampled it yet, but it smells delicious."

"Thanks, but I'm not very hungry," she answered.

"I stopped by that little bakery and picked up some tiramisu for you. Surely you won't pass on that."

"Maybe later."

"But it's tradition."

"Not right now."

"Is there anything I can get for you?" he asked.

"All I want is to take a shower and go to bed."

"Sounds good to me." He nuzzled her neck as both arms encircled her waist.

"Will, please." She wrestled free from his grip, clearly conveying her desire to be left alone.

Rebecca collected her garment bag and small carry-on, then headed upstairs. Will picked up the large suitcase and followed her, guessing that further interaction would have to wait until morning. Behind their bedroom door, she wasted no time and went straight to the shower. He wanted to slip into the shower and taste the warm droplets on her skin, feel the soft curves of her hips and breasts beneath his fingertips. They hadn't shared any sort of real intimacy in weeks. After a minute's debate, knowing she wanted anything but, he turned and made his way back downstairs.

****

Frantically, Holly searched her purse, sighing with relief when her fingers wrapped around the card key. Her heart pounded with anticipation. They'd kept their distance from one another all night, stopping and chatting only briefly within the safety of a large group of party-goers. A tall blonde hung on his arm; Isabella is only an accessory, he promised her, but she'd kept a close eye on them, anyway. Though she had absolutely no reason to be jealous, she just couldn't suppress that most human of emotions. Of course, it had all been part of the plan. She would arrive via a borrowed press pass to mingle while he would make the tabloids scramble to discover the identity of his new mystery lady. Hopefully, with a little luck, their secret affair would remain just that—a secret.

She swiped the key quickly, checking the hallway

once more before vanishing inside his suite. It was now almost two o'clock in the morning, and she'd taken three different cabs to three different locales just to throw off any late-night paparazzi. A photo of the two of them had been snapped at a Feed The Children fundraiser in Chicago the month before. Though they were flanked by several other prominent figures, all brandishing large smiles and champagne flutes, there was speculation that the wealthy financier might have eyes for the beautiful, albeit married, Mrs. Deming. The image garnered a spot in several questionable publications, with a host of ridiculous captions. So ridiculous that even Zander, with all his jealous tendencies, had to laugh it off as bogus. The guilt in deceiving her husband had reached its zenith, but she couldn't deny the greater feeling that guided her every thought. She was desperately in love with Jack and tired of living the lie.

Once inside, she locked the door and tiptoed to the bedroom. The dark suite was lit with only bits of moonlight streaming in. Standing beside the windows, her coat and dress fell quietly to the floor. She slipped into bed, spooning her chilled body against the warmth of his. They hadn't seen each other for a few weeks, and the distance between them had been almost debilitating. All the sneaking around, everything covert and stealth—she didn't know if he could take it anymore.

"You feel so good." Her fingers danced along the contours of his back. "I know it's only been three weeks, but it feels more like three months."

"It's not right."

"What's not right?"

"Making you hop from cab to cab in the middle of

the night. Trying to coordinate our work schedules so we just happen to be in the same city on the same night." He touched her cheek and ran his finger lightly along the line of her jaw. "My God, you are so beautiful, Holly. And you deserve more than this. So much more."

He kissed her deeply. The physical connection they shared was on a completely different level than she'd ever experienced. She needed him like the most basic of necessities. Food. Water. Air. Jack. In two days, she'd board a plane back to her life in Australia. She and Zander would be spending a month-long holiday together at their beach house. The thought of being away from him was eating her alive. The look in Jack's eyes told her he felt the same way.

"Marry me," he whispered. "Leave Zander and marry me."

"Jack, I—"

"Don't say a word..." He pressed his finger against her lips. "Not unless that word is yes."

****

"Where's Rebecca?" Georgia inquired.

"She's turned in for the night." After perusing his options, he grabbed a beer from the door of the fridge.

"What?" She looked at Will. "Did you tell her what I made for dinner?"

"I told her."

"And?"

"It'll have to wait 'til tomorrow, Georgia." He twisted the top off and tossed it on the counter near the sink.

"But it's her favorite."

"It'll still be her favorite tomorrow. She just wants

to shower and go to bed."

"I guess she's pretty tired, huh?"

"Among other things." He rolled his eyes.

"Can I ask you a question?"

"Shoot."

"What's with you and the brew? I mean, every time I open the door of the refrigerator, there's something new in there. Most of them I can't even pronounce."

"Just trying out a new hobby." He took several sips from the bottle in his hand. "This one's from Japan. It's a Scotch Ale."

"A Scottish Ale?" Georgia cocked her head to one side. "From Japan? Isn't that a bit of a contradiction?"

"Live dangerously, Georgia." Will smiled.

"I did. It got me arrested and in rehab for eighteen months, remember? Besides, you know I hate beer." Her face screwed into a look of disgust.

"Hey, I've got a few phone calls to make and a proposal to review before my nine o'clock. After that, I'm heading up."

"So you're not eating either?" Her shoulders fell in disappointment.

"Let's just say I'm on a liquid diet tonight." He raised the bottle in Georgia's direction.

****

The downstairs clock chimed eleven times as Will pulled his sluggish body up the stairs. He tried to be quiet as he approached their bedroom.

"What are you doing up?" he asked, surprised to find her wide awake and on the phone.

"I know, I know. First thing in the morning." She nodded in Will's direction.

All I want is to take a shower and go to bed? Bullshit!

"I'll email you a copy as well. Will that do it?" She laughed. "Well, you know me, whatever it takes to make you happy. I'll let you know tomorrow. Goodnight."

She hung up the phone and then turned toward Will, speaking with a nonchalance he hadn't heard from her in weeks. "Drew wants me to email these last three chapters first thing in the morning."

"So you haven't been asleep?"

"Not yet. My editor asked for these before we left for London. I'm so far behind." She sorted through several stacks of papers strewn about their bed. "Drew promised her they'd be ready tomorrow, so I don't really have a choice."

"I see," he answered, feeling the resentment build inside him. "You are something, you know that?"

"Oh, I'm sorry. If you're ready to go to bed, I can move my work downstairs…"

"Oh, I'm ready to go to bed." The anger in his voice was unmistakable, fueled by a string of lonely nights and several strong Japanese ales. "In fact, I wanted to go to bed hours ago…with my wife."

"Will, I'm not in the mood to—"

"Can you be this self-absorbed?" He laughed sarcastically. "Can you really be this inconsiderate of other people's feelings?"

"I can't help it if I have a deadline. I would think you of all people would understand—"

"Three hours ago, you were completely exhausted. So much so that you wouldn't even let me touch you. So what did I do? I left you alone, just as you requested.

Believe me, it's not what I wanted. Then I come up here and find you working? Do you think that little of me?"

What started as sarcasm quickly grew into a war of words, with Will hurling a slew of hateful comments with expert precision. Rebecca stood her ground firmly, but the argument escalated into a full-blown shouting match.

"Georgia made a special dinner to celebrate your homecoming! I even stopped and picked up your favorite dessert because that tradition is important to me! And call me selfish, but I wanted to spend some time with you because I honestly can't remember what that feels like!" He continued to shout, "What the hell is going on? I mean, there was a time you couldn't wait to be with me. We went to great lengths just to spend a few minutes together. And now I have to take a number behind your goddamn literary agent?" He shook his head in disgust. "You know, I think I'd actually feel better if I thought you were sleeping with Drew. At least you'd be acting on emotion. But I don't even rate ahead of three chapters of some meaningless work of fiction!"

He had never spoken to her with such malice, never looked at her with such antipathy.

"I know you think this is nothing more than some fit of jealousy over your book," he added, not giving her the chance to interject. "Well, I'll let you in on a little secret, Mrs. Best-Seller List." He leaned across the bed and locked his eyes on her. "I don't give a goddamn about your book."

Rebecca said nothing but stood and collected her things, hands shaking.

"Guys?" Georgia called softly from behind their bedroom door. "Rosalie just called. It's really important that Rebecca call her back."

Will crossed the room and opened the door. "What?" he snapped.

"It's your mom. She's called Will's cell phone half a dozen times over the past few minutes. I didn't want to answer it, but I thought it might be important. Maybe something about Leland. And since you two were…" She glanced warily at Rebecca.

"What did she say? Is my father all right?" Rebecca asked.

"It's not your father. She just said that she needs to talk to you."

Georgia held out the cell phone. Rebecca didn't move.

"Well? Are you gonna call her back or what?" Will glared at her.

"Not when we're in the middle of—"

"It's never stopped you before. Just make the fucking call."

Will stomped out of the room. Rebecca and Georgia stood staring at one another until the slamming of a door broke the silence between them.

****

"Will?" Rosalie answered on the first ring.

"It's me, Mom. Is everything okay?"

Rebecca listened as her mother delivered the unexpected news. As Rosalie spoke, Rebecca wrote down the particulars on a small notepad bearing her monogram, wiping tears with the back of her hand.

"Sweetheart, I'm so sorry. Maybe I should have waited and called you in the morning."

"No, I'm glad you called. It would have been harder to wake up and see it on the internet. I just can't believe she's gone. Part of me thought that she'd..." Rebecca's voice cracked as more tears trickled down her cheeks.

"Live forever? I think we all thought that. She lived a good, long life with no regrets that I could see. And she loved you very much."

"I can't believe it. We were just talking about her, too." Rebecca reached for a tissue from Will's bedside table. "She was a good person. A *really* good person."

"She certainly was," Rosalie agreed.

After the call with her mother, Rebecca made several more. The airlines, the hotel, the rental car agency they preferred. With all arrangements made, she hung up the phone, and as she did, Will reappeared in the doorway. By the look on his face, she could see their fight was far from over.

"What was so urgent?" he asked.

"Gloria died this morning. She had a stroke."

"Gloria who?" Will didn't immediately recognize the name.

"Glass. Kelly's mother."

"Oh." He quietly slipped his hands into his pockets, unsure what to say. "I'm sorry."

"I've, uh, booked us on a United flight that connects in San Francisco." Her mind reeled, struggling to put every detail in its proper place. She glanced back over her notes, finding a tear stain on the edge of the page.

"You booked us on a flight for what?"

"For her funeral."

"We're not going to Gloria's funeral."

"Yes, we are."

"No, we're not," he repeated, only with a much firmer tone.

"Maybe you're not but I am," she stated definitively.

"I'll be damned if I'm going to let you get on a plane and fly to Sydney fucking Australia! You're not going."

"I'm not discussing this anymore." Rebecca's focus turned back to her laptop. "I'm going. How you choose to react is up to you."

"So, let me get this straight. You breeze into town for a day or two, and as soon as the phone rings, you jet off to London with Drew. Then, Daddy Dearest calls and you're off to Atlanta. You spend a week and a half playing nursemaid to a man who has more than enough money to hire a fleet of healthcare professionals. Then, when you finally decide to come home, you're too exhausted to make love to your husband but you'll hop on a plane and fly twenty goddamn hours to be with Kelly?"

"This is not about being with Kelly. My God, Will! His mother died!"

"People die every day!" he yelled.

"Gloria was an important part of my life at one time!" she shouted back, feeling a revulsion toward him that she'd never experienced.

"And at one time…" His cold eyes zeroed in on hers, a mix of loathing and lament. "So was I."

Chapter Seventeen

Zander threw the broken knee guard into his locker with angry force. He rummaged through his gear bag until he found a suitable replacement.

"Hurry up. You've got sixty seconds." A tall gentleman gave him a supportive pat on the back in passing. "They're not going to wait on you, even if you are the star player."

"I'm coming," Zander replied, securing the guard in place.

"If you'd just take it easy out there, then maybe—" the man suggested.

"We're winning, aren't we?"

"It's an exhibition match, for Christ's sake. You're trying to kill every shot. If you're not careful, you'll kill yourself in the process."

"I'm just giving the crowd what they paid for, Nash."

"There's a big difference between intensity of play and cheap shots, Z."

"What the hell's that supposed to mean?"

"It means you better watch it with that elbow on Steele."

"Hey, I don't have to tell you that Jack Steele plays for keeps." He looked the man squarely in the eye as he closed the door of his locker. "And so do I."

The two men jogged back to the field where the rest

of the team waited. The final match in the Chukkas for Charity season came down as everyone had predicted. Zander Deming's team versus Jack's team. The weather was beautiful and the crowd that had gathered to watch the world's finest players, past and present, was the largest ever assembled at the famed polo club.

Zander mounted his third pony of the match, swinging his graphite mallet near-side several times. As he made his way back onto the field, he spotted Jack adjusting the chin strap on his helmet. Nash was right. He had gone after Jack from the moment the wooden ball hit the grass. No penalty had been called...yet, but it was only a matter of time. Backing off was not his style. He was aggressive and competitive in every area of his life. Work and play. And though he hated to admit it, he'd already lost one trophy to Jack Steele.

He searched the crowd for his wife. She was easy to find, hair blowing in the breeze. Standing with a group of polo wives, she wore her signature Ray-Bans and a solemn expression. Although her eyes were hidden, by the position of her head, Zander knew both her attention and heart were directed across the field, fixed on Jack.

****

Rebecca examined herself in the mirror. Dark circles had captured her green eyes and taken them prisoner. Her rosy, flawless skin looked pallid and thin. Sleep had not come easy the night before as she'd tossed and turned, replaying Will's hurtful words over and over in her head. Alone in their bedroom, she'd waited for her husband's return, wondering when he'd give up and slip into bed beside her. He never did. When the light of morning finally forced her tired eyes open, she knew that they would exchange goodbyes instead of apologies.

"All set?" Georgia asked, pulling her jacket up around her shoulders.

"I think so." Rebecca inspected her baggage at the bottom of the staircase.

"This is it, huh? Just Shamu here?" Georgia reached for the oversized black and white suitcase.

"And my carry-on."

"I want you to take this, too." She held her cell phone out to Rebecca.

"Oh, Georgia, that's very sweet of you, but I can't take your—"

"It's not a choice. You don't have yours and I don't want you out there without one."

She smiled, knowing it was fruitless to argue. "Thank you. Mine should be here in a day or two. You use it until I get back."

"There's nothing I like more than an even trade." Georgia winked. "Now, let's get you to the airport."

Rebecca said goodbye to Dizzy while Georgia waited in the car. Standing at the front door of their beautiful home, she draped a coat over one arm and took one last look around. She ran through her mental checklist, realizing she had everything she needed...except Will.

There was little conversation on the way to the airport. The verbal showdown the night before had stripped her need for conversation of any kind. Thankfully, Georgia didn't press her, leaving the radio to keep the mood light. Yet with each mile, she couldn't deny a strange feeling tugging on her heart—a need to share a loving, supportive word with her sister-in-law before vanishing inside the busy airport.

"I ordered the flowers online this morning. They'll be delivered on time, no problem," Georgia said. "They're gorgeous, too. A big spray of lilies and eucalyptus, just like you wanted."

"Thank you. Lilies were Gloria's favorite."

Georgia had proven to be a lifesaver on more than one occasion.

"I also called the hotel to confirm your reservation. They'll send a car for you, too."

"You didn't have to do that."

"I know I didn't. I wanted to."

The last leg of their journey together was spent in silence. She felt Georgia's eyes every few minutes, stealing a glance in an effort to engage, but Rebecca kept her thoughts and words to herself.

As they crossed onto airport property, Georgia spoke again. "I've been searching for something to say. Something to end the unhappiness and make it all go away."

"I'm so sorry you had to bear witness to our bad behavior."

"Why are you apologizing when my shithead brother is the one at fault?"

"We're both at fault."

"Yeah, well…" Georgia huffed.

She pulled up to the curb in front of the United Airlines terminal and helped retrieve the bags from the trunk.

"I can't thank you enough…for everything." Rebecca turned to her.

"I wish I knew what to say to make this better."

"Georgia, you've been wonderful. You don't have

to say anything."

"There's nothing I can say. You were a marriage counselor. I'm sure you already dissected this from every conceivable angle."

"All couples fight."

"If you start with that 'fighting is healthy' bullshit…" Georgia rolled her eyes.

"Will and I are going to be okay."

"You better. You're the only role models for a normal relationship I have."

"But no pressure, right?" Rebecca cracked a small smile.

"He really does love you. He's never loved anyone the way he loves you."

Rebecca lowered her eyes, searching her heart for a reply. It was the first time she'd stopped to consider Georgia's feelings and the uncomfortable position they'd trapped her in. For weeks, she'd tiptoed around them, holding her tongue and giving them space. Rebecca never thought about how their lack of marital harmony might impact Georgia.

"I know he does," Rebecca said.

"Promise you'll call as soon as you land?"

"I promise."

They shared a warm embrace. Rebecca turned and waved before disappearing into the traveling masses.

****

At the gate, Rebecca gripped Georgia's cell phone in her shaky hands. Twice she tried to get up the nerve to call Will, and twice she'd failed at the task. There had been no further exchange between them following her decision to leave. Georgia had mentioned that he'd spent the night on the sofa in the study and departed at dawn. She'd wanted to talk to him face-to-face, hoping for some sort of reconciliation or consideration at the very least, but got neither. Waiting to board a plane bound for the other side of the globe, the need to say goodbye to him increased tenfold. She watched the bodies moving around her, remembering a turning point goodbye early in their relationship.

They sat inside his car, knowing they had just minutes. The airport shuttle would be arriving soon, taking her away from him for the last time. They'd spent another stolen weekend holed up inside a Boston hotel suite, living off room service and each other, completely oblivious to the outside world. Despite the quiet moments that defined their time together, a troubling silence existed between them. He reached for her hand, moving her wedding ring back and forth.

"Are you okay?" Will asked.

"I'll be fine," Rebecca answered.

"I love you. You know that, don't you?"

"I know," she whispered.

"After tonight, we won't have to say goodbye."

Rebecca didn't respond but watched as his hand slid over hers. Just a short plane ride separated her and what was left of the life she lived with Kelly. Would her desire for a divorce come as a surprise to him? As certain as she was of her love for Will, there was no denying the heartfelt pain of severing ties with her husband. She wasn't in love with Kelly and hadn't been for some time, but there was a tender side to Kelly Glass. A thoughtful, caring man who could make her laugh. A man that, despite his physical strength and audacious nature, could love deeply and without limits, if only he allowed himself to do so.

"After tonight, I won't have to watch you fly back to Kelly ever again." Will touched her cheek and smiled.

An airline employee announced the first boarding call, bringing her mind out of the past. The window of opportunity was closing fast, and only a few minutes remained before she'd be required to silence the cell phone for the duration of the trip. With a deep breath, she placed the call.

"Is she gone?" Will asked, answering on the first ring.

"It's not Georgia," Rebecca whispered, heart racing. "It's me. She lent me her cell phone for the trip. They're boarding the plane now. I just wanted to call and—" Her heart raced.

"Get my blessing?" he interrupted.

"Apologize," she gently corrected.

Will made no response, leaving his wife to wait on the line for what seemed like an eternity. She knew immediately what his silence meant. The call would not yield the two outcomes she desired most: understanding and forgiveness.

"Are you still there?" she asked after a moment.

"You're not getting the first…" His tone was still filled with anger. "And I couldn't care less about the second."

"Will, if you would just listen for a—"

The phone went dead just as another boarding announcement was made.

Chapter Eighteen

It was afternoon when Rebecca's exhausted body fell into bed. The trip had been quiet and uneventful. Thankful to have arrived without incident, and true to her promise, she called Georgia. Not much was said, and her husband's name was not mentioned. Now alone in the suite, she was ready to grab a few hours of rest before showering and taking a cab to the viewing. She called down to the front desk to request a wake-up call.

No one in the Glass family was aware of Rebecca's arrival in Sydney. She'd tried several times to reach Lily in London with no success. She tried to find a listing for Kelly online but found none. With eyes closed, she tried to imagine the look on her ex-husband's face when they saw one another. Would he be polite? Upset? Indifferent? Kelly was the king of unpredictability, and thus, as she drifted off to sleep, she cautioned herself to be prepared for anything.

****

Rebecca paid the fare and exited the cab, smoothing the wrinkles from her black dress as she climbed the stairs to one of the most historic places of worship in all of Sydney. Though she'd been there dozens of times, the English-style gothic architecture never failed to impress her. It had been her former mother-in-law's second home. A woman of deep faith, Gloria Marchand Glass had given millions over the years to further the congregation's works. It came as no surprise that those who loved her would pay their final respects in the cathedral that had brought her a lifetime of joy.

Inside the ornate church, Rebecca made a polite inquiry and was promptly directed to the crypt where Gloria's body rested for public viewing. Walking briskly, she exchanged smiles with a number of visitors, all of whom seemed to follow her to the same destination within the cathedral. As she approached the entrance to the crypt, she could see a long line had formed. Gloria, while not a political figure, was indeed an icon of sorts and revered by most. The money her father had amassed from his years in mining and exports made her one of the wealthiest women in the world at the tender age of twenty. She quickly married Kelly's father, a well-to-do American doctor, giving birth to Kelly a few years later. Together, they increased their fortune and worked to better the lives of those less fortunate. They invested in hospitals, churches, schools, and cultural centers. Even the accidental death of her husband, Denis, didn't stop her quest to end the world's suffering. And now, with her own death, Rebecca wondered if Kelly would step up to carry on the tradition and his mother's work.

She stood nervously in line for several minutes. What would she say when they finally met? It had been years since she'd looked into his deep brown eyes. They'd crossed paths only once since she and Will had married. Rebecca could still remember when he and Will exchanged handshakes inside Heathrow airport. It had easily been the most unnerving moment of her life, watching both her former and current husband engaged in small talk. Pangs of guilt were deep and intense when she shook Kelly's hand one last time before leaving to board their flight.

The line inched forward for another five minutes before Rebecca's feet touched the terrazzo tiles down in the crypt. Again, she faced another lengthy wait as Gloria's casket was positioned at the end of the long, flower-lined corridor. A man dressed in a dark suit made his way down the line, offering words of comfort and cream-colored cards bearing Gloria's image and the accolades of her life. Rebecca took the card with a nod and read through the list of vast accomplishments, overcome with pride and emotion. Gloria had a hand in numerous charities and, with the help of her husband, saved thousands of lives in third-world countries. Rebecca concentrated on the outdated photograph and smiled again. It was one of her favorite pictures of Gloria and, ironically, the man given credit for the photograph was none other than her father, Leland Graham. He'd been traveling in the outback, snapping a series of shots for an upcoming spread in National Geographic. Dressed in safari chinos, gaiters, and a plain white shirt, he captured Gloria doing what she did best—giving aid to those in need.

Rebecca watched the front of the line, scanning for signs of a familiar face. Nearing the casket, she could see the only figures near the body were that of security. Kelly was nowhere. A part of her felt a twinge of disappointment as she stood at the velvet rope in front of Gloria's casket, hoping that they would have been able to see one another before the service. Bowing her head, she said a silent prayer for peace before turning and making her way out of the crypt.

****

Under different circumstances, Rebecca would have loved dining on a private hotel balcony above the lights of Sydney Harbor. Tonight, she had no appetite for five-star cuisine or an incredible view. The few hours she'd slept had worn off, and all she wanted was to crawl back into bed.

Collecting the tray, she moved the remains of dinner into the hall outside her suite. Searching through the suitcase for her favorite silk PJs, she mentally counted the hours between Sydney and home. She eyed the borrowed cell phone on the bedside table, wanting to call Will all day, but deciding against it, knowing he wasn't interested in anything she had to say.

She finished up her nightly routine and returned to the bedroom. In the corner, she spied her laptop sitting on the floor, which she retrieved before sliding in between the sheets. For several minutes she read through and responded to several book-related emails, startled when the quiet was interrupted by a ringing phone. Her heart fell when she realized it was the hotel phone and not Georgia's cell.

"Hello?" she answered warily.

"Excuse me, Miss? You're in my seat," a man said rudely.

"No, I don't think so." She smiled, instantly recognizing Kelly's voice as they replayed the moment when they first met.

"My ticket says Row M, as in *move*."

"Well, this is Row N, as in *no way*. You're in the wrong row, sir."

"Becks…" He spoke her nickname in a serious tone. "I can't tell you how much it means to me that

166

you're here. I knew you'd come."

"But how did you know that I was here? And staying at this hotel?" she asked.

"An old business associate of mine said he saw you at the viewing. As far as the hotel goes, what you lovingly refer to as tradition, I call predictability. There's only one hotel in Sydney that fully meets your seal of approval."

"How are you doing? Really?" she asked with genuine concern.

"I'm okay. The last few days have been a blur. You'd think my mother was the Queen with the amount of pomp and circumstance going on. I mean, she was an incredible woman and very deserving of all the fuss, but you know her. This is the last thing she ever wanted. Her will specifically stated a quiet funeral. It's been anything but quiet."

"Just focus on making it through tomorrow. Once the service is over, things should quiet down."

"It was sure nice of you and Will to fly down for this."

"Actually, Will wasn't able to come. Just too many irons in the fire right now. He sends his apologies and his condolences. He had enormous respect for your mother and the impact she made on the world," Rebecca said, stretching the truth.

"Listen, a small group is gathering at the cathedral for a light meal with the clergy before the service tomorrow. Just family and a few close friends. I'd like for you to come."

"That's very thoughtful of you, but I don't know if I—"

"I'd really like to see you before the service. And I

know Lily would too."

"So Lily made it in?"

"She got in yesterday morning."

"I tried to call her at her flat but never got an answer."

"She was probably with Maks."

"Did she tell you that we ran into each other in London a couple of weeks ago?"

"Called and left me a message right after she saw you. It made her day."

"I know I don't have to tell you, but she's beautiful, Kelly. Absolutely beautiful."

"You know something? She said the same thing about you."

Rebecca struggled for an appropriate response. There was something different about the man on the other end of the line, though she couldn't describe it.

"Where are she and Evelyn staying?" She quickly changed the subject.

"Evelyn's not here. As a matter of fact, I don't even know if she knows."

"What?" That surprised Rebecca.

"She's in seclusion…sitting on some rock, probably worshiping a cactus in the desert. Lily called and left several messages for her, but we never heard back."

"Oh, Kelly, I'm so sorry."

"I'm not. My mother had love and compassion for so many in this world…but Evelyn…well, let's just say they were never very close. And the tension between Lily and her mother is at an all-time high. It's better this way."

They spent several minutes discussing old friends

and acquaintances who had contacted Kelly in the wake of Gloria's death, names she hadn't heard in years. The more she listened, the more it became apparent that the prideful, arrogant man who once shared her life and her bed had changed in ways she couldn't have imagined. There was a calm humility about him that he'd never shown.

"Hey, I know you're tired so I won't keep you."

"Kelly," she started. "Is there anything I can do for you? Any last-minute errands or details before the funeral? Anything at all?"

Another quiet moment developed between them, making Rebecca hold her breath. She'd envisioned everything from civility to silence but certainly hadn't imagined that their first verbal exchange in nine years would be so relaxed and comforting. They spoke as easily as two old friends, without a hint of jealousy, guilt, or animosity. It was both wonderful and strange…and the soothing nature of his voice made her realize just how lonely she was.

"Just knowing you're here for me…it's all I really need," he said softly.

****

A gathering of family and a few close friends for a light meal turned out to be an exquisite dining experience of about one hundred guests. A black limousine collected her from the hotel precisely at ten o'clock, but because of heavy traffic in the area, she was one of the last to arrive at the cathedral. Standing at the doorway of the massive private hall, she felt as though entering a wedding reception. The mood of those present was light and cheerful. *Now, this is what Gloria would have wanted*, she considered. No tears.

No heavy hearts.

Her eyes traveled around the room, hoping to find Kelly and Lily.

"Excuse me?" A gentleman approached her. "May I help you?"

"Yes, I'm looking for Kelly or Lily Glass."

"Your name?" He pulled a clipboard from underneath his arm.

"Rebecca Albright."

After a moment's searching of the lengthy list, he located her name.

"Of course, Mrs. Albright. Mr. Glass has requested a special place for you at the family table. Right this way."

Rebecca followed the elderly gentleman through a maze of round tables toward the back of the hall. They made their way to a long rectangular table along the back wall where she spotted Lily chatting with several familiar faces.

"There are place cards on the tables. I believe you're just to the left of Ms. Glass." He pointed.

"Thank you."

The gentleman bowed, leaving her alone amid the crowd. She continued to scan the room, eager to find Kelly. A second later, a hand gently touched her shoulder. She turned around and looked into the eyes of her ex-husband.

She froze, silently studying the shell of a man standing before her. The mass of jet-black hair she expected to see was thin and pure white. His face, drawn and ashen. The once masculine frame that moved with confidence was now almost skeletal. And his eyes...those deep brown eyes that once penetrated a very private part of her life, were lost inside hollow, dark circles. Rebecca's heart pounded as she tried to process the physical changes that had warped his body and robbed him of his youth since their last meeting. He was almost unrecognizable.

Sensing her shock and discomfort at the moment, he shared a sweet smile and wrapped his arms around her. He hugged her tenderly, and Rebecca felt her heart break as she pulled his frail body close.

"Thank you so much for coming," Kelly whispered in her ear.

Chapter Nineteen

The celebration of Gloria Glass's life lasted for close to two hours. From government officials to big names in the entertainment industry, many offered words of thanks and comfort, few of which reached Rebecca's ears. Seated two rows behind him, she could not focus on anything other than her former husband. She stared at the back of his head with a sick feeling gnawing at her insides. Something was wrong with him, she had no doubt. And she had every intention of finding out exactly what had turned this once larger-than-life man into a shadow of himself.

They rode separately to the burial where Gloria's body was placed in the ground beside her husband, Denis Blackwood Glass. The priest shared a poem that Gloria herself had penned about love and forgiveness, and the importance of giving more than one might take. Rebecca fought to center her attention, but just like in the cathedral, she couldn't help but steal looks in Kelly's direction.

The priest offered a final prayer before the cloud of mourners, all cloaked in black, quietly made their way toward Kelly and Lily, sharing hugs and goodbyes. Rebecca stood with a group of solemn-faced individuals, several of whom she recognized from her past life, and waited to extend her love to the family. It took several minutes, but the crowd eventually thinned, and Rebecca embraced Lily once more.

"Your grandmother loved you so much," she whispered in the young woman's ear. "You were by far the most beautiful flower in her garden."

"I know she did." Lily held her tight, smiling through her tears.

With their arms linked together, the two women walked toward the waiting caravan of limousines.

"Lily! Becks!" Kelly called out.

She turned around at the sound of her name. Kelly headed toward them, wearing a look of both exhaustion and relief.

"Is it all settled?" Kelly asked, looking into his ex-wife's eyes.

"I'm sorry…" Rebecca shook her head in confusion.

"I haven't asked her yet but since you're here, I'll let you do the honors." Lily gave her father a knowing nod as she and Maks continued on.

"Ask me what?" Rebecca inquired.

"Dinner. Tonight. Just the four of us."

"Oh, Kelly, surely you don't feel like going out—" she began.

"Not out—in. At my place. Just a quiet evening, nothing fancy. Unless Maks specializes in fancy because he's volunteered to be our chef."

She hesitated. "It's been such a long day and—"

"It would really mean a lot to me if you joined us."

"Are you sure? It's been an emotionally draining day," she questioned.

"We'll make an early night of it, I promise." He touched her arm warmly.

****

Rebecca arrived right at eight, still not quite sure why she'd agreed to come. Was she about to be blindsided by their painful past, or would the night simply be a casual evening of reminiscing? She hoped, of course, that it would be the latter, even though she had an agenda of her own.

Lily and Maks created culinary magic, and the party of four dined amid breezes and city lights on his terrace. It didn't take long for their collective laughter to relax her. By the time Kelly refilled her wine glass, she'd forgotten the apprehensions that had plagued her during the ride to his luxury waterfront apartment. Kelly touched them with stories of his childhood and the woman he was privileged to call his mother. Rebecca couldn't deny it; her former husband had a gift for captivating his audience. Some of the stories she'd heard before, only now he delivered them with a completely different flavor. His words were softer and more meaningful. At one point, as he narrated a favorite memory, he held eye contact with Rebecca, and she felt something for Kelly Glass that she hadn't for a long time: love. Not a romantic love, but the love of two souls who had shared a unique journey.

Rebecca volunteered for dish duty after dinner, but Lily flatly refused, pushing her father and former stepmother into the living area. She took a moment to inspect the room while Kelly fetched a couple of cappuccinos. The style of the space surprised her. It had nothing in common with the cool, sleek designs that he'd favored during their marriage. The furnishings were warm with a relaxed, curl-up-for-awhile feel. Along one wall, floor-to-ceiling shelves held hundreds of books and treasures from his travels. She scanned several of the titles, surprised by his choices in reading materials.

"Feel free to take one." Kelly returned, a coffee cup in each hand. "That is, if you'd like something to read besides a room service menu. In fact," He held a cup out to her. "I just finished a great book I think you'd like."

"Who are you?" She shot him a sideways look.

"What do you mean?"

"I mean, the Kelly Glass I know doesn't read. He's the 'let's just rent the movie instead' kind of guy."

"Well, I guess you could say that I've grown up a bit since those days."

"Homer. James Joyce. Kafka?" She read several authors' names aloud.

"Oh, God, no. I don't read those." He laughed. "Those are just to impress the women I bring up here. They're actually hiding the decades of Playboy I have stacked behind them."

"That sounds more like it." She nodded, taking a seat on the inviting leather sofa.

He turned his eyes away from her, running a bony finger along the spines in search of a particular title. "Gimme a second. I know it's here."

Rebecca watched his hands moving methodically over each book. In fact, she'd watched them closely throughout dinner. The strong hands that once tied a host of sailing knots with precision held his fork gingerly as he picked at the food on his plate. His robust appetite was missing, and he passed each time the bottle was offered, opting for water instead of wine.

"What genre are we talking about?" she asked.

"Um…" He pulled a book from the shelf and

joined her. "I guess you'd call this realistic fiction."

He placed the book on the sofa between them with a grin. Rebecca couldn't contain her laughter.

"Now I think I should caution you…there's a character in this book who will probably turn you off."

"Really?" she questioned.

"Zander, I believe, is his name. A completely self-absorbed, arrogant asshole."

"Is that so?"

"Oh, this guy's a piece of work. Egocentric. Braggadocious. Sexy as hell, but a devil nonetheless," he quickly added with a wink.

Rebecca dropped her eyes from view for a minute, feeling a pain in her heart as she ran a hand over the cover of her novel. Were his comments in jest…or was he acting in classic Kelly fashion? Using humor to disguise his true feelings?

"Listen, Kelly…" She took a deep breath.

"You don't have to defend yourself. All's fair in love and fiction."

"I don't want you to think, well, what I mean is…are you mad?"

"Mad?" He laughed loudly. "Hell no, I'm not mad. I'm honored."

"Really?" she asked, still unsure of his feelings.

"Really." He reassured her, placing a hand atop hers. "Don't forget that in the end, Zander Deming turned out to be a pretty nice guy."

"He certainly did."

Their quiet moment was interrupted by Lily taking last-minute requests before closing the kitchen for the night. Kelly asked for a top-off of his coffee, but Rebecca declined once she noticed the lateness of the hour.

"I can't believe it's so late. I know you all are exhausted." She eyed her watch.

"You're not thinking of leaving now, are you?" Kelly asked.

"I honestly don't know how you're still awake."

"You know me…" He gave a sly grin. "I do all my best work at night."

"Kelly Forrester Glass!" Lily yelled. "That is not the image I want in my head when I fall asleep. Would you at least wait until I'm in bed before you start trying to hit on your ex-wife?"

The foursome spent another fifteen minutes talking before Lily yawned and called it a night. With a kiss to both of them, she slipped off to the guest room with Maks.

"She's amazing. Her mother's looks and her father's smarts," Rebecca commented once they were alone.

"She's a great kid," he replied with a sigh. "Not everything in my life has been a mistake."

"Lily is definitely your best work."

"Listen, if you're ready to call it a night, I understand. I can have a cab here in five minutes, or I'll take you back to the hotel myself. Whatever you prefer."

"A cab will be fine. I've had a wonderful time."

"You know, I do have some business to discuss with you. The will and whatnot. But it's late and I know you're tired—"

"The will?" she said, surprised.

"I didn't mention it last night. It didn't seem like the appropriate time. I wasn't sure how long you were planning to be in Sydney. Hell, I never even considered I'd be discussing the will with you in person." He cleared his throat. "Will you be around another day or two? Because if you are, I'd really like to show you your inheritance myself."

"Show me? My inheritance?" she remarked curiously.

"It's not something you can appreciate from a piece of paper."

"What are you talking about?"

"Now if I told you, it'd take all the fun out of it, wouldn't it?"

"Can you show it to me now?"

"I would, but it's about a five-hour drive from here."

"Five hours?" Rebecca's eyes widened.

"But lucky for us, I've got access to a helicopter. We can be there in about an hour."

"Where is 'there'?"

"A little place I call Anembo." He looked at her with soft, sincere eyes. "That's an Indigenous word that means—"

"A quiet place." She finished his sentence.

"Just like my Lily. Beautiful and smart." He raised his coffee cup in her direction.

"Speaking of quiet places"—she cautiously changed the subject.—"I heard you gave up the city for life on a boat?"

"I did."

"But you live here?" She glanced around the room.

"When I have to. Otherwise, Edna and I are out on open water." He took another sip of his cappuccino.

"Edna?" Rebecca raised an eyebrow. "A new lady

in your life?"

"Not exactly new. We've been together for about nine years, give or take."

"Was she at the funeral today?"

"No, no," he answered with a quick shake of his head. "She's not big on crowds. Prefers a more intimate gathering, if you know what I mean."

"Oh." Rebecca nodded.

"But I'd love to introduce the two of you."

He placed his cup on the coffee table and casually crossed the living room. He returned a moment later, wearing the largest smile she'd seen all day. Taking his seat once more, he wrapped his hands around a beautiful acoustic guitar and strummed it softly.

"Rebecca, this is Edna."

"Edna?" She examined the instrument suspiciously.

"My one and only."

"Okay, now wait just a minute…" She placed her cup on the table, shaking her head in disbelief. "Kelly Glass does not play the guitar. The slots and the ponies maybe, but definitely not a guitar."

"This is the new and improved Kelly Glass. Poet, Renaissance man, and guitar player extraordinaire." He grinned, playing a snippet of an old seventies tune.

Their conversation quieted as Kelly filled the room with soft, beautiful notes. Rebecca listened in amazement, seeing his weakened fingers come to life as they moved with graceful motion over the strings. After a minute, she fixated on his face, finding lines of concentration along his furrowed brow. *Who is this man?*

"*But how I miss the girl…*" he sang.

Rebecca looked into Kelly's eyes as his final notes drifted away. "You are unbelievable."

"If I had a dime for every time a gorgeous woman said that to me…" he joked, playing a quick flamenco rhythm with a grin.

"How on earth did you come up with the name Edna? I'm sure there's a story there," she asked.

"Well, you know me. There's always a story. I wasn't the one to name her. Actually, it's an acronym. The guitar was given to me by a buddy of mine—a guy named Elliot. Edna stands for 'Elliot's drunk, not asleep.' We've weathered quite a few storms together."

He played a montage of her favorite songs—everything from Glen Campbell to The Guess Who. Her eyes traveled the length of his body once more, head to toe. While the man before her bore a resemblance to her former husband, the similarities between them were purely physical. One was a loud, gregarious man who commanded control of everything and everyone around him. The other, a quiet, gentle soul offering friendship and acceptance. As if by the flip of a switch, everything in their collective past disappeared. Kelly Glass, a man who defined a turbulent period in her life, had become the man she always hoped he could be.

He played the final chords and when silence once again filled the room, Rebecca felt that same pain return. Only this time, the emotions were more intense. Now it was time to broach the subject that had controlled her thoughts all day.

"When were you going to tell me?" she asked, looking him squarely in the eye.

"About what?" He played dumb.

"Oh, c'mon. You should've said something when we spoke last night."

"Right. How would that have gone, exactly? 'Oh hi, Becks. It's me. Listen, we'd love for you to join us for brunch before my mother's funeral. And by the way, you're getting two corpses for the price of one.'"

The flippancy of his words, coupled with a weak smile, made her heart sink.

"How sick are you?" she asked warily after a long pause.

"I don't really know," he answered.

"What do you mean, you don't really know?"

"I didn't stick around long enough to find out. The doctor said two words—aggressive chemo. That's when I decided to cash in my chips."

"So, you're telling me that you have no idea what type of cancer you have?"

"Cancer is cancer, Rebecca. It doesn't matter what type." His gaze wandered until landing on her again.

"You're giving up? Just like that, without a fight? The Mayo Clinic and MD Anderson have incredible doctors—"

"Who will poison my already poisoned body? Lying in a hospital with a needle in my arm doesn't quite fit my lifestyle. It's hard to navigate the deep blue sea when you don't even have the strength to stand up."

"Kelly, you've always been a fighter—competitive in every area of your life. I don't understand why you won't fight this."

"A wise man once said that when the game is over, the King and the pawn go back into the same box. A few months or fifty years from now, I'm still going in that box…and I'm going to do it on my terms."

She stared at him, heart beating fast, without a clue of how to respond. He never gave her a chance, changing the subject and bringing the evening to a close.

"I have to fly to Auckland tomorrow to tie up some loose ends for the estate."

"Okay."

"Will you be here when I get back? I'd really love to show you a small slice of heaven that's been left in your care." His expression was gentle and genuine. "It would mean the world to me and my mother."

"I don't have a set return date."

"So, you'll stay?" he asked, his eyes filling with hope.

"I'll stay," she replied, offering a smile to please him.

Chapter Twenty

Will walked through the double glass doors, giving his tie a final adjustment. The outer office was silent, and the desk where the receptionist kept vigil stood vacant. He debated for a moment, unsure whether to take a seat and wait or go right on in. Seconds after contemplating his options, she strolled casually through the intricately carved wooden doors, stopping short when noticing him.

"Mr. Albright?" Charlotte said, surprised. "What are you doing here?"

"It's Will, remember? I have a six o'clock appointment with the head of the firm. Some old codger named Charlie." He grinned.

"Was that tonight?" She rifled through her briefcase. Within moments, she located her day planner and pulled it into view. "I could've sworn I had you down for tomorrow at four."

"I'm pretty sure we said today. If you have other plans, tomorrow will be fine."

"I'm so embarrassed." She flipped through the pages of her calendar.

"Don't be. It's an honest mistake."

"I'd say we could meet now but I don't even have your paperwork here. I've been working on it personally the last couple of nights."

"Burning the midnight oil?"

"A little." She smiled.

"Well, as long as you're giving me your undivided attention—my project, that is."

"I think you'll be really pleased with the changes we discussed for the façade on the east side, as well as the redesign of the Albright logo."

"You've yet to disappoint me. I'm sure I'll love it."

"Can we reschedule for tomorrow?" She placed her calendar on the outer desk, checking it against her secretary's. "Wait, I have a better idea. How would you like to accompany me to a birthday party tomorrow?

"Didn't we just celebrate your birthday?" he asked. "I distinctly remember a host of foreign beers and a heated discussion on the use of designated hitters in the American League."

"It's Slats's birthday. You remember the bartender from the restaurant? The older gentleman?"

"Of course."

"He always knocks off early on his birthday. Likes to have dinner with his daughter and grandkids. He and I have a celebratory drink before he clocks out for the night. It's kind of a tradition."

"Well, I wouldn't want to intrude on your tradition."

"Are you kidding? Slats would love it. If there's one thing that man can't get enough of, it's an audience."

"I'd love to join you, but only if you agree to a working dinner afterward—my treat."

"Deal." She offered an outstretched hand.

****

An old Boston tune came on. Jack reached for the knob on the dashboard, turning the stereo up as loud as it would go. Cruising along the winding road, he slammed the gearshift forcibly into place. The headlights of his sleek roadster cut through the dark October night, and his mind raced as fast as the engine. He took each curve with devilish delight, pushing the machine to its limit. Every mile gained equaled one minute closer to her. Closer to Holly.

They hadn't seen each other for ten days. Ten long, painful days, as Holly and Zander began the task of dividing up their vast estate. Multiple investments, properties, and half a dozen homes they shared around the world, all the subjects of great debate. In the end, she gave up, opting for a life with Jack against any sort of monetary gain that would result from the pending divorce. She signed her Mrs. Deming holdings away, save for their cottage on Martha's Vineyard and a house in Aspen.

They'd fought more than ever since Holly had dissolved her marriage. Suddenly, with Zander out of the way, their life seemed to be more difficult—the rumors, the press. Everywhere Holly went, someone was on her heels looking for a comment or photo. The quiet nights spent holed up together in dark hotel rooms were no more. At times, Jack wished they'd left things as they were. He longed for the nights of secret meetings and wrapping his arms around a woman who wasn't fully his.

The music reached its crescendo and he pressed the accelerator to the floor. The wind blew in his hair, and he remembered the expression on Holly's face after sharing their first kiss in her hotel suite. It brought a smile to his face but one that was quickly wiped away, illuminated by the lights of the tractor-trailer truck

185

swerving dangerously into his lane.
****

The party of three sat in a corner booth, toasting good health and good fortune with tankards of the old man's favorite. Slats entertained them for a full hour before donning his hat and bidding them goodnight. Will stood and shook the bartender's hand, realizing for the first time that he and Leland were a lot alike. Both genuine. Both real.

"I don't know, Chuck. This one seems too good to be true." Slats slipped his hands into his pockets. "Well-groomed, good manners." He looked Will up and down. "Nice shoes, too."

"I didn't know I was here for inspection." Will gave Charlotte a wink.

"We're business associates, Slats. I work for Mr. Albright." She adjusted the collar of his jacket. "But thanks for sharing your observations."

"You must be one smooth customer, because it's you who should be working for her," he said with a grin.

The old man turned on his heel and shuffled out of the crowded bar, not bothering to look back. Will sat, shaking his head for a moment. Charlotte buried her head in her hands in embarrassment.

"I am so sorry about that." She looked up at him.

"It's okay, really," Will said.

"I guess I should have warned you ahead of time." She nervously rolled up the corner of her cocktail napkin. "It's the old man's mission in life to find me a man."

"I'm sure his heart is in the right place, but I doubt you need any help in that department."

"Slats has a heart of gold, absolutely. You know, he even flew his newly divorced son out here to meet me a couple of years ago."

"You're kidding?"

"Wish I was. He had this idea that we were perfect for each other. Slats was determined to make a match."

"What happened?"

"Well, he talked about his son all the time. A big investment guy in New York. Very successful. Slats is so proud of him, as a father should be, right? Anyway, he flew out for a weekend. We met, had dinner, went to a concert; he was super nice, but there was no real chemistry."

"You know what I think?" Will's lips curled into a sly grin.

"What?" she asked.

"I think that old Slats O'Brien has a tremendous crush on you."

"Oh, c'mon…" She tried to fight back a grin. "He's a little old for me, don't you think?"

"That's the only thing that keeps him in check. He'd like to be having dinner with you tonight. Alone. Sans the daughter and grandkids. Since he can't, he wants to make damn sure that whoever's arm you're on has his personal seal of approval."

"Don't be silly…" Charlotte rolled her eyes.

"I'm totally serious. You don't see the way he looks at you? The man is smitten."

"I've never given him any reason to think that I…or that we…"

"He doesn't need a reason, Charlie."

Slats's replacement approached their table. "Another round, Ms. Cross?"

"Not right now. Anything for you?" She looked at Will.

"Just the check," Will smiled up at the young man.

"Slats is taking care of your tab tonight, sir."

"See what I mean? Taking care of you even in his absence." Will nodded at Charlotte.

"Whatever you say." She rolled her eyes once more.

"Shall we?" Will asked, motioning toward the dining room.

"Of course. I need to snag my notes from the car. Why don't you get our table and I'll meet you there? Two minutes?"

He stood and pulled out her chair. "I'll walk out with you. It's dark and—"

"My car is just across the parking lot. I'll be fine," she reassured him.

"You're sure?"

"I'm a big girl, Mr. Albright. Cut my own meat and everything." She winked.

They parted company at the bar's main entry. Will secured the attention of the hostess with a friendly wave. She'd reserved a table under her name, and he was seated immediately. A waiter approached him and, after a moment of perusing the wine list, he ordered a bottle of their best Zinfandel. Looking around, he recognized quite a few faces—colleagues, competitors, and, more importantly, a couple of women he knew to be purveyors of the latest gossip. He acknowledged a couple of suited gentlemen with an indiscreet nod. A knot formed in the pit of his stomach, and he wondered what looks would be cast his way when his beautiful dinner companion arrived.

"Will?" A man stopped beside his table.

"Trent! How are you?" he asked, his gaze drawn to the woman beside him.

"Fine. Fine. I didn't know you were a regular here, too?"

"A business dinner with my architect."

"That's right. How's the project coming?"

"Hammering out the particulars as we speak," Will replied.

"Will Albright, I'd like you to meet a friend of mine. This is Rachel Fleming."

"Nice to meet you." Will shook her hand.

They spent a minute catching up. He noted a certain nervousness in his old friend, as though he'd been caught with his hand in the cookie jar. *He's getting back out there. Good for him!* The two men exchanged another handshake before the couple disappeared across the crowded restaurant.

The waiter returned with a bottle in hand, and Will watched as he extracted the cork. After a small sampling and a nod of approval, the gentleman filled two glasses and left with a bow. With his eyes toward the door, Will watched the crowd as he sipped his wine. He waited several minutes before acknowledging the sixth sense that gripped the hairs on the back of his neck. *What's taking her so long?* He was just about to go in search of her when a uniformed police officer appeared, walking with deliberate steps in Will's direction.

"Will Albright?" the officer asked quietly.

"Yes. Is something wrong?"

"Would you mind following me outside, sir?"

"Is there a problem?" Will asked, pushing his chair

away from the table.

"A woman named Cross asked that I come and get you."

"Is she all right?"

"She's gonna be okay, once the paramedics are done."

Chapter Twenty-One

Will followed the officer out to the valet stand, heart beating fast, where he found Charlotte sitting on the curb. Blood trickled down her right cheek and her left arm lay limply across her lap. He rushed to her side.

"Charlotte! Oh my God, what happened?" He kneeled down and placed a supportive hand on her shoulder, noticing even more blood on her blouse. Hand in his pocket, he pulled a handkerchief into view and pressed it to her head.

"Ms. Cross was in the wrong place at the wrong time, I'm afraid. Rounded the corner and came face to face with him," said the officer.

"Who?"

"Some guy in a hooded sweatshirt with my laptop and gym bag," she said.

"Popped out the back window behind the driver's side," the officer added.

"My God, you could have been…" Will stopped, afraid to verbalize the obvious.

"Paramedics are on the way," the officer confirmed.

"I don't need an ambulance. I told you, I'll be fine," she protested.

"She's a big girl, you know. Can cut her meat by herself and everything," Will told the officer, connecting with Charlotte's frightened eyes.

More police cars and emergency vehicles appeared as a large crowd of diners looked on. Will checked the status of his own car while Charlotte submitted to the probes and prods of the paramedics. Several units patrolled the area immediately surrounding the restaurant, looking for any sort of clue. The attacker got away with Charlotte's items, as well as a portable gaming system and a few bucks cash from another car in the area. Will paced for what seemed like forever, and after a half-hour, they finally cleared Charlotte to go.

"I don't care what she says, she's pretty shaken up," the officer confided to Will out of earshot.

"I know she is." He ran his hand through his hair, visibly shaken himself.

"Will you see that she gets home? My partner cleaned the broken glass out of her car but she's in no shape to drive. We dusted for prints but got nothing. I think she's gonna have to write this one off."

"Of course."

The drive to Charlotte Cross's home was quiet. Aside from the occasional 'turn left at the light and take a right at the stop sign', she said little. The gash above her eye required a thorough cleaning and a few stitches, which cut through her perfectly shaped dark eyebrow. She flipped down the sun visor and examined the wound in the light of the small mirror with an annoyed sigh.

"Maybe Anastasia makes house calls," Will joked, making reference to the woman who tamed the brows of LA's rich and famous.

"I doubt she can fix this." She flipped the visor back up.

"The important thing is that you're okay. You are okay, aren't you?" he asked.

"I'm fine," she answered in a tone that said anything but.

"I wish you'd let me take you to the hospital. I'd feel better if we got your wrist x-rayed."

"It's not broken." She looked down at the light blue sling that held her left arm.

He followed her directions for another five minutes before they arrived at her home. He pulled her black Mercedes sedan up the cobblestone drive, stopping at a large, black iron gate on the south side of the house. He walked her to the front door where she tried to wrangle her key in the lock but couldn't control her still-shaky hand. Will sensed her frustration, covering her hand with his own as he helped guide the key in place. With a turn, he opened the door and followed her inside.

She turned the lights on as she walked through the house. Immediately, Will was drawn to the rich terracotta color that bathed the walls. It was dramatic and unexpected, yet warm and inviting.

"Your house is beautiful." Will inspected the massive rustic beams that crisscrossed the vaulted ceiling. "How long have you lived here?"

"About two and a half years. The place needed a lot of work, and I needed a project, so here I am."

"I don't know what it looked like before, but you've done a fabulous job." He walked the perimeter of the room, admiring her choice in European antiques.

"Would you like some coffee?" she offered.

"How 'bout I get the coffee? And maybe some Tylenol?" he suggested.

"I could use a little something, I guess." She ran a

finger lightly across her stitched brow.

"If you've got some peroxide and a saltshaker, I'll take care of that stain on your blouse, too."

"I appreciate your willingness to help, really, but I've caused enough chaos in your life for one night. You didn't sign on to play chauffeur or nursemaid, and I don't want to tie up your evening any further."

Though her voice was soft and her words sincere, Will realized she wasn't herself. Her hands were still shaking, and a very real fear held fast in her blue eyes.

"So, you're trying to get rid of me, is that it?" He folded his arms across his chest.

"Well, no…" she answered, his actions helping her find her smile again.

"Then point me in the direction of your coffee maker so I can get to work."

He found everything he needed in the sleek, professional kitchen and waited in the living room with a fresh pot until she returned from the bedroom. He recognized the same yoga-style pants she'd worn the first time they met. Only this time, she'd paired them with an oversized Vanderbilt University sweatshirt. *Mark and Jonathan were right. No way in hell is this woman fifty.*

"You've done this before," she commented, pointing to the neatly organized tray of coffee and cake.

"Read about it in a book once. And I found these in the cabinet beside the spice rack." He placed a small medicine bottle on the tray beside the coffee pot.

"Thank you."

She watched as he poured them each a cup, then reached over and accepted it. Will continued to admire the details of the room as he blew into his steaming cup.

"You're quite the art collector."

"It's the art history major in me, I guess. I've always loved art. Impressionism, mainly."

"I was looking at your photos"—he motioned toward a large built-in shelving unit to the right of the stone fireplace—"And with the Vandy shirt, it all makes sense. You're from Nashville, aren't you?"

"Born and raised," she confirmed.

"You've met so many of the greats—Johnny Cash, Loretta Lynn…"

"My father was a music producer. He spent time with all the bigs. He was in the room when Patsy Cline recorded 'Walkin' After Midnight'."

"What about your mom?"

Charlotte thought for a moment. "She's known throughout Davidson County for her incredible peach cobbler. Chet Atkins used to order one from her for his birthday every year but that's where her fame ends."

"Aside from giving birth to a beautiful and talented daughter?"

"She wouldn't argue that point."

They sat in silence for a minute or two. Will's mind scurried for light-hearted topics to keep her thoughts in a happy place. It was then he noticed the absence of her sling.

"Didn't you forget something?"

"What?"

"Your sling." He pointed to his own wrist.

"It's just a sprain."

"You should wrap it up at least."

"Really, it's okay."

"Are you always this stubborn?" he asked, leaving his cup on the tray before crossing the room.

"Yes. Where are you going?"

"I'm on a quest for a first aid kit."

"In the same cabinet beside the spice rack. Try the second shelf, behind the vitamins."

"Got it."

He was back in a minute, whistling as he entered the room. Taking a seat beside her, he went to work, carefully wrapping her injured wrist.

"That's not too tight, now, is it?"

"It's perfect." She held her arm up, inspecting his work.

"Are you ready to take one of these?" he asked, reaching for the bottle of pills.

"Those really wipe me out. I better wait."

"Wait? For what? It's late and you should rest."

She ran her finger across the row of stitches on her brow again, closing her eyes for a moment.

"I'm really sorry about dinner," she offered after a pregnant pause. "I promise to make it up—"

"Charlotte, do not apologize. But next time, promise you'll let someone walk you to your car, okay?"

"Okay."

"It's like the officer said, no neighborhood is safe anymore."

The conversation stalled and Will noted the far-off look in her eyes. Though her physical wounds were relatively minor, the emotional trauma, he knew, would haunt her for a while. The bone china cup in her hand began to shake. Will quickly took the cup from her and returned it to the tray.

"Is there someone you'd like me to call? A friend maybe, or your brother?"

She shook her head, fighting back tears. The fear in her eyes touched a place inside him that had been dark for a while. He was overcome by a desire to comfort her as well as his own selfish need for a real, human connection.

He scooted over next to her and took her in his arms. "Hey, it's okay. I'm here. I'm not going anywhere."

Her body melted against his and together they sank back into the pillows on the sofa. He held her for a long time, running his hand through her hair while she released the tears she'd held inside.

"My name and address are written inside my laptop case. That means he knows where I live."

"You heard what the officer said. He's not interested in you. He's looking to pawn your computer and make a few bucks. Probably looking to score some drug money, that's all. I'm sure he dumped your case and bag at the first available trash can."

"Yes, but what if he—"

"Charlotte," Will pulled back. "You're home. You're safe. The doors are locked. The guy got what he wanted. He's not coming here. Okay?" He brushed a tear from her cheek with his thumb.

"Mr. Albright, I…" She pulled his hand away from her face, tears still falling.

"Why won't you call me Will?" he whispered.

He fought to keep his emotions in check, but he was failing. His mind raced with sinful thoughts. He imagined touching her, kissing her—loving her. Sitting just inches from her, Will contemplated crossing that line. If he did, there'd be no turning back.

"I'm afraid." She looked at him, fear evident in her

eyes.

"Afraid of what?" He cupped his hands around her cheeks, wiping away more tears.

"Of falling in love with you," she whispered.

Their lips touched, and instantly, a sensual rush coursed through him. It didn't take long to move from the cozy living area to her darkened bedroom. She pushed his jacket off his shoulders, letting it fall to the floor. Running her hands across his chest, she stopped at the first button on his shirt. She struggled for a moment, the bandage on her wrist an obvious hindrance. With a smile, he pulled her hand away and finished the task. Charlotte watched as he freed each button, letting her yoga pants fall to the floor beside his jacket. She slipped her uninjured hand under his open shirt, walking her fingers across his back. He found her lips again and kissed her deeply. His body pressed against hers. They stood for several moments, lost in each other before she took his hand and led him to her bed.

Will pressed her against the softness of down pillows. His hands disappeared beneath the Vanderbilt sweatshirt; her skin soft against his fingertips, and he explored the contours of her body. A tiny sliver of light coming from the bathroom illuminated her face. Though she said nothing, her expression spoke volumes. He looked down at her, gently tracing the tiny row of stitches on her brow. He kissed it lightly before his lips traveled down her cheek. Stopping at her neck, Will buried his face in her hair. She whispered his name as his warm breath filled her ear. He pulled her closer, and she whispered once more.

"Promise you won't say goodbye. Promise you'll

just stay with me."

****

Will stood at the large vessel sink, refusing to look at himself as the repulsion inside grew. Handfuls of cold water on his face and neck did nothing to relieve the numbing pain. Both hands steadied against the cool marble countertop, needing stability for his weakened legs and morals. At any moment, he knew his heart would pound through his chest, and he'd die a coward's death right there on Charlotte's bathroom floor. Alone. Without Rebecca. Tiny drops of water hung in his hair and fell from the tip of his nose. After several moments of silent damnation, he summoned the strength to look in the mirror.

The image of the man he found staring back was more than he could take. He struggled to draw a cleansing breath, but the air around him had stopped. In fact, everything in his perfect life had stopped. His dress shirt, unbuttoned and wrinkled, clung to his frame. A million beads of sweat on his back and chest sent chills over his entire body. Lying in the next room, a desirable, scared, and confused woman waited—a woman with deep blue eyes who would hold him all night, if that's what he wanted.

"Promise you won't say goodbye. Promise you'll just stay with me."

It was those words that transported him back in time. Suddenly he was on his yacht in a dark marina, begging a beautiful, married woman to make the same promise.

"Will? Are you okay?" Charlotte asked from behind the closed bathroom door.

"I just need a minute," he said, still focused on the

reflection of a man he now loathed.

He waited a moment, curious if she would enter or let him be. Thankfully, she made no further response, and he stood at the sink a minute longer, his mind reeling. He'd lived a large portion of his life on the edge but never had he stood atop a cliff so deadly. A cliff that would disfigure not one life, but three. Though he'd stopped short of losing himself entirely, the intense guilt he felt made his body feel as lifeless as if he'd jumped.

He washed his face once more and dried it on the tail of his shirt. The dark circles that held position under each eye were nothing compared to the lines of remorse that now cut across his forehead. *Please, God. Just let me get out of here.* He fought for another breath, and when he finally felt stable enough to stand on his own, he began to button his shirt. As he did, something caught his eye, and his focus shifted from the man in the mirror to an enormous painting on the wall behind him. Slowly, he turned, the blood in his veins turning cold with shock. Hanging quietly above Charlotte's porcelain claw-foot tub was a familiar impressionist image of a young girl, riding a sorrel horse on a deserted stretch of beach. In the bottom corner, the signature of an artist he knew well.

Rosalie Rutledge Graham.

Chapter Twenty-Two

The night wind blew through Rebecca's hair. The lights of a hundred yachts glimmered on the harbor, taking her back to a place in the past—a time filled with regattas and champagne and falling in love with a smooth-talking sailor. The same sailor who now entertained her as they closed out the final hours of a very long day in the moonlight.

Dinner with Lily and Maks had been quiet, certainly not the constant chatter that surrounded the foursome just two nights before. Rebecca could see the fatigue on Kelly's face in the way of dark circles under each brown eye. He shuffled his body with caution, and she could tell he was experiencing some type of pain. The hours spent roaming the bush had taken a toll, though he'd never admit it. Following dessert, she stated her need for a taxi and a hot shower, ready to end her ex-husband's suffering and call it a night. But Kelly wouldn't hear of it, announcing that the final nightcap of the evening would take place aboard his brand-new luxury cruiser, *Cashin' In*.

They'd been together since dawn, traveling to and from the magical place he lovingly called Anembo. She could hardly believe her eyes when his helicopter touched down at Wigilopka Wildlife Reserve—five thousand acres of rugged beauty, and Gloria Glass's final legacy. A labor of love she cultivated with her son, and the place that, upon Kelly's death, Rebecca learned, would be left in her care. They'd explored vast terrain while the head of the operations, Terrence McBride, played chauffeur and tour guide. Rebecca watched with wonder as both he and Kelly narrated the various sites around the reserve currently under construction—the animal hospital and rehab center, an education and multimedia center, and staff housing. A twenty-two-room guest house was also under construction for those who desired an extended stay where they might view dozens of native creatures and be amongst nature. It was more than Rebecca could have imagined, sincerely touched by the pride glistening in Kelly's eyes.

It was almost four o'clock when they returned to the helicopter pad on the east side of the property. They'd traveled down the eight-mile stretch of dirt road in silence as Rebecca tried to process the enormity of her unexpected gift.

"Kelly…" She shook her head in disbelief, taking one last look as she climbed into the Bell Jet Ranger. "It's the most amazing place I've ever been in my life. I just don't know what to say."

"You don't have to say anything. The smile on your face says it all."

Now, hours later and back on his boat, her thoughts had moved on from the wildlife reserve to the man seated before her. She watched as he played the guitar, his gaze bouncing from his fingers on the strings to her face every few seconds. Each look conveyed a peaceful sort of contentment that tugged at her heart.

"What on earth possessed you to start playing the guitar?" Rebecca broke the silence. "You were never interested in music."

"Actually, it was Evelyn's idea, in a roundabout sort of way."

"Evelyn?" Rebecca was surprised.

"She came to my rescue, I guess you could say, at a time when I really needed a friend. I was pretty strung out; Evelyn intervened. On Lily's behalf, of course. I could either get cleaned up or lose Lily. And you know the rule—don't fuck with Evelyn or her fleet of attorneys. So, I did what every obscenely rich son of a national treasure does. I checked myself into a posh rehab for aging brats. Found a little Jesus and a lot of sobriety. Roomed with a famous country music singer who taught me a few licks. And that…" he strummed a funny little melody, "Is how I learned to play guitar."

It was with this confession that Rebecca's gaze moved to a two-tone medallion hanging from a braided leather cord around Kelly's neck. She'd noticed it earlier that day and meant to ask him about it, but in the excitement of exploring the reserve, she had forgotten. The triangular symbol on the gold and silver pendant was one she'd seen before. After hearing his story, she recognized it as the symbol for Alcoholics Anonymous.

He changed chords and began playing once more. She instantly recognized the tune and couldn't help but smile.

He threw a wink her way, cleared his throat, then strummed and sang the first few verses of what he knew was her favorite song by The Eagles. Rebecca's foot bounced in time with the beat. When he reached the chorus, she joined him, singing a harmony that eventually ended in their shared laughter. Kelly stopped playing for a moment.

"Wanna know a secret?"

"Of course."

"I always pictured us on a beautiful boat like this. Just the two of us together on a night like this one. I never dreamed that when it happened, I'd be on my deathbed, and you'd be wearing another man's ring."

"That's not funny." She shook her head, not amused by his comment.

"It wasn't meant to be. Truth isn't always humorous."

"Kelly, I really wish that you wouldn't—"

"Talk about my impending death?"

She sat stunned by his lackadaisical attitude. Was he just pretending? Playing the brave hero for the woman he once called wife?

"You want to know the beautiful thing about death, Becks? It's that you can say and do anything you want—within reason, of course."

"And that includes making stupid, tasteless comments?" She shot him a look.

"Well, you know me. I'm gonna make those regardless."

His fingers returned to the strings, and he played the intro to another Eagles song. She downed the last few drops of wine from her glass. Silently, she sang the lyrics of the famous hit to herself, thinking of a man on another continent, seven thousand miles removed.

As if he could read her mind, Kelly steered the conversation into choppy waters.

"So, when were *you* going to tell *me*?"

"Tell you what?"

"Oh, c'mon. Give me a little credit. There are only three givens in life: death, taxes, and the fact that Will Albright escorts his lady everywhere, no matter the distance."

"He's in the middle of an enormous—"

"Hostile takeover? Multi-million-dollar merger?" Kelly interrupted sarcastically.

She looked away, heart pounding in a violent rhythm. *Am I that transparent?*

"Really, Kelly…" She smiled, trying to play it off. "Will wanted to come, but he just couldn't get away."

The last of her words faded away as she watched her ex-husband shake his head disapprovingly.

"The only way two people can keep a secret is if one of them is dead. And since I'm standing in the batters' box swinging for the afterlife, let's dispense with the charade. You've never been a very good liar, Rebecca. You know, that's something you took quite a bit of license with in your novel, too. Holly was a great liar." His dark eyes held her with an intensity that caught her off guard. "You never were."

His words, while not spoken harshly, were filled with an honesty that seemed to stop the air around them. For weeks, travel and press had pushed the truth to a dark corner of her life, the truth that her marriage was officially in trouble. She'd used her newfound success and her father's recent accident to avoid facing it. But now, alone with Kelly on a boat, she had nowhere to run.

"You wanna know the hardest thing for an alcoholic to do?" He placed Edna on the white leather seat beside him and moved in closer to her. "Admit he's got a problem."

He reached for her hand and held it tenderly. She couldn't speak, the weight of her inner self struggling to get free. One tear fell, followed closely by another. In seconds, she found herself enveloped by his familiar arms, rocking her as gently as the waves around them. They held each other under the cloudless November sky. His arms felt good around her. They said nothing but listened to the sounds of water lapping against the sides of the boat.

"He's hurt you." Kelly rubbed her back softly.

"No," she confessed. "We've hurt each other."

"Do you want to talk about it?"

"I don't even know where to begin."

"Is it because you're here with me?"

"That's part of it."

"Is it the book?"

She sighed. "That's a lot of it. The traveling, the press junket."

"So, the little woman's not home when Big Daddy breezes in from the office, is that it?"

"Even when she is home, she's not really there."

"How would you make it better? I mean, you're a best-selling author, right? How would you write your way out of it?" he asked.

"I honestly don't know."

"Becks, you have to do better than that." He rested his chin on her head. "Do you still love him?"

"Yes," she whispered.

"Enough to stop writing? Maybe go back into the counseling business?"

She froze, feeling as though he'd sucker-punched her in the stomach. Her body stiffened, and Kelly must have sensed that discomfort. He released her and moved back, giving her some breathing room.

"About twenty-five years ago, a man interviewed my father and asked him if he ever got jealous of my mother's success. You know, my father made a lot of important contributions to medicine. But he was never really in the trenches to the degree my mother was. While he was operating inside a sterile hospital, my mother was shoveling manure, bottle feeding some orphaned animal, or building a mud hut in the middle of nowhere. Anyway, this interviewer asked my father if he got jealous of all the attention placed on my mom, and if he ever wanted her to just give it up—her causes, I mean. I remember this vividly because the entire room just stopped. My father sat there and thought for a moment. Then, in the calmest voice possible he said, 'She was carrying a torch when I met her, and she'll carry it long after I'm gone. If she has to give something up, let it be me. I'm just one person. Her torchlight touches thousands.'"

Rebecca digested his words and the significance of his story. Deep down, she knew Will would never ask her to walk away from writing just as she would never ask him to walk away from his career. They'd fallen in love with each other in every sense from the word go. Physically, emotionally, and spiritually; neither would ever challenge the choices they'd made to fulfill their personal goals. Yet the hurt he inflicted the night before her departure still burned. More so than his words, the look in his eyes pierced her inside, creating an emptiness that ruined every night of sleep since.

"Will hates you, Kelly," Rebecca finally said, and her tears began to fall once more.

"I know he does…but he loves you. He loves you in ways I never could. I knew it the first time you danced with him, after the LA to Honolulu race. God, if I'd only put my drink and my pride down long enough to dance with you myself."

"I never meant to hurt you. It's just that we—"

"I know you didn't. Baby, it wasn't you. I'd been hurting myself for a long time. Don't make the same mistakes I made, Rebecca. Don't let jealousy and pride drive you away from the most important thing in your life. Let your words die on the page, and let his money rot in a bank. That's not what matters. That's not what the couple on the dance floor cared about. I watched those two together that night—the looks and the laughter they shared. What you and Will have together is worth fighting for."

The weight of his words pressed against her heart. The man who caused years of anguish and unhappiness now spoke with tenderness, delivering words that filled her with hope.

"I don't know how you do it, but every moment I spend with you, I'm more and more amazed."

"I have that effect on so many women. It's a curse, really."

"Kelly, I'm serious. At times today, during lunch especially, I honestly didn't know who you were. The way you spoke with such passion about the reserve and wanting to leave something behind for the benefit of others…" Her voice cracked. "I'm really proud of you."

"You know, the good Lord's ability to love and forgive is surpassed only by his ability to create irony. I've spent the last ten years trying to become the kind of man I know you always wanted me to be. A man who can give and receive love without consequence. A man who can let the world happen without having to control every aspect of it. And now here we are, and the few remaining moments I have left are just drops of rain in a very big ocean. If only I'd learned these lessons long ago."

He brushed her hair off her forehead, then pressed his lips tenderly against it. The boat continued to rock gently, and Rebecca realized that this would be the last night they'd spend together.

"I'm so afraid for you." She reached and touched his cheek, running her fingers softly along his jawline.

"Afraid of what? Of my dying?" He laughed and pulled her back into his arms. "Oh, baby, I'm not. Not anymore. In fact, my breath could leave my body at this exact moment in time, and I'd die a more peaceful death than I ever imagined because you've helped me cross the final item off my bucket list."

"And what's that?" she asked, feeling a warmth for Kelly Glass she prayed would never leave her.

"To lie under the stars holding the only woman I ever truly loved."

Chapter Twenty-Three

Her name is Charlotte. Her name is Charlotte. Her name is Charlotte.

The captain turned on the 'fasten seatbelt' sign, putting an end to Rebecca's short but telling dream— one containing images of her husband's hands and mouth greedily devouring the body of another woman. She took a moment to collect herself, wiping sweat from her neck and brow with her sleeve.

The flight had taken two hours longer than expected, with an unforeseen mechanical problem. Her last-minute decision to leave Austin and fly back to Atlanta landed her in coach, forcing her to engage in polite conversation with the chatty woman beside her. Phyllis Larson, mother of four, talked incessantly from the moment she'd taken her seat. The subject she'd had to endure for the majority of the flight was that of a hot, new novel—one whose author bore a striking resemblance to Rebecca. She'd tried her best to be courteous, though she contributed little to the exchange. Talking was the last thing on Rebecca's mind. Luckily, the woman pulled her book from her knitting bag and spent the final hour of the trip reading. It'd taken a while to convince Mrs. Larson that she wasn't Rebecca Albright, celebrated writer and overnight media darling. Lack of sleep coupled with a thousand tears after Will's shocking confession made it easy to pull off the charade. Skipping make-up and hiding behind a pair of glasses added another layer to her anonymity.

"I guess we'll be on the ground soon," the woman commented.

"Umm…" Rebecca nodded.

The flight attendants made final preparations for landing, collecting empty cups as they moved their carts along the center aisle of the plane. Rebecca turned toward the window, staring into clusters of clouds. In a few minutes, she would touch down and head for the nearest rental car counter, hoping to sort out her heavy thoughts in the drive between the airport and her quiet hometown suburb of Havenbrook.

What am I going to tell my parents? She'd tried for hours to answer that question. Now time was running out, and she still hadn't alerted them of her arrival. In fact, no one knew her present whereabouts. She'd stumbled through the Austin darkness just hours before, the compass that once guided her life spinning out of control. She drove around for hours, finally bedding down at an airport hotel because returning home was not an option. Now, with daylight and a thousand miles between them, Will's fateful declaration of his tryst with another woman pierced her heart with painful and unexpected precision.

"She was hurt and scared and alone and I—I mean, we…" Will's voice trailed off.

A long and heavy silence chilled the air. Rebecca held her breath, processing everything he'd said. There has to be some mistake, *she told herself.* This can't be happening. *She searched his eyes for the tiniest sliver of reassurance, but the look on his face was undeniable.*

"We didn't have sex," he added with remorseful

211

eyes. "I realized things were getting out of control and I stopped."

"And I guess you want me to somehow thank you for that?" she asked through tears, as their cornerstone of trust fell into a black chasm.

The captain's voice echoed once more on the intercom, commanding the flight crew to take their seats as they began the descent. Mrs. Larson continued to read, and Rebecca composed a mental checklist until the plane stopped at the gate.

"Gosh, I hate to stop," the woman said, storing the novel back inside the knitting bag. "This is the most intense part of the whole book. You know, the part where Zander shows up, only Holly thinks it's Jack. And then Zander has to tell Holly that Jack was critically injured in the accident. Can you imagine?" She shook her head. "I actually feel sorry for Zander, the way Holly falls into his arms, completely grief-stricken."

"Yes, I remember that part." Rebecca's eyes connected briefly with the gregarious stranger.

"I mean, here he is, on his way to confront them and catch them *in flagrante delicto*, so to speak, and he happens to be the first one on the scene after Jack rolls his car. And then the flashback he has, seeing the look in Holly's eyes as she watched Jack give his speech at that dinner. He knew! He knew even then that Holly was in love with Jack. And now he's faced with the greatest dilemma of his life: let his wife's lover die on the side of the road or do the right thing and save another man's life.

"He could have just gotten in his car and driven away, and that would have been the end of his problem, right? But no. What does he do? He not only pulls Jack's body out of the car, but he holds him and talks to him, begging him to fight, until emergency crews arrive." She released another heavy sigh. "I thought I was Team Jack all the way but after that, I don't know. I mean, how could you not fall for Zander after he shows such compassion? It's just so completely unexpected."

"Life is full of the unexpected," Rebecca confirmed with a heavy sigh.

****

With little explanation to her parents, Rebecca collapsed in her old bedroom. Her tired body bypassed dream state, and she awoke to feel as though she'd slept through decades of her life. Lying in bed, listening to the familiar creaks of her childhood home, she found that the new day brought zero clarity. She slipped from the bed and into a parka and an old pair of rain boots, then tiptoed outside, hoping the fresh air might provide some comfort.

A long walk to clear her mind ended in the one place she'd sought for years when the answers to life's questions were seemingly beyond her grasp. The worn, wooden slats were littered with an assortment of leaves. A late-night storm had blown the crisp remains of autumn up along the boat dock, and it took Rebecca several brushes of her gloved hand to clear off a suitable spot on which to sit. Winston, her father's faithful beagle, poked his head around the nearby trees and bushes, uncovering nothing of substance. Winter was on its way, and the bleak landscape around her oddly resembled the current state of affairs inside her private life.

She sat and, with half a smile, watched Winston play Tug O' War with a vine that was lifeless from the season's chilly temperature. She peeked at her watch, knowing it was only a matter of minutes until her mother and father would be up and in search of answers to the questions she'd avoided.

Despite the beauty of the estate, she could only see a series of grainy images she'd created in her head— pictures of her husband, sharing intimate moments with someone else; meeting her for dinner at what had once been one of Rebecca's favorite restaurants; comforting her after the parking lot attack and driving her to her Tarrytown home; disappearing behind the bedroom door.

Her feet dangled off the end of the dock as she tried to put a face to the name. The nightmare began with four words. Just four little words, spoken with a guilty tongue, still pounding inside her head as she imagined Will running his hands through this Charlotte woman's hair. Feeling her skin beneath his fingertips. Exploring her body with his lips.

"I see my secret spot is no longer a secret," a voice called from behind.

Rebecca turned, surprised by the presence of her mother.

"Oh, Mom, I hope I didn't wake you. I tried to be quiet."

"You didn't wake me. I've been up since five. It's been sort of my ritual since I've been here. The mornings are just too beautiful to sleep in." She sat on the end of the dock beside her daughter.

"I don't imagine you have many mornings that look like this in the Big Apple, huh?"

"Not even close. Don't get me wrong, there are so many things I love about New York—the arts, the culture; Bobby, my favorite bagel vendor near Rockefeller Center. But the quiet doesn't exist in the city. Not the true, peaceful, I-can-really-hear-myself-think kind of quiet like this."

"It's everything a secret spot should be."

"Sadly, we're not the only ones in the know. Your father surprised me down here a couple of days ago."

"Dad came all the way down here? But how did he—"

"Oh, believe me, he won't do it again. Not after the sermon I preached. He scared me to death. I turned around and there he was, standing with his cane in one hand and a picnic basket in the other. I don't know how he managed it by himself. I know he's getting stronger every day, but the distance alone is tough, even for me."

"A picnic basket?" Rebecca smiled.

"My favorite coffee and Melba's cranberry muffins. We had breakfast right here on the dock. Of course, your father pouted when I refused to let him take the boat out."

"Sounds like things are better between the two of you? In fact, I thought you'd be back home by now."

"I guess you could say we've buried the cornucopia." Rosalie smiled.

They sat side by side, taking advantage of the serene backdrop as the sun continued to climb. Rebecca's heartbeat quickened. Her parents hadn't pressed for details of her unexpected visit. Of course, every time she made eye contact with her mom, it verified just how wise a woman she was. She'd never been able to keep a secret from her. Today would be no different.

"Your father talked to Kelly," Rosalie finally said, her gaze fixed upon the glass-like surface of the water.

"What? When was this?"

"He called here a couple of days ago. Thanked us for the flowers we sent for Gloria and also to see how your father was doing. Said you told him about the fall and his surgery. They actually talked for a long time."

"Dad and Kelly talked?" Rebecca couldn't hide her shock. "What on earth about?"

"I don't know. Everything. Deep-sea fishing, college football, the old times, when your father photographed Gloria all those years ago. Of course, he told your father how much he appreciated your presence at the funeral. Said he wouldn't have made it through without you."

"That was very thoughtful of him."

"Suspiciously so," Rosalie agreed.

Rebecca dropped her head, returning for a moment to their final, tearful goodbye. The pain she felt for Kelly was now magnified a thousand times over. His life was coming to an unexpected close. Thinking back to the moments spent beneath the stars, rocked by the gentle waves, she remembered his tender plea. *Don't let jealousy and pride drive you away from the most important thing in your life.*

"He's dying, Mom. Kelly's dying."

"What?" Rosalie's head snapped in her daughter's direction.

"He has cancer."

"Oh my god." She shook her head in disbelief.

"It's really bad."

"Oh, sweetheart, I'm so sorry." Rosalie slipped a supportive arm around her daughter. "What type of cancer?"

"I don't know. He wouldn't tell me. Something aggressive. Pancreatic maybe? You wouldn't even recognize him if you saw him; I bet he doesn't even weigh a hundred and seventy pounds. His hair's as white as Dad's."

"One seventy? I can't even picture it."

"When I walked into the private reception before the funeral, I froze. All through the service, I just kept staring at the back of his head. He's like a ghost. I don't know how else to describe it. Only, it's just his body that's diminished. His spirit…" She began, feeling a familiar lump return to her throat. "His spirit is stronger and more beautiful than you could ever imagine."

"We are talking about the same Kelly?"

"Do you know he hasn't had a drink in over ten years? He's completely sober. And you should hear him play the guitar. He's a master musician, Mom, like he was born to play. And then there's the reserve."

"The reserve?"

Rebecca took a deep breath and exhaled loudly. "Remember when I ran into Lily in London and she said that Kelly had dropped out of the rat race?"

"Yes, you said that he'd sold off his major interests and spent all his time on his yacht."

"Actually, he rolled everything over into a wildlife reserve with Gloria. It was a joint project. Their first and only mother-son philanthropic endeavor. They were beginning to put on the finishing touches when she passed away."

"Kelly Glass hunts exotic animals, he doesn't save

them."

"He does now. He's arranged for the reserve to go to me when he…" Rebecca's bottom lip quivered.

"It's okay." Rosalie pulled her in.

"We connected on levels we never found when we were married. All the jealousy and trying to strong-arm everything around him…gone. It's all gone. What's left is a gentle, caring, attentive soul. I can't stop thinking and wondering—what I mean is, if the Kelly Glass I just spent time with in Sydney had been the same Kelly Glass I married years ago…" She paused and swallowed hard. "And now, after everything that's happened with Will."

She stopped, her words replaced with tears. Rosalie increased her grip, pulling her daughter's body even closer. She held Rebecca in her arms, letting her release the barrage of emotions that had taken over recently.

"I'm right here, sweetheart. I'm right here."

"I don't know what to do, Mom."

"I know this is hard on you. All the stress of traveling plus the interviews and the book signings. Losing Gloria and then seeing Kelly. But you and I both know that this goes way beyond your trip to Sydney."

The tears fell harder but Rebecca didn't say a word. Saying it out loud, even to the woman who loved her no matter what, would make it all too real. Deep down, she wanted to tell her mother everything, every agonizing detail of Will's confession from the flat tire in the rain and the run-in at the tennis club to a business meeting with an unexpected detour in Dallas. She wanted to tell her about late-night birthday toasts in a dark, crowded bar that led to playful texts and portraits sketched on cocktail napkins. A knight in shining armor…and a night in another woman's arms.

"What's her name?" Rosalie pulled away, looking into her daughter's glassy green eyes with deep empathy.

"Charlotte," Rebecca whispered after a long pause. "Her name is Charlotte."

****

"Are you in love with her?" Rosalie asked, though she feared his answer.

Leland stood in the doorway of the bedroom they had shared for years, hands tucked inside his pockets. His posture alone was enough to convict him. The suitcase on the bed in front of Rosalie spelled it out, leaving little doubt in his mind. He knew with complete certainty that he could do nothing to stop her from leaving. He'd justified his actions for so long that he could no longer decipher truth from fiction.

"Leland! Are you in love with Claudia?" she shouted, as tears etched lines upon her cheeks.

"My God, how could you even ask that? Of course I'm not in love with her. It's over. I ended it. It was a mistake; a hugely regrettable mistake and it's over," he said firmly, as if his statement of truth would be enough to negate months of lies.

"A mistake?" she yelled. "A mistake?! Running a red light? That's a mistake. Forgetting to set your alarm? That's a mistake. But sleeping with your wife's best friend? For an entire year? That's not a mistake, Leland. That's a goddamn affair!"

Chapter Twenty-Four

Georgia stood at the bottom of the stairs, exchanging confused looks with the dog at her feet. For two days she'd tiptoed through the house, waiting for something to give. The anguish caused by Rebecca's departure was unrelenting and tense. She wondered if and when her brother would emerge from his bedroom suite to rejoin the land of the living.

In the time that she'd lived with them, Georgia had witnessed a fair share of disagreements and arguments. Like any couple, Will and Rebecca Albright suffered the occasional bump, but all-out fighting was a foreign concept in what many considered an ideal marriage. To Georgia's knowledge, they'd never climbed into the ring in all their years together—not the way they had two nights before. While she hadn't heard the exact exchange, the tears she saw in two sets of eyes as Rebecca hastily collected her purse and keys confirmed what she'd suspected. Someone had crossed a very dangerous line.

She'd tried her best to stay out of Will's way. Trays of food left outside the bedroom door went untouched; phone messages continued to pile up, all ignored and none from Rebecca. Georgia feared her twin brother had been living out of a bottle for the better part of forty-eight hours. They hadn't spoken to one another since the painfully quiet dinner following

Rebecca's return from Sydney. Frankly, she couldn't take it another minute. With a nod in Dizzy's direction, she swallowed hard and walked upstairs.

Without bothering to knock, Georgia opened the door and took a few steps inside. The room was dark, and it took a moment to make out his silhouette. He was flat on his back, staring up at the ceiling. Georgia waited for some sort of acknowledgment. With a deep breath, she sat on the edge of the bed, an understanding ear at the ready. Will neither looked her way nor responded. Georgia's heart sank when she saw the empty bourbon bottle on the bedside table, alongside his wedding ring and a wrinkled piece of paper.

"*With one kiss we find all the tomorrows suspended in a fleeting moment / Never to be wholly relived / Encompassing and engulfing yet carried away with faint clouds / And the hope of one day to regain the light that nourishes and sustains / And gives without hesitation, the peace I have found / Without definition or reason, in you.*" Will spoke in a whisper, his eyes still focused on the ceiling overhead.

"Will, what the hell is going on?" Georgia asked, puzzled.

"I never told you about the first time I saw Rebecca, did I?" He spoke in an eerily calm voice.

"Sure you did. It was at that club in Hawaii, after the race. The night you danced together, right?"

"That was our second meeting. Only, I didn't realize it at the time. We actually met years before."

"When was this?"

"Back in my Navy days when I was stationed at Kings Bay."

"You met Rebecca then?" Georgia asked,

221

confused. "But you were just a kid. She would have been a baby."

"They had this amazing house on Saint Simons, right on the water. I only went there one time, right after Rebecca and I got engaged. Her father sold it not long after that. Anyway, they'd just spent two weeks there and were headed back home. I was on a special errand for my commanding officer, and I got a flat tire on the highway. The spare in the car I'd been issued was flat, too. I was stranded and, of course, there were no cell phones back then.

"Leland and Rosalie stopped and offered to give me a ride to the nearest service station. We loaded up the tire in the back of Leland's brand-new car. I'll never forget it. I rode upfront with him, and Rosalie sat in the back with Rebecca. She was maybe nineteen or twenty, and fast asleep in the back seat. I got in the car and took one look at her and thought, 'Wow! She's a knockout!' Her hair was long then. She was wearing a white sundress and a pair of designer sunglasses like she'd just flown in from Monte Carlo or something. Her feet were bare, and I remember that she had a Band-Aid wrapped around one of her toes."

"Listen, Will, I got a pot of hot coffee. Come downstairs and—"

He continued, "She never woke up. Of course, I was only in the car with them for about ten minutes. We found a station on the Interstate. Leland said he'd wait and take me back to my car, but I hated to take up any more of his time. I told him that I needed to call the base and let them know what had happened. I asked if I could borrow a pen and a piece of paper. He gave me his pen and Rosalie tore a sheet of paper out of

Rebecca's journal. I remember this so vividly. I was standing outside the car on the passenger side watching Rosalie through the window. She flipped through this little pink and green floral notebook for a minute, looking for a blank page. Rebecca was completely unaware of what was going on. Rosalie finally ripped a sheet out. It had writing on one side, but the back was blank. She handed it to me with a reassuring smile and said, 'She'll never miss it.'"

"And the writing on the back of the sheet…that was…" Georgia understood, putting the pieces together.

"Rebecca's poem." Will sighed again, dropping the wrinkled scrap of paper on the bed. "I've carried that piece of paper around in my wallet for years. Each time I read it, it takes me back to that day and the beautiful young poet sleeping soundly in the back of a silver Lincoln."

"Wow, Will, that's one hell of a story." Georgia shook her head.

"You know, I thought about that girl for years. I always wondered what color eyes she had. I could remember every detail about her: her hair and her skin, even that Band-Aid. But her eyes? They were a mystery until I held her on that dance floor and looked into those magical green eyes of hers for the first time." Will smiled. "At that moment, I knew I'd found the very light that nourishes and sustains, and gives without hesitation, a peace that is found, without definition or reason."

The end of Will's story triggered the return of the same uncomfortable silence that had imprisoned them for two days. Georgia picked up the piece of paper and reread the poem, clearly written in Rebecca's hand. A few letters, she noticed, had changed over the years. The tails on her y's were not quite so grandiose, and her s's were no longer as curly. But they were definitely Rebecca's words.

She placed the poem on the bedside table beside the empty bottle. "After you and Rebecca started seeing each other, her parents didn't remember your name?"

"I don't think we even exchanged introductions that day. He just called me by my rank."

"But they know, right? That you were the guy on the side of the road?"

"You know the old saying…that if you make a wish on a star, and you tell someone, it won't come true? Well, I never told them. Even Rebecca doesn't know."

"Listen, Will, I don't know what's going on, but I know you, and I know Rebecca. There's nothing in this world the two of you can't work out."

"It's over, Georgia," he whispered.

"What?" she answered in shock. "You're drunk. It's not over."

"When you let a third party into your relationship…" He finally looked at his sister.

"What are you saying?" She studied Will's eyes and the defeat that resided behind them. "Are you telling me that Rebecca and Kelly…?"

"It wasn't Rebecca." He closed his eyes and exhaled loudly. "It was me."

Georgia's hand shot to her mouth.

"Just go, Georgia."

"What have you done, Will?"

"Get out, Georgia!"

"No! I'm not leaving until you tell me what

224

happened."

"I kissed Charlotte!"

"Charlotte who?"

"Charlotte Cross—Charlie—the head of the architecture firm."

"You have everything, Will. Every goddamn thing in the world. Why? Why would you do that?"

"It's none of your business. Please, just get out of my room!"

"Get up." She shoved his body as hard as she could, but he didn't move.

"I swear to God, Georgia, touch me one more time…"

"Get! The! Fuck! Up!" She stood and yelled as loudly as she could, emphasizing each word.

"Goddamn it, Georgia!"

"You think you'll get her back like this?"

"Leave me alone!"

"No! I'm not leaving this room! I'm not playing the sweet, supportive sister anymore, either. You're going to get up out of that bed, take a shower, and make your life right again. You're going to drive over and apologize to that Cross woman for wasting her time and being an absolutely worthless piece of shit, and then you're going to work like hell to bring your wife back home."

"She left! God, don't you get it? If she'd wanted to work this out, she would have stayed. I laid it all out there. Everything that happened—the one hundred percent God's honest truth. You think that was easy? Do you?"

"You wanna know what I think is easy? Curling up with a bottle and checking out. And before you play the 'well-you-know-all-about-that-don't-you' card, keep in mind that I never, *ever* cheated on my husband. Recovering addict? Yes. Adulterer? Not even once."

Chapter Twenty-Five

Rebecca was eager to curl up on the inviting leather chair but shivered when she entered the study. An empty fireplace and a wall of windows created a chill, initiating a quest for a blanket. Scanning the room, she stopped at the large trunk in the corner near the television. Carefully lifting the lid, she peeked inside and found what she needed folded neatly on top—a soft wool blanket in a masculine plaid bearing her father's monogram. She pulled it from the trunk, surprised by what was hiding underneath. An oversized photo album she didn't recognize resting upon stacks of old books and magazines. With a quick check over her shoulder, she reached for the album.

Page after page, she examined images of their family from the comfort of her father's favorite chair. Holidays, vacations, birthdays, graduations... A complete history of the Graham trio. Some photos she hadn't seen in thirty or more years. Shots of her swimming in the ocean, picnics down at the dock, and learning to drive the old red T-bird. Her photographer father had captured her entire young life on film. There were some beautiful shots of her mother, too, reminiscent of the photo hanging above the fireplace. She stopped for a moment and gazed at a picture of her mother, unable to ignore the pain she felt inside.

In the back of the album, she made an unexpected

find. A small brown mailing envelope containing dozens of photos she hadn't seen in forever. Photos of a fresh-faced bride and the dark-haired man with an impish grin. She studied the bride for several moments. She was young, twenty-something. Perfect hair. Perfect smile. Perfect. Kelly stood proudly by her side, his arm wrapped firmly around her waist, surrounded by family and close friends. The photographs were beautiful—she couldn't deny it. But something was missing. They just didn't seem real. They looked as though they'd simply been pulled from the pages of a bridal magazine. Their expressions didn't match. While his face shone with a smug smile, her smile conveyed a different sentiment, though she wasn't sure what. Perhaps that young woman knew even then that their union was a mistake.

"Are you planning on tying up my chair all afternoon?" her father teased, leaning on his cane in the doorway of his private study. "It's nap time, you know."

"Sorry, Dad." She closed the album.

"Taking a trip down Memory Lane, are we?"

"I was looking for a throw in your trunk and came across it. Some of those pictures I've never even seen before."

"Melba and I spent an entire weekend going through box after box of old photos. I found that album in the hall closet and tried to organize a few."

He sat on the sofa and motioned for her to join him. The room fell silent as Leland flipped through the album. Rebecca held her breath with every page he turned, confused by her feelings.

"Do you remember this one?" He pointed to a picture of a teenage Rebecca standing on a trampoline, wearing a green bikini top, frayed denim shorts, and a frown.

"Remember it? It was the longest day of my life."

"You were a little upset with me that day if I recall." He laughed.

"Upset? I was mad as hell. I was exhausted. We'd been out there for hours, and you wouldn't let me quit."

"That's because you were so close. I knew you could do it if you'd just relax a bit. And I was right. You mastered the back tuck. It was beautiful."

"It was borderline abusive," she corrected.

"I guess that's why you spent the following afternoon showing off your new trick to all our guests?"

"And you spent the afternoon bragging to everyone about what a great coach you were."

"That was a wonderful weekend, wasn't it?" He pushed his glasses up from the end of his nose, taking in the details of the outdated photograph. "I miss the old barbecues we used to have."

"Funny…I don't remember this one."

Rebecca reached out and tapped her finger on another photo. She wasn't in the shot, one that featured her father and mother, along with their former best friends. Seeing the woman that came between her parents made Rebecca's heart skip a beat. She couldn't help but think back to the heart-to-heart she'd shared at the dock and her mother's hauntingly honest words.

"Before you walk away from the life you've built with this man, I want you to think about something. I want you to think about how you're going to feel years down the road, when you run into Will, and he's with someone else. Maybe it'll be across a crowded ballroom or inside a busy airport terminal. Maybe he'll

see you, or maybe you'll just watch him, unnoticed, in the company of another woman. And when you see the man you loved above everything, sharing his life with someone else, I wonder if you'll ask yourself the same question I've asked myself all these lonely years," Rosalie spoke softly, eyes welling with tears.

"What question is that?" Rebecca asked, her own sympathetic tears now falling for her mother.

"Why didn't I do more to try and save my marriage?"

"But how do you rebuild that kind of trust, Mom?"

"You have to be strong enough to do what I wasn't able to." She brushed her daughter's hair off her forehead. *"You have to forgive. I know you've probably preached that day in and day out in your professional life, but it's almost impossible to practice in your personal life."*

"This was taken at the beach house?"

He nodded.

"Was this before or after you started sleeping with Claudia?" she asked coolly, her heart pounding furiously.

Leland said nothing but slowly closed the album and returned it to the coffee table. He removed his glasses, rubbing his eyes with a bony finger. Rebecca waited, unsure of the response. She braced herself for an old-fashioned shouting match, the kind they had regularly after her mother's departure from their everyday lives. Just as the news of her father's infidelity shocked and stunned her, his reaction to her unexpected question surprised her even more.

"Despite all his strength, at the end of the day, a man is still just a man," he muttered.

"And just what the hell is that supposed to mean?" Rebecca stood, arms folded across her chest, ready to unleash on her father.

"It means that there's nothing you can say, no accusation you can make, or damning words you can deliver that I haven't already inflicted upon myself."

"No, Dad, that's not good enough." Rebecca raised her voice. "I want an answer. A mature, honest answer!"

"I don't owe you an answer!" he snapped, glaring at her with angry eyes. "This is between your mother and me. It had nothing to do with you."

"You drove my mother away!" she shouted back. "It has everything to do with me!"

"Your mother was suffering from severe depression, Rebecca. Our relationship had been strained for a long time."

"She'd buried her mother after a long battle with dementia. Then, her studio burned to the ground. Then she finds out that her husband is having an affair with her best friend and business manager? If that doesn't spell severe depression, then I don't know what—"

"I'm not going to sit here and argue with you about this," he interrupted.

"Of course you're not. If you did, you might have to admit just how weak you really are. She protected you all these years. There were times when I couldn't stand to look at her because I thought she'd hurt you. You sat back while I crucified my mother year in and year out for choosing the art world over us. And you said nothing. Nothing!"

Rebecca's words echoed throughout the house. Seconds after they were spoken, she sank back into the sofa, head in her hands, crying the tears of a frustrated and hurt young girl.

"If I could take back every night I spent away from her, don't you know I'd do it in a minute? Losing your mother was the most devastating thing to ever happen in my life. I knew what would happen once you learned the truth." He passed a wrinkled hand through his hair. "That's the honest, mature answer, Rebecca. It may be that of a coward, but it's the truth. I didn't tell you about Claudia because I couldn't bear to lose you, too."

Chapter Twenty-Six

The valet motioned for her to stop, but Holly waved him off. She pulled up to the automated ticket register, pressed the button, and drove through. As luck would have it, she found a parking spot just around the first corner. She collected her cell phone and book, pulled on her favorite jacket, and made her way to the main building.

The elevator arrived on the ninth floor, and she stepped out into the harsh fluorescent lights. A group of a dozen or so people was already assembled in the waiting area. It was immaculately clean but not inviting. However, what the hospital lacked in décor they more than made up for in expertise. The intensive care unit of the neuro-trauma wing was award-winning, run like a highly professional and well-oiled machine. She wanted nothing but the best for Jack.

She signed in at the nurses' station and affixed a family visitor badge to her shirt. She wouldn't be allowed in to see him until eight-thirty. The ward was stringent on the amount of time family members were allowed to be with patients. There were six visitation periods set up throughout the day and she planned on being at every one of them. Now she had forty-five minutes of waiting to fill. The cafeteria, she decided, was probably her best option to kill time. She honestly couldn't remember if she'd eaten dinner the night before.

Back in the elevator, she hit the button to return to the main floor. Quietly, she studied the cover of her new book—the last in the famed Dragon Tattoo *series. She prayed it would be just as engrossing as the others she'd read to get her through the afternoon between visitation periods.*

When the doors opened, she froze. He was the last person she expected to see.

"Zander?"

"Hi, Holly," he said softly.

"What are you doing here?"

"Making up for lost time."

"What do you mean?"

"Can we go somewhere to talk?" he asked.

"I'm on my way to the cafeteria. We can talk there."

They were surprised to find the dining area full at such an early hour. Holly found a tiny table stacked with dirty dishes in the back. She cleared and wiped it down while Zander stood in line for their breakfast. She helped herself to coffee from the self-service drink bar and poured a cup for him as well—cream, no sugar. They returned to their table at the same time.

They sat in silence for a couple of minutes. Holly stirred a packet of sugar into her coffee mug and watched him, filled with guilt and remorse for what might have been.

"Have you seen him this morning?" he inquired.

"The first visitation isn't for another hour."

"I saw him last night."

"You were here last night? When? I didn't see you and I was at the last visitation."

"It was very late, and you were already gone. I sweet-talked one of the nurses into letting me see him. I was only with him for a few minutes. The nurse was right there with me the whole time. He looks a little better than I expected. I don't think he'll be happy with the lopsided haircut they gave him, though."

She knew in her heart he was only trying to lighten the mood, but she just wasn't ready to make jokes of any kind regarding Jack's condition. Her fork fell to her plate along with a stream of tears. She felt Zander's strong arms around her two seconds later.

"He's gonna make it, Hol. Jack Steele doesn't give up—on anything."

Holly's tired body melted into his, and for a good five minutes, she allowed herself to be comforted by the man she'd hurt most.

"Why, Zander? I just don't understand."

"Accidents happen. It's no one's fault. He's getting the very best care—"

"No, I mean why are you doing this?" She pulled away and looked into his eyes. "I lied to you. I had an affair with another man—a man who would be dead right now if it hadn't been for you. You saved Jack's life...and now here you are, saving mine. Why?"

Zander reached and held her hands. She was still wearing her wedding ring. He touched the large diamond, moving it back and forth across her delicate finger. After a moment, he looked up and held her gaze. He swallowed hard, then spoke the truest and most painful words he'd ever said to his wife.

"It's really very simple. You love him, Holly...and I love you."

****

235

Will sat inside his car at the end of Charlotte's driveway, nervously drumming his fingers on the steering wheel. The sun was shining. Just another beautiful day in the state capital. He watched the house for several minutes, noting the neatly trimmed hedges that lined the cobblestone walkway. He hadn't noticed them before, though he remembered so many other details of her home with painful clarity.

He hadn't spoken to her since that night. Minutes after their encounter, he emerged from the bathroom and quickly fled on foot. He muttered the only sentiment he could, leaving her and the words "I'm sorry" at her door. He'd wandered around in the dark for half an hour before summoning a Lyft. Shamefully unable to return home, he hid out inside his office, finally pinning down a few hours of sleep. It wasn't until Georgia arrived the next morning with a suspicious and disapproving look in her eyes that Will truly realized the magnitude of what he'd done.

Another ten minutes passed before he gathered his courage and collected a pink-and-white striped box from the passenger seat while exiting the car. He walked determinedly up to her door, feeling his heartbeat increase with each step. He hadn't bothered to rehearse any sort of speech, opting to let honesty guide his words. He owed her that much. With a cleansing breath, he raised his hand and knocked lightly.

After a moment, he heard her call "Yes?" from behind the closed door.

"Charlotte, it's Will."

"Just a sec."

He listened as she worked her way through a number of locks. His heartbeat pounded in his ears the moment the door opened and their eyes met.

"Hey," he said, his voice barely above a whisper.

"Hey," she repeated, motioning him inside with her left hand, the majority of which was hidden by a pink fiberglass cast.

"So, I guess it's…" He pointed to her arm.

"Broken. Just a hairline fracture, but the doctor wants to keep it in a cast for a couple of weeks regardless."

"Well, I'm glad you decided to get it x-rayed."

"I didn't have a choice. Ben loaded me up kicking and screaming and drove me to the orthopedist."

"Good for Ben." Will smiled and held up the box. "I stopped by that bakery you told me about. They were all out of your favorite marble cake. I made an executive decision and went with the coconut. I hope that's okay."

"That's why you make the big bucks. Coconut is my second favorite." She returned his smile.

He followed her into the kitchen where she promptly offered him coffee. They exchanged the usual pleasantries before taking their cups back into the living room. This time, however, he kept his distance and took a seat on the sofa across from her.

"The cake looks delicious. You really didn't need to—" she began.

"I know I didn't need to. I wanted to," he said with a nod.

"I actually have something for you."

"You do?" he asked, surprised.

"Let me get it. I'll be right back."

She slipped out of the room, leaving Will alone. He checked his watch, knowing that his presence was required at an important meeting in ninety minutes—one that had been rescheduled numerous times. But rushing was not an option. Charlotte deserved more than a drive-thru apology.

"I used your trick." She waved a small, neatly folded cloth in his direction.

"Trick?"

"Peroxide and salt. The blood came right out." She placed his handkerchief on the table and then sat beside him.

"Listen, Charlotte, I want to talk about what happened the other night."

"You don't owe me any sort of explanation." She looked away.

"Actually," —he touched her hand, forcing her to stop and look at him— "I owe you an explanation and an apology."

They spent an hour talking openly, like two old friends. He held nothing back, sharing his jealousy toward Rebecca's success and the guilt he felt upon his initial attraction to her.

"A part of me wanted to hurt her because of the hurt I was feeling."

"We all feel that way at one time or another. It's human nature to want to lash out. You're not perfect, Will. There's no such thing as perfect."

"But it wouldn't be hurting just Rebecca." He locked on her eyes once more. "I would never want to hurt you. You're a beautiful, intelligent, desirable woman. But the truth of it is, I love my wife, Charlotte. I've loved her from our very first moments together. I don't want to lose her."

"You don't have to say another word. I

understand." She gave a reassuring nod.

They talked a few minutes more, a lighter feeling thankfully filling the room. Will glanced at his watch, knowing that it was time to go. She led the way to the door and turned to him.

"I put Seth Culver back on your project. He's up to speed on everything, and I personally guarantee you will be one hundred percent satisfied with the final product. I thought that, under the circumstances, it would be best if you and I limit our professional contact."

"Thank you." He nodded. "Mark's gonna run point for me from here on out. I have a host of talent to oversee this project. They certainly don't need my help."

"I'll let Seth know."

"Well..." He extended his hand. "Take care of yourself."

"I will. You too." She shook his hand.

They stood facing each other, neither knowing what to say. In another place and time, maybe they would have built something lasting together. But in his heart, Will knew that he wanted to spend his one-and-only life with the woman who unlocked worlds inside him that he never knew existed.

"It's funny..." she said, looking at him with serious eyes.

"What's funny?"

"The very thing that attracted me to you is the very thing that..." Her voice trailed off and Will noted the emotion in her eyes. "You're that kind of man, Will Albright. There aren't many like you left. Business, pleasure, personal—it's just your character."

"I don't know what you mean." He shook his head.

"You don't cheat at cards. You don't cheat on your taxes. And in the end, you don't cheat on your wife."

Chapter Twenty-Seven

The unnerving silence throughout the house meant only one thing: they'd sentenced themselves to an afternoon in solitary, each in search of much-needed alone time. If history held true, Rosalie guessed that Rebecca had ventured off down a collection of back roads. And Leland, she knew with a high degree of certainty, was probably sorting through his emotions while organizing his garden shed.

She hadn't heard every word of their heated exchange, though she had a pretty good idea of what transpired between father and daughter. The look of shock on Rebecca's face as she'd filled in years' worth of lies and omissions was still fresh in her mind, and she wondered what details Leland had shared. She knew it would happen one day—divulging what really happened between herself and her former husband and why she moved to New York. Though she shared the heartbreaking truth with her grown daughter, the hurt in Rebecca's eyes reflected that of an innocent girl.

Rosalie grabbed one of Leland's old jackets from the hall closet, pulling it around her shoulders as she set off in the direction of the greenhouse. Sunset was on her heels, and a chilly wind nipped at her. She held the jacket closed with one hand, keeping the other wrapped firmly around a thermos of hot coffee. A pair of clogs on her feet, she carefully navigated the rocky pathway, a little out of breath by the time she reached the door. Standing still, she watched him for a minute through the small window. Sitting behind an oversized workbench, he quietly cleaned a pair of shears. It was a task she'd seen him complete countless times during their years together and one that made her smile. Leland Graham was by far the most fastidious human she'd ever met. Not that the recent condition of his bedroom closet would confirm such a fact, but when it came to his personal interests—gardening, antique car restoration, fly fishing, photography—he was beyond obsessive about the condition of his gear. Flies meticulously tied and stored, lenses inspected and re-inspected following a shoot; he was a man of order. And now, looking at him through a thin sheet of glass, she held her breath, a feeling of deep remorse churning inside. An emotion that confirmed just how much she still loved him.

At that moment, he stopped and looked up at her as if stirred by the same feeling. Their eyes met and he gave her a knowing smile, waving her inside.

"I thought I might find you out here," she said, closing the door gently behind her.

"I've needed to get to this all week." He turned his eyes back to his task.

She walked around the table, positioning herself beside him. He didn't look up but kept right on working. She placed the thermos in front of him with a sigh.

"I brought you some coffee. Dinner will be ready in about an hour," she announced.

"Is it that time already?" he questioned. "What's Melba cooking up tonight?"

Though he tried his best to sound cheerful, she

knew he was anything but. There was a tension in his voice that he couldn't hide with small talk.

"Nothing. I took command of the kitchen, remember? I gave Melba the night off. I hope that's okay?"

"That all depends on what you're serving." He looked up.

"I played it safe." She smiled. "My roasted chicken with fennel."

"Safe is good. Nothing wrong with safe."

His focus returned to his chore as he moved the oil-soaked cloth across the metal blades in deliberate strokes. As he worked, Rosalie's gaze wandered around the small room. Images of their daughter hung on every wall—a complete pictorial history of their only child's upbringing.

"It hardly seems possible." She zeroed in on one particular photo of a seven-year-old beauty, missing a front tooth but smiling brightly. A blue ribbon held high above her head—the first of many that day.

"What's that?" Leland asked, looking up and following her gaze.

"That summer we spent in the country." She pointed up at the photo. "Rebecca's first swim meet at the club. How can that be…" She paused for a quick calculation. "Thirty-seven years ago?"

"She was something." Leland smiled up at the photo of his daughter. "The little thing swept every event."

"That's because a tough old man coached her well."

"She didn't need coaching. She was born for it."

"My God, she was beautiful, wasn't she?" Rosalie

grinned at the picture of her young daughter again.

"How could she be anything but? She looks just like you."

After all those years, he could still get to her. Rosalie could never decide if it was what he said or the sound of his southern accent and the way he emphasized certain words. Whatever it was, it always elicited the same internal response. Her heart beat a little faster, racing back to golden times when they spent hour upon hour wrapped up in each other.

"Are you all right?" she asked pointedly after several moments of silence, ready to address the real reason she'd sought him out.

He looked away without responding but continued to focus on the shears.

"Leland?" She called his name.

The response to her query began as a loud exhale. He folded the cloth in half and tossed it up on a shelf. Inside his coat pocket, he retrieved a fresh one and after removing his glasses, began to rub each lens with care. Rosalie studied the lines on his face and the silver in his hair, though all she saw was a dark-haired young man who'd swept her away years ago.

"Why did you wait?" he inquired, his head still down.

"I'm sorry?"

"Rebecca built a rock-solid wall of resentment between the two of you. You could have taken it down in one fell swoop. Of course, I could have too. Should have." He shook his head, exhaling once more. "I selfishly took the easy way out because I was afraid of losing both my girls. Every time Rebecca spent a weekend or holiday with you, I wondered if you would tell her the truth. Drove myself mad with worry, which is nothing compared to the pain I caused you." He looked up, his eyes connecting with her in a way no one else ever could. "But you never said a word about Claudia or the affair. Not one word until today. Why?"

It was the first time he'd ever used the word 'affair' to describe his year-long relationship with her former best friend and business partner. For years, it'd been nothing more than a mistake. And now, hearing the softness in his voice, the honesty with which he spoke, she saw him for what he truly was—a man with fears and faults like everyone else.

His questioning caught her off guard and she paused for several moments as she considered her answer. It was a simple one, she realized after only a few seconds. A simple, logical, yet painful truth.

"I was just her mother. You were her hero..." She took a deep breath, wishing to God she could rewind the years and start over. "I knew your fall from grace would be far greater than mine."

"After everything that happened between us, and everything I put you through, you protected me." He reached for her hand, gripping it tightly. "Why on earth would you do that?"

"When you love someone..." She gave his hand a tender squeeze. "That's what you do."

****

"Graham residence."

"Leland, it's Will. Sir, I'm sorry to call so late. I really need to talk to Rebecca, and she's not answering her cell phone."

"Rebecca's not here," Leland said. "She left for New York first thing this morning."

"New York?"

"Book business. Should be back in a day or two if she and Drew can—"

"I've been on the phone with Lily and an inspector with the AFP all night."

"Lily? Kelly's Lily? What's wrong? What happened?" Leland asked.

Will filled him in on the particulars of the phone call from Rebecca's former stepdaughter, a call bringing news no one expected. Rosalie poked her head into the study and Leland motioned emphatically for her to stay. She took a seat on the sofa beside his chair, trying to decipher the context of the call. His responses were cryptic and his expression perplexed; both clues that the late-night call did not bring good news.

"She's staying at Rosalie's. You've got the landline number, don't you?

"I don't think this is the type of news I can deliver over the phone—not when she's alone. And not after everything Lily told me. It would be different if she was there with the two of you, so that you and Rosalie might…" He sighed heavily, running a hand through his hair as he tried to formulate a proper game plan. "Listen, I'll call a buddy of mine. He's given me access to his plane whenever I need it. As soon as our flight plan gets approved, we'll be on our way."

"You're flying to New York? Tonight?"

"Not tonight, but first thing in the morning. I really don't think there's another way. This is not the sort of thing I want to tell Rebecca over the phone. Not when she's alone in New York."

"Is there anything we can do?" he asked.

"Maybe you and Rosalie could give Lily a call. I

think she'd really like to talk to you both."

"Of course." Leland grabbed a pen from the small table beside his chair, jotting down the number in the margin of a discarded newspaper. "Anything else?"

"Listen, Leland, if Rebecca calls…"

"We won't say a word until we've heard from you."

"Thank you, sir."

****

"Sweetheart?" Rosalie tapped on the door of her daughter's childhood bedroom.

"Come on in, Mom."

"Do you want to talk about it?" Rosalie asked after a minute of silence.

"No. We said everything we needed to say. We're gonna be okay."

"Your father loves you so very much. You know that, don't you?"

"I know. He loves you, too. He's never stopped."

Rosalie dropped her eyes from view. She twisted the tiny diamond ring around her pinky finger for a moment. Rebecca had never gotten the full story on the ring but knew it connected her mother to her father in ways her wedding band never did.

"Mom…forgiveness doesn't have a shelf life. It doesn't expire."

Rosalie remained silent, the ring still spinning. Rebecca reached and took her mother's hand. "It's not too late for either of us."

Rebecca couldn't stop thinking about the conversation she and her mother shared two days before. Will was just a phone call away, so why couldn't she make the first move? They hadn't spoken in days. She'd spent that time in deep reflection, evaluating her life as Mrs. Will Albright. It wasn't perfect by any stretch, but she couldn't imagine a life without Will. It was time to make a move and begin the process of rebuilding her happily-ever-after. She'd made peace with her mother and forgiven her father, and she knew in her heart it was time to offer Will the same.

With the phone to her ear, she dialed the number to their home. Her heartbeat increased steadily with each ring as she anticipated the sound of his voice on the other end. After four rings, however, the call rolled to voicemail. She hung up and tried his cell but was met with the same disappointing outcome. She wanted to leave a message, but didn't know what to say. She hung up a second time, her heart pounding out of control.

The dark, empty thoughts that had stalked her for days returned. Her mind began to spin a noxious tale as the walls of her mother's apartment seemed to close in around her.

Where is he? Why doesn't he answer? I've waited too long. He thinks I'm not coming back. He's probably with her. He's with Charlotte. It's over. I've lost him. I've lost everything.

Chapter Twenty-Eight

The cab ride into Manhattan found Will questioning his decision to arrive without a formal announcement. He thought about calling Rebecca but feared he'd be forced to reveal the news. Saying it over the phone was just not something he could bring himself to do. Apart from everything they'd been through, he wanted to be there beside her when she learned of her ex-husband's grisly death.

After forty-five minutes of traffic, Will finally arrived at his mother-in-law's building. According to the security guard in the lobby, Rebecca hadn't left the building. He stashed his bag behind the main desk and grabbed coffee from a small bakery around the corner. He returned a few minutes later and took the elevator up to the fourth floor, his heart drumming an intense rhythm.

The elegantly appointed hallway was quiet. He walked down the long, carpeted corridor, stopping when he reached Rosalie's door. Balancing two cups of dark roast in one hand, he sighed and knocked softly with the other. He placed one ear against the door, straining to hear signs of life inside the apartment. He drew back when he heard a series of locks being opened.

Rebecca opened the door and froze, her eyes filled with a mix of surprise, anger, remorse, and relief.

"Hi," he said softly.

"Hi," she responded in the same low tone.

"May I?"

"Oh, of course, I'm sorry." She stepped back away from the door.

Once inside, Will took a moment to collect himself. It'd been two years since he'd visited Rosalie's place. Nothing appeared to have changed; it was still as warm and inviting as he remembered. He shifted his weight back and forth, looking for a place to empty his hands.

"Coffee?" he asked.

"I was actually in the kitchen on a quest for the very thing when you knocked."

"Rebecca, there's something I need to talk to you about."

"I can't do this right now, Will. I have a meeting with Drew at his office. Can we please wait and—"

"Rebecca, this isn't about us, and it can't wait."

"What is it?" she asked, unable to mask the alarm in her voice.

"Can we sit down?"

"Oh my God, is it Georgia?"

"Georgia is fine," he said reassuringly. "Please…"

He motioned to the sofa and waited for her to take a seat. He'd tried for hours to decide how he was going to tell her. And now, seeing the panic in her eyes, he knew it would not be an easy task. He sat beside her, their bodies almost touching. He drew in a deep breath and released it slowly.

"I got a call last night…from Lily," he said, looking down and twisting his wedding ring around his finger.

"He's gone, isn't he?" she whispered, trying to fight back tears. "Was he…was Lily with him? Was he in a lot of pain?"

"Rebecca…" He spoke her name softly, swallowing hard as he prepared himself to deliver the painful particulars of his death. "Kelly drowned."

"What do you mean, he drowned? Kelly had cancer, and he was—"

"A small, unmanned sailboat was reported off the coast."

"But he doesn't sail anymore. He doesn't even own a sailboat. He has this beautiful cruiser that he…" Her voice trailed off.

"Marine Area Command responded and found a large pool of blood on and around one of the steel cleats, along with several bloody hand and footprints. Investigators think he fell and hit his head on the cleat. The blow was severe enough that he stumbled around a bit as he lost consciousness, and that's probably how he fell overboard."

"What did the autopsy say?" she asked after a lengthy pause.

Will didn't answer but lowered his head into his hands with another heavy sigh.

"Will? The autopsy?"

"His body hasn't been recovered. I doubt it ever will be. He was out in deep water," he said in a whisper.

Out in deep water. It's where Kelly Glass had lived his entire life. Rebecca said nothing but slumped against Will's body. Tears tumbled hard and fast. He cradled her in his arms and rubbed her back with a loving touch.

"I didn't want to tell you over the phone. I am so, so sorry."

****

Rebecca sensed that something was wrong the night before. Lying awake in her mother's bedroom, she'd felt an eerie sort of cold fog roll across her body—one that brought Kelly's image into her mind with strange clarity. The feeling was so strong that it pushed her out of bed and to the phone at two a.m. She'd tried both his cell and his Sydney apartment but to no avail.

Part of her feared that alcohol would be the culprit, that somehow the death of his mother—coupled with the advanced state of his cancer—had initiated a dangerous backslide. It was a reality she wasn't prepared to accept.

The shock of the news tore through her, leaving Rebecca with only one conclusion: it had to be a mistake. That Kelly Glass might be floating lifeless in the Pacific Ocean was entirely surreal. The man spent the better part of his life whipping the waves of the world's oceans into submission. No one was a more accomplished sailor than her ex-husband, Will included. And now, if the reports were true, the woman that fascinated him most, his mistress of rolling swells and mysterious beauty, had taken him down into her watery depths and refused to let go. It was too cruel an irony.

She thought back to their last night together, spinning yarns and singing to the stars from the back of his yacht. Despite his weakened state, he retained his full-bodied sense of humor and the ability to poke fun at himself. *Why, Kelly? Why in God's name would you venture out alone?*

Of course, she already knew the answer to that question. There was only one reason that he did anything—because he felt like it. Kelly moved and did as he pleased for most of his life without a drop of regard for such concepts as safety or self-respect. He was ten feet tall and bulletproof, even when his body said otherwise. She closed her eyes and dropped her head, offering a prayer for the man that she'd loved once upon a time. A man she'd done her best to hurt, but who still loved her regardless.

****

The twenty-two-hour flight to Australia was grueling and quiet. They slept intermittently, engaged in small talk, and traded magazines to pass the time. Will stayed in contact with those searching the area where Kelly's boat was found. When they landed a day later, they were met with a disappointing report. Rescue boats, world-class divers, helicopters, and dozens of volunteers gave their best efforts, but the outcome had not changed. The news of Kelly's death was now all over the media. Every local channel and newspaper displayed the same outdated photo of him, holding the large silver lighthouse trophy after taking first place in the Newport Bermuda Race. A picture, Rebecca remembered, that held a special place on the wall of his mother's study for years. It was a great shot, and she was thankful that a more recent photograph had not been leaked to the press.

They bypassed their hotel and took a taxi from the airport to Kelly's apartment instead where his grown daughter waited. Rebecca had spoken only briefly with Lily following Will's arrival in New York. She was surprised by the young woman's calm demeanor when she finally looked into her big, brown eyes. They sat together for several hours, their fingers lovingly intertwined, while a fleet of attorneys swarmed around them, sorting out every last detail. Police reports were examined and re-examined; terms like 'death in absentia' and 'coroner inquest' were tossed about, leaving Rebecca with a monster headache. They were all exhausted and in need of a good night's rest. So, at the recommendation of Kelly's physician, Rebecca escorted Lily down the hall, ready for some one-on-one before she and Will returned to their hotel.

Behind the closed guest bedroom door, Lily popped a sedative and slipped into pajamas. Rebecca sat down on the bed beside her, offering her a hand and a sweet smile.

"Is there anything you need before we go?" Rebecca asked.

"I don't think so."

"You've been remarkably strong through all this. Your father would be so proud." She brushed Lily's hair off her forehead.

"I can't tell you how much your being here has helped, and your husband. He's been my angel through all this. The way he sprang into action after I called... He gave me hope when no one else could."

"What do you mean?" Rebecca asked.

"Authorities called off their search after twenty-four hours. They didn't have enough manpower. Something about wind conditions and the depth of where the boat was recovered. When I called your house, I was a wreck. Will listened and said he'd assemble the necessary teams to continue the search.

He promised to do everything in his power to find my father." She reached for a tissue and blotted fresh tears from the corners of her eyes before continuing. "Rebecca, I'm not a little girl. I don't have any grand illusions about my father walking through that door, laughing and telling us some fantastic tale. He was physically unable to control that boat. I knew it, and I begged him not to take it out. Just a quick out and back. That's what he promised."

"But why would he do it? He could barely get on and off his yacht without a helping hand."

"I think he wanted to see if he had a shot at sailing in the Hobart Race next month. After Grandmother died, something happened to him. And then, after seeing you..." She sighed heavily, running her hand along the edge of the sheet.

"What are you saying, Lily?" Rebecca studied the young woman's eyes. "He wasn't drinking again, was he?"

"No, it wasn't that. In fact, it was totally the opposite. You renewed his spirit, Rebecca. Do you know that after you left, he contacted several doctors to discuss treatment options?"

"He did?"

"Said he wanted to make the most of the time he had left. He even called my mother and offered to take the three of us on a Mediterranean cruise, because we'd never really taken a proper vacation as a family."

"Well, that certainly sounds out of character."

"Being together with you and sharing his work on the reserve..." She looked into Rebecca's eyes with total honesty. "You gave my father the will to live."

Rebecca had no idea how to respond. Part of her

was embarrassed and part was filled with pride.

"You don't have to take my word for it." Lily opened the bedside table drawer and pulled a small envelope into view. "I'll let him tell you."

Instantly, Rebecca recognized Kelly's handwriting. Her name and address were printed neatly on the front. It only lacked the necessary postage to make the journey from Australia to Texas.

"I found the letter on his desk. He'd addressed the envelope but hadn't put the letter in it. I folded it and put it inside. I promise I didn't read it."

"I don't know what to say," Rebecca confessed.

"You don't have to say anything. I know my father's body will probably never be found. But knowing you and Will have put your lives on hold to help bring some sort of closure to this…and knowing how my father felt about you and the happiness you gave him during these last days…well, it's something that a thank you just won't cover."

"We care about you, Lily, and we promise we'll always be here for you."

"I love you, Rebecca." Tears returned to her eyes. "I always have."

"And I love you too, sweetheart."

They shared a warm embrace, breaking only when a soft knock sounded on the door.

"Come in," Lily called.

"I'm sorry to interrupt. Rebecca, the cab is here. I told him to wait, so there's no rush. Whenever you're ready." Will gave her a nod.

"All right. I'll be right there."

"Lily, if you need anything—anything at all—do not hesitate. You know how to reach us," he said.

"Will, I don't know how to thank you."

"You and Maks can thank us by getting some rest." He shared a warm smile.

****

Little was said in the cab between Kelly's apartment and the hotel. Rebecca hadn't asked where they were staying, yet she wasn't surprised when they pulled up in front of her preferred hotel in the historic district. Will checked in while Rebecca waited with their luggage near the elevators. Minutes later, they were standing inside a beautifully appointed suite on the top floor.

"Would you like me to pour you a drink?" he asked, perusing a selection of fine spirits in the mini-bar.

"I don't think so." She shook her head, already out of her shoes.

"Are you hungry? I could call down for room service."

"I'm fine, really. A bath and bed, that's all I have the strength for."

"I told the gentleman that we'd like the late seating for breakfast. We should try to be downstairs a little before nine. Is that too early for you?"

"No, nine is okay."

"Because I can change it if you'd rather have a tray sent up here."

"Will…" She focused on his eyes, wondering if hers looked as tired as his. "Nine o'clock will be fine."

"All right. I'll leave your room key right here."

He tossed a black plastic card on the glass top table in the living area and turned toward the door.

"Where are you going?" she asked, confused.

"To my room. I'm next door."

"Oh." She gave a nod.

"I just thought that, well, under the circumstances…"

Their sleeping arrangements hadn't even crossed her mind. How could it, when her thoughts had been solely focused on Kelly and Lily for well over twenty-four hours?

"Right."

"The last thing I want is for you to feel uncomfortable or pressured in any sort of way."

"Thank you," she said.

"Listen, if you need anything during the night…"

"I know."

"I guess I'll see you in the morning, then."

He walked toward the door where his bag sat waiting.

"Will, wait," she called out.

He stopped and turned around. "What is it?"

"Lily told me what you did. Organizing your very own rescue effort." She paused and bit her bottom lip. "All those calls you made on the way to the airport, I thought you were talking with local authorities about their ongoing investigation. I had no idea that you'd coordinated and funded the entire operation."

"Well, you can't imagine the fear in that girl's voice when she called."

"It's the most honorable thing I've ever known you to do."

She watched as Will drew a deep breath. Had her words surprised him? In her heart of hearts, she'd never paid him a greater or more heartfelt compliment. Part of her wanted to go to him, to wrap him up inside her love and kiss away all their pain. But the distance between them was still great and she'd made a silent vow to not move too quickly.

"I didn't do it for honor." His eyes showed only sincerity. "I did it because it was the right thing to do. You love Lily…and I love you."

Chapter Twenty-Nine

Becks,

Man, has it really been three days since I put you on a plane back to Texas? It seems like years since we were together. But that's how it is with a good thing, isn't it? It goes by too fast. This whole ride has been too damn fast.

I've spent every night since you left thinking about the conversations we had while you were here. Dinner with Lily and Maks at my place. What a great night! The trip to the reserve. I've never been so proud to share something so close to me. Only you could understand and appreciate its importance. Thank you for that. Oh! And the night out on my boat. In a word— flawless. The whole experience—you, me, Edna— underneath the stars and singing our way through our mottled past. It was the singular greatest night in recent memory. We covered a lot of ground and exhumed a number of ghosts in our short time together. Seeing you again stirred up so many memories of the special times we shared. Do you remember the little ski resort in Cortina? My God, you looked incredible on the slopes. And the week we spent exploring Austria? The hills were definitely alive back then, weren't they? What about our bike tour through Spain? I don't really remember it (blame it on the Amontillado Sherry!). Then there was the first night we spent in our first house. Magical. That night was pure magic. How adorable were you when you made us your first home-cooked meal? Who knew spaghetti could burn? What I'm trying to say (and I'm probably failing miserably) is that the best times of my life have your name written all over them.

Oh, Becks. You were so beautiful then. Vibrant, determined. You're even more beautiful now. I was a self-absorbed SOB and still am to some degree. I really was proud of you. I only wish I told you more often what you meant to me. And since I didn't, I want to take this opportunity to say the words that have haunted me from the minute I left you at the airport.

Three days ago, the odds were stacked against me. I'm terminally ill. I have cancer, the ultimate death sentence. But just the sound of your voice touched a place inside me that hasn't seen the light of day in years. I suddenly feel renewed, reborn, and ready to step forward and make the most of the time I have left. I thought I was ready to say goodbye to this world. I'd made peace with my prognosis and didn't want to be a burden on anyone. Then you fell back into my life in what has been a dark time, bringing that special light that can only be found in your smile, your warmth, and your honesty. Ever since you left, I've fought to stay focused on it. You are the sun, Rebecca. You are my sun.

I contacted several specialists—two here in Sydney, one in Houston, and one in New York. It may be too late. In fact, I'm probably well beyond my expiration date. Nine lives only sounds like a lot for a mangy cat like me. I'll be flying to New York in two weeks to meet with Dr. Freeman from Sloan-Kettering.

If you happen to be on the east coast, I'd love to meet up for dinner. I promise to be on my best behavior (well, sort of). I wonder if that little Italian place near the Winter Garden Theater is still there? We raised a few glasses there, didn't we?

In all seriousness, your love and friendship have inspired me to try. I don't know what the future holds, but I know exactly what lies in the past. Mistakes. Regrets. But also love. I have an incredible daughter. How I got so lucky with that one I'll never know. I also have a circle of wonderful friends who've stood by me when I didn't deserve their loyalty. I've made a ton of money and experienced some of the most amazing things this world has to offer. Hopefully, there'll be a little more where that came from. I want you to know that some of the greatest blessings in my life are centered around you, and for the gift of those tender moments, I thank you.

Well, I've rambled on long enough. Don't know when I last sat down and wrote an authentic letter. Maybe I'll try it again one day. In the meantime, the canvas is calling my name. Surely there's a little salt left in an old sailor like me. Saw a pretty little twenty-three-footer in the marina that needs a little love. You know, we can all use some.

I love you, Rebecca Rose Rutledge Albright. Thank you for giving me back something I'd lost for a very long time. Please give my best to Will. I pray the two of you have found your way back to one another and are stronger and more in love than ever. I think Neil Diamond said it best: sometimes being lost is worth coming home.

All my love,

Kelly

Rebecca finished the letter for the third time, drying her tears with the belt of her robe. It was so raw and honest, as though he'd been sitting right there with her. She could hear his voice in every single line. It wasn't fair. He was everything in death that she'd longed for during their life together. Yet it was through his suffering that she realized just how fine a line she teetered on. She studied the large diamond on her left hand. Two rings had taken up residence there but only one had truly connected with the deepest recesses of her soul. She eyed the clock beside the bed as she reached for the phone. Her heart was beating furiously, and she held her breath as she waited for him to pick up.

"Rebecca?" he answered in a sleepy tone.

"Will…" she whispered, a large lump forming in her throat.

"Babe, what is it?" he asked, his voice echoing with alarm.

"Kelly's dead," Rebecca's voice cracked as she glanced down at his letter. "He's not coming back. And his precious Lily…"

"I know. I'm so sorry," Will replied softly.

"I just don't understand why all this is happening. What is happening to my life?"

"Rebecca, I want you to listen to me, all right?" His voice took on a commanding yet still gentle tone. "I want you to hang up. Okay? Just hang up the phone. I'll be right there."

"I don't want to end up like my parents, Will. I just can't do it."

"I promise it'll be okay. I'm coming. Right now.

Hang up."

She didn't respond but followed his orders. Seconds after ending the call, she heard a quiet knock on the door. She slipped from the bed, wiping her tears away. Millions of words had built up inside her. From the intense expression he'd worn all day, she knew that her husband had stored up hundreds as well. With her hand on the doorknob, she took a deep breath. She stared down at the cold marble floor for a moment, flooded with a dozen emotions at once. *What if Will had been the one in that boat? What if I'd never seen him again?*

She opened the door and found him waiting, standing in the hall in a matching hotel robe. They stood there for a minute, encased in silence as they looked into each other's wounded eyes. So much had happened between them. So much that should have brought them closer together—his thriving business and her literary success. But their collective accomplishments had driven a dangerous, hurtful wedge between them, one that now seemed so trivial.

Her bottom lip began to quiver. "He's not coming back. See, he wrote me this letter. There's this doctor, he's in New York…you know, I burned his dinner this one time, and then I thought about the time you were in that motorcycle accident and those old barbeques down on the beach…and then that's when I couldn't—"

Her words stopped making sense and she struggled for a breath as her tears came in full force. She couldn't fight it anymore and she didn't want to. Without a word, he pulled her trembling body to him. Being back in Will's arms was like coming home. They hadn't shared a moment this real, this honest, in forever. She didn't want it to end.

"Tell me I haven't lost you forever. Tell me I haven't destroyed everything between us," Will whispered.

There was a vulnerability in his voice she hadn't heard in months. Days before, she had silently cursed his name—lonely, confused, and doubtful of any real reconciliation. Now, feeling his arms around her, she was ready to forgive. They belonged together and had since the moment he held her on the dance floor. They were far from perfect, but they had something worth fighting for. Kelly had shown her that. She felt perfect when she was with him, and that was all that mattered.

"I want my life back." She reached up and touched his cheek. "*Our* life. I don't want to be lost anymore."

He took her hand and kissed her fingertips. "I love you, Rebecca. Only you."

They disappeared behind the door of her suite. Will called down for a pot of decaf. Minutes after the room service attendant arrived, they settled onto the sofa. Side by side, they began to put the broken pieces of their lives back together. Rebecca backed up two weeks, sharing the details of Gloria's funeral and her quiet moments with Kelly. She expected a fair amount of jealousy from her husband, but he listened with a gentle ear, softly rubbing his hand across her shoulder. A few tears returned, especially when together they read Kelly's letter. Rebecca shocked him with the truth of her father's yearlong affair and the lessons in forgiveness that she and her mother decided to embrace. Will revealed several telling sessions with Georgia and the decision to remove himself from the building project. Rebecca held her breath as he disclosed the details of visiting Charlotte's house a second time, still unable to draw a clear picture of the woman who almost came between them.

They talked well into the night, sharing more of themselves than they had in months. There were no accusations. There was no blame. After two and a half hours, they agreed to let go of the guilt as well, knowing they'd never move forward, otherwise. They had both made mistakes, but their ability to forgive—truly forgive—came in the form of the promise they'd made to one another years before. The promise of forever, for better or worse.

The coffee pot now empty, Rebecca yawned, and Will followed suit. Jet lag took firm control of their tired bodies, and they knew it was time to call it a night. Taking his hand, she led him to the bed. They slipped between the cool sheets and each other's arms without a word. A peaceful sigh escaped her as her body found the familiar contours of his. It was her safe place, the warm spot in her life where she felt the most secure. He pressed his lips against her head and pulled her close. They lay together in the quiet of the suite for several minutes, their hearts beating in an almost identical rhythm.

"Rebecca?" Will broke the silence between them.

"Yes?" she answered.

"Would you really give up writing?" he asked.

"Will, we just spent hours agreeing to close this subject."

"This is the last time I'll bring it up, I swear."

"If I thought that's what you wanted then yes, I would give up writing."

"Forever?" he questioned.

"Yes."

"Why?"

"What do you mean, 'why'? If that's what it would take to make you happy, then that's what I'd do. I need you more than I need to write. It's not like it's been my life's work. This whole thing started on a dare, remember? I like writing, but I love you."

He turned over to face her, his finger tracing the outline of her jaw.

"I want you to know something. I'd never, *ever* ask you to give up something you're passionate about— something that brings you happiness and makes you feel special or validated. And definitely not something that showcases your talent. You're an incredible writer, and the world deserves to know you."

They held each other's gaze for a moment. The sincerity in his eyes was more than enough—not that she needed much convincing. Giving herself to Will was all she ever wanted. His arms encircled her waist, and in another second, his mouth found hers.

"My God, Rebecca..." he said. "I was so afraid that I'd never hold you again."

Her heart skipped a beat. A week earlier, she'd fallen asleep in her childhood bedroom wondering the very same thing. Her mother had given her a lot to think about. Would she really be able to have a life without Will in it? Just one look into his eyes had given her the answer, one that had been there all along.

"Please don't ever let me go," she whispered back.

Chapter Thirty

Rebecca and Will said goodbye to Lily after a week in Sydney, their final afternoon spent exploring recent progress at the wildlife reserve. Much had been done in the short time since her first visit, and again she marveled at the depth of her ex-husband's vision. With a sound plan in place, they vowed to return once a year, leaving oversight of the day-to-day operations in the capable hands of the reserve's manager.

The body of Kelly Forrester Glass was never found. On the plane ride back to the States, it occurred to Rebecca that it was exactly the way he would have wanted to go. The ending he would have written for himself, if given the choice—one shrouded completely in mystery. The stuff of legends.

Leland and Rosalie held Thanksgiving dinner for them, and they celebrated together as a family on the last day of the month. Georgia joined them, and together with Rosalie, their combined culinary talents garnered applause and rave reviews. Rosalie smiled as she placed the picture-perfect bird on the table.

"You haven't lost your touch, Rose," Leland said with a grin.

After dinner, once Georgia had placed the last dessert on the buffet, Leland stood, glass in hand, and cleared his throat.

"Well, it hardly seems that a year has passed, but

it's indeed that time again." He smiled at his former wife. "The time when we honor a long-standing Graham tradition. This year I've selected a poem from the great Ralph Waldo Emerson which I would like to recite."

He pulled a pair of glasses from the pocket of his shirt, along with a small scrap of folded paper. He cleared his throat a second time and read the words of the famous poet aloud.

"*For each new morning with its light, for rest and shelter of the night, for health and food, for love and friends, for everything thy goodness sends.*"

He shared a smile with everyone around the table, and once more applause filled the room.

"Rose, honey, it's your turn." He sat back down.

Will and Rebecca exchanged another knowing glance. It was beyond obvious. The constant stream of niceties and pet names that flowed without hesitation between the couple formerly known as Mr. and Mrs. Leland Graham left little doubt. The flame that died decades before had been rekindled to a warm, comfortable fire. Rebecca hadn't seen her parents this happy in years, and it filled her heart with joy.

"I can't believe you!" Rosalie said, feigning outrage.

"What?" Leland grinned.

"You peeked at my poem, didn't you?"

"I haven't the faintest idea what you're talking about."

"So you're telling me that of all the poets in all the world, you just happened to select one by Emerson?"

"And what's wrong with that?" he asked.

"*My* poem is by Emerson."

"Well, of course it is." He winked in his daughter's direction. "Great minds think alike."

Rosalie stood and read her poem aloud, smiling warmly at her former husband when she took her seat again. He reached across the table for her hand and squeezed it with affection.

"Sweetheart?" Rosalie looked hopefully at her daughter.

"I hate to be the one to break tradition but I completely forgot. I'm so sorry."

"Oh, that's all right," her father reassured her.

"Uh, Leland?" Will interrupted. "I have a poem I'd like to share."

"You do?" Rebecca looked at him, clearly surprised.

"It's not exactly Thanksgiving-specific…" He pulled his wallet from his pocket. "But it's something I give thanks for every single day."

"Who wrote it?" Rebecca inquired.

"An angel in a Lincoln Continental," Georgia interjected with a mischievous smile.

"Well, my curiosity is more than piqued. Let's hear it," Leland urged with enthusiasm.

Will began with a small tale. "There was a young naval cadet traveling off base on assignment for his commander. Well, he had a blowout on the highway, and as luck would have it, his vehicle was minus a spare. He was stranded in between towns. No cell phone, no nothing. Luckily, this family stopped. A beautiful family. The father offered a ride, which the cadet gladly accepted. They loaded up the damaged tire and off they went. It wasn't very far to the next town, and within a few minutes, they'd located a gas station.

The cadet thanked them and said he'd find a way back to his car. The family drove away but not before sharing this poem with the young officer."

He unfolded the piece of paper with care, watching his wife from the corner of his eye. He didn't really need the hard copy; he'd committed every single line to memory. After reciting the lines, he looked up, his eyes connecting with Rebecca's. The wheels inside her head moved at lightning speed. He'd thought about this moment for years, and it didn't disappoint.

"I know that poem,"—she shook her head, trying to jog her memory—"Where do I know that poem?"

"You know it because you wrote it—Band Aid and all." He tossed it on the table in front of her.

Dumbfounded, she reached for the worn piece of paper, immediately recognizing the handwriting of her younger, inexperienced self...a girl who dreamed of falling in love and discovering the world.

"Where did you get this?" she asked.

"Years ago, I was stationed at Kings Bay. My tire blew, and you three were on your way back—"

"From our place at Saint Simons," Rosalie interrupted, shaking her head in disbelief. "That handsome young man was you?"

"My God, it *was* you," Leland agreed.

"You were asleep, and I needed a piece of paper. Your mother tore this from the back of one of your journals," he confirmed.

"And you saved this? After all these years?" Rebecca questioned.

"Some things in life are absolutely worth saving."

****

They took a long walk, Winston and Dizzy in tow,

and ended up down at the dock. Will tossed a few pebbles into the dark blue water, watching the ripples slowly work their way across the surface. Rebecca sat down on the last wooden slat, boots dangling off the edge. A minute later, he took his place beside her and reached for her hand.

"You want to know something? The last time I sat on this dock, I was convinced that it was over between us," Rebecca said.

"How do you feel now?" he asked, gently rubbing her thumb with his own.

"Like we're just beginning." She rested her head against his shoulder.

They sat together for a while, enjoying the quiet landscape. Rebecca's mind replayed the scene at the dining room table and the surprise gift her husband had given all of them.

"What did you mean, 'Band-Aid and all'?" she asked curiously.

"You had a Band-Aid wrapped around your toe. I'll never forget it. You were wearing this white sundress and these enormous sunglasses, like you were hiding from the paparazzi or something. For years I wondered what color eyes you had."

"You're making this up." She gave him a suspicious look.

"It's one hundred percent true. Ask your mother. I know you don't remember but she does."

Silence returned and Will continued to rub her thumb. The sun was beginning to set on what had been a perfect day—a day in which she'd given thanks numerous times. In less than four weeks, they would return to the sights and sounds of Christmas at her family home. She had a feeling it would be their most memorable holiday yet.

"Uh, they're green, by the way…just in case you wondered." She batted her eyes at him playfully.

"I'll make note of that." He winked.

A word about the author…

Suzy England fell in love with fiction the minute she picked up her first Judy Blume book in third grade. A retired elementary educator and native Texan, she lives in Houston with her husband. She's the proud mom of two adult children and dog mom to her Havanese, Ivy. Suzy is the author of the novella, THE WEEKEND (Silver Phoenix, 2019) and rom-com, CHASING MR. CROWN (a Wattpad Paid Story, which has amassed over 1 million reads). When she's not writing, she's binge-watching British television, listening to true crime podcasts, or cheering for her alma-mater, The University of Texas at Austin. www.suzyengland.com

Thank you for purchasing
this publication of The Wild Rose Press, Inc.

For questions or more information
contact us at
info@thewildrosepress.com.

The Wild Rose Press, Inc.
www.thewildrosepress.com

CPSIA information can be obtained
at www.ICGtesting.com
Printed in the USA
BVHW051738190123
656651BV00009B/187

9 781509 246076